THIEF IN THE NIGHT

Trembling Fenella stepped from the coach and out into the soft moonlight.

For a brief moment her heart seemed to stop as she saw the man who stood before her.

She looked at his face and saw its upper part masked above his smiling lips.

She looked at his hands and saw a pair of long-barreled pistols pointing directly at her.

Then she saw his face come closer and she closed her eyes and felt his lips upon hers . . .

. . . and she knew that this man who dressed like a thief and spoke like a Lord was out to steal not only her gold and her jewels, but her now wildly beating heart as well. . . .

THE INNOCENT DECEIVER

More Regency Romances from SIGNET

THE INNOCENT DECEIVER

by Vanessa Gray

A SIGNET BOOK
NEW AMERICAN LIBRARY
TIMES MIRROR

PUBLISHER'S NOTE

This novel is a work of fiction. Names, characters, places, and incidents are either the product of the author's imagination or are used fictitiously, and any resemblance to actual persons, living or dead, events, or locales is entirely coincidental.

Copyright © 1980 by Vanessa Gray

SIGNET TRADEMARK REG. U.S. PAT. OFF. AND FOREIGN COUNTRIES
REGISTERED TRADEMARK—MARCA REGISTRADA
HECHO EN CHICAGO, U.S.A.

SIGNET, SIGNET CLASSICS, MENTOR, PLUME, MERIDIAN AND NAL BOOKS are published by The New American Library, Inc., 1633 Broadway, New York, New York 10019

First Printing, October, 1980

1 2 3 4 5 6 7 8 9

PRINTED IN THE UNITED STATES OF AMERICA

1

"My dear Fenella," said Lady Dorton, reaching for her fourth buttered muffin, "how dreadful it must have been!"

It was July 6, 1813, a bright sunny morning. The sun streamed through the windows of Lady Dorton's morning room, bathing the heavy silver urn and the Wedgwood tureens on the mahogany sideboards in clear light.

The ample proportions of the tureens were repeated in the rounded contours of Lady Dorton, a kindly, amiable woman, fond of her comforts, and well-disposed toward the world.

Fenella Morland, sitting opposite her godmother at the round breakfast table, crumbled her muffin absently in her fingers. It had indeed been dreadful—but not precisely in the way her godmother thought.

"But the worst of it was," explained Fenella, anxious to put her friend Caroline Lamb in the best possible light, "that Lord Byron all but sneered, if you can believe it!"

"I can believe it," said Lady Dorton with unaccustomed vigor. "A shocking pair. Breeding isn't all, my dear. I cannot help but take comfort in the strict discipline your grandmama insisted upon. Had I not the utmost confidence in your proper behavior, and your elevated mind, I should not have allowed you to go about London in someone else's care. Although I have the highest opinion of Lady Baltford's sense," she finished in some confusion.

"My dear godmother," said Fenella dutifully, "I should not wish you to make yourself uncomfortable on my behalf. Lady Baltford indeed is most careful. It surely was not her fault that Caro Lamb and Lord Byron—"

"Dreadful!" interrupted Lady Dorton, her eyes shining with suppressed excitement. "Tell me again just how it was!"

Fenella could see the entire scene at Lady Heathcote's as though it were imprinted upon the inner surface of her eyelids. "As soon as Lord Byron came in," she began for the third time, "Caro began to cry—"

Caro Lamb, taking an unexpected fancy to Fenella Morland, in London for her first Season, had poured out her heart to her new friend. At impassioned length, she spoke of her enraptured devotion to Lord Byron, the brooding, sulky lion of the hour. The course of Caro's love did not run smoothly. Fenella had refrained from confiding overmuch in her godmother, for Lady Dorton's view of what was *comme il faut* bore little resemblance to the realities of life as seen by Lady Caroline Lamb. Caught up in the excitement of an illicit love affair—once removed—Fenella thrilled to Caro's exaltation, became sunk in despair when Byron scorned her friend.

Now she continued her heavily censored narrative. "She sobbed, and clutched me, begging me to take her to her husband—"

"Was he there?"

"No, he wasn't," Fenella said. "And I knew that Caro would die rather than let Lady Melbourne take charge, and I did not know quite what to do."

"My poor child!" sympathized Lady Dorton, her eyes brimming with tears of sensibility. "What *did* you do?"

"I could do nothing! Caro simply *sped* into the next room, where the punch bowl was, don't you see, and took one of Lady Heathcote's best glasses and broke it. On the edge of the table. I think there must still be pieces of glass caught up in the linen—"

Even Blake, Lady Dorton's butler, was caught up in Fenella's narrative. She was aware of his unsuccessful pretense of inattention, for even his bent back was eloquent of rapt interest. The advent of Miss Fenella had been a boon to the bored servants of Lady Dorton, for her lively sorties into Society, often related in their hearing, had provided new interest in the servants' hall. Blake was storing away every word of Fenella's tale.

"What a shame!" exclaimed Lady Dorton, sipping coffee. "Now the set is incomplete—and all for a foolish notion!"

"I doubt that Caro thought about Lady Heathcote's set of crystal," said Fenella drily.

"Doubtless she did not. A very thoughtless child, I always considered her. Her mother had not the slightest notion of how to bring up a child! Lady Bessborough herself has little moral discipline." Having delivered herself of the required strictures, she said, "Did Byron see this?"

"He couldn't help but see it," Fenella explained. "But he could have stopped her. She began then to stab at her wrists, and cry and shriek——"

Fenella's eyes filled with tears. She was truly fond of Caro, the most enchanting creature she had ever known, and to see her in such distress of mind was most upsetting. Even though Lady Melbourne had by dint of force held her daughter-in-law's hands from wreaking further damage on herself, and had carried Caro away and put her into the Melbourne carriage, Fenella still felt a pang in her heart as she had the evening before. And Byron, standing there with that superior sort of sneer on his full lips——

"I shall never read another word he writes!" exclaimed Fenella with emphasis. "He is totally heartless!"

Lady Dorton pursed her lips in a show of disapproval. She was an easygoing woman for the most part, and had welcomed her lively goddaughter with enthusiasm. She had found the child most biddable, of impeccable decorum, and entirely trustworthy. She was aware now, however, that she had perhaps trusted the young girl too far, for Caro Lamb, even though highly connected, was not the kind of companion Lady Dorton wished for Fenella. She vowed she would keep a closer rein on her, and even though this meant stirring herself unduly to go into society, yet for the sake of Fenella's grandmother, she would make whatever effort was needed.

"There is no need to read anything of Lord Byron's," she said soothingly. "I must confess that *Childe Harold* is not my idea of the most elevating literature."

"But," pointed out Fenella, "you did read it."

Lady Dorton laughed. "Oh, yes, to the very end. But I did feel that I wanted a warm bath afterwards, with *plenty* of soap!"

Fenella's thoughts already moved forward. "I am to be at Devonshire House this afternoon," she began doubtfully.

Lady Dorton said at once, "You must send your excuses. I shall do it for you. It is out of the question for you to be seen with any of Caroline Lamb's family, and the world knows that her aunt the Duchess will make any kind of excuse for the poor girl. No, Fenella, I wish you to attend me this afternoon. I shall make a round of calls that are in truth overdue. We shall take the brougham, with the top laid back, I think, so that your whereabouts are clearly seen——"

All morning Lady Dorton bent her efforts to undoing the

possible damage. She had not troubled dear Fenella with the implications that she herself, well versed in the ways of the world, saw in the unfortunate *contretemps* at Lady Heathcote's. Lady Caroline Lamb was totally lost to convention, and it was most *unfortunate* that Fenella had been drawn into the fringe of that circle. Lady Dorton herself was impervious to Caro's charm, but she was shrewd enough to know that such attraction was real enough. Fenella, dear child, simply had not sufficient experience to recognize the meretricious nature of Caro's attraction. Fenella was far too innocent, and Lady Dorton must think for them both.

She was a woman of her world, and although she did not wield substantial power in the level of society in which she moved, yet she had a certain standing and counted friends of worth and good sense.

Fenella, without quite knowing how it came about, was busy for the next few days in outings to Richmond, drives in Hyde Park at the fashionable hour of five in the afternoon. She went to teas, ate biscuits, and what Gunther the pastrycook called, "Fine and Common Sugar Plums." With Lady Dorton, she traveled into Wigmore Street to visit Clark & Debenham's establishment, looking at, but not purchasing, cottage twills, sarsnets, bombazines, and stuffs, as their notice proclaimed. She did not enjoy the airless shop of W. H. Botibol, where not a window was opened lest the moving air disturb the ostrich feathers that formed the plumassier's stock in trade.

She made, in Lady Dorton's company, unexceptionable visits to the menagerie in the Tower, to the Royal Academy where the swirls of color that Turner considered art were hung, and even to purchase new hats for her godmother.

Hugh Napier, a wealthy young man with Scottish connections, often rode beside Lady Dorton's carriage in the park, and Charles Portland came to Fenella's side, but there was no sign of Lord Byron, or of the Lambs, William or Caroline. Fenella had little time to ponder, but she was conscious of a lack of excitement in her days. How fortunate Caro was, in spite of her deep unhappiness, thought Fenella. To give all one's heart and soul to a love, even though a forbidden passion, must be the most exciting emotion one could feel—and she could certainly not see Hugh Napier in the light of a love past discretion!

Lady Dorton gave her little freedom. But after five days,

when it was rumored that the Melbournes had packed Caroline off to Brocket with William to act as nurse and jailer as well, Lady Dorton relented. With Caro out of London, Fenella was safe from the tarnish of her company.

The invitation from Lady Tregwyn came that morning. Lady Dorton opened it absently, congratulating herself silently on the undiminished number of invitations that came to Dorton House. It was clear that Fenella's reputation was unstained, even though she had been seen often with the unspeakable Caro Lamb in the past weeks. Trust the good sense of Society, thought Lady Dorton, to place blame where it belongs. But yet, an uneasy recollection of occasions when good sense seemed to have deserted the arbiters, so to speak, troubled her like a soft summer breeze passing lightly over a pond, leaving only a few ripples behind.

"She's owed me a party for a long time," muttered Lady Dorton, reading the missive, "and I thought she would never get around to repaying me. I was quite out of patience with her—"

"With whom, ma'am?" asked Fenella, docilely. She had become accustomed to Lady Dorton's elliptical way of speaking, beginning with unidentified pronouns and ending with conclusions, all taking for granted that her listeners knew precisely what she was talking about. Fenella had long since given up trying to keep up with Lady Dorton's swooping mind, and contented herself with questions sufficient, not to elicit facts, but merely to indicate interest.

"Lady Tregwyn, didn't I say?" Lady Dorton flourished the cream-colored vellum. "Cynthia Tregwyn wishes us to join her at a supper party at Vauxhall Gardens this very evening. There will be"—Lady Dorton referred to the paper in her hand—"half a dozen or more, no one of any seriousness, for the party is only to acquaint her nephew, up from Cornwall, with the fantastic attractions of the capital. Trust Cynthia Tregwyn to state the obvious."

Fenella's eyes shone. "Shall we be going, ma'am? I have seen the Gardens at night only once, but I should dearly love to go again. Do say we shall?"

Lady Dorton had had a sufficiency of confining stays and too-tight slippers over the past five days. She had stirred herself to go about with Fenella in tow for a purpose—and she was gratified to note that her intention of presenting Fenella unsmirched to her world had been accomplished. She set her heart now on lapsing again into the indolence that suited her temperament.

"But it's tonight!" exclaimed Lady Dorton, and then, catching sight of Fenella's lips held tightly to mask her disappointment, relented. "Well, one more night shouldn't do irreparable damage to my ribs, I should imagine."

Fenella's delight shone in her eyes. She was not one to complain, and even Lady Dorton was aware of her godchild's sweetness of disposition. But Fenella could not look forward with any degree of anticipation to another evening spent with Lady Dorton, without company.

Lady Dorton usually dozed in her chair from just after dinner until the tea tray was brought in, waking at every slightest sound, even the hushed whisper of Fenella's soft-soled slipper on the Turkey carpet. A long, boring evening in prospect, until Lady Tregwyn's welcome invitation.

"Now, child," said Lady Dorton, indulgently, "we shall go, for I could not bear to see your disappointment."

"I'm a great trial to you, ma'am," said Fenella meekly.

"Not at all, my dear. But your companions I could not say as much for. You cannot guard your reputation too carefully, my dear, lest all consider you as flighty as Lady Caroline, and then you will see all your offers whistled down the wind. Once the word gets out—"

Fenella objected. "But what word could there be, ma'am? I have truly done nothing—"

"I know that," said Lady Dorton, placing her hand on the other's. "But appearance, although I daresay it is not quite Christian to believe in rumor, is all in all, and—Well, enough said. You will begin to think that I believe all that I hear. I assure you that is not the case."

Fenella did not press the matter further. She knew that her actions had been of a pristine innocence, no matter what construction might be placed on them. It was a small comfort that Lady Dorton did not take right against her. She was grateful for her godmother's immediate support, and she knew well the force of the visible presence of Lady Dorton's respectability at her side. Lady Dorton had mentioned in the most specific terms the likely result of Lady Caroline's outrageous scene at Lady Heathcote's. A snub in public—and one might as well die. There would be no recovery from a direct cut, and if one led an exemplary life for fifty years thereafter, yet it would all be for naught.

But during the past week Fenella thought she might as well be sequestered in Morland Manor in Essex, night after night watching Grandmama napping while Aunt Kitty bent over her embroidery, as to sit in a similar chair in Lady Dorton's similar salon, watching her godmother dozing.

The day passed well enough, hot for July, and clear. The promise of fine weather for the evening held good, and at last Fenella decided on her amber gown, with only a touch of gold embroidery braiding on it. The color looked exceptionally fine on her. She allowed only her crown of auburn hair to set it off. She had few jewels, and none of them suited with this strong color.

She went along to her godmother's room to seek her approval. She tapped at the door, and Cooper, Lady Dorton's sour-faced maid, opened. "Come in, Miss Fenella," said Cooper, "but you'll not like it."

"Like what?" said Fenella, nervously. She knew Cooper blamed her for the drastic alteration in Lady Dorton's self-centered life, a life that pleased Cooper for there was little required of her but the simplest of dressing and coiffing.

"See for yourself," said Cooper sourly, adding as an afterthought, "Miss."

Indeed, the sight that met Fenella's eyes was one to dismay even a stout heart. Lady Dorton was still clad in her peignoir, and her intended gown lay unnoticed on the bed. But Lady Dorton herself had collapsed into a chair, her color an alarming ashen, her eyes closed.

Cooper snatched up a fan she had apparently just laid down, and set herself to vigorously fanning her mistress's face.

"My dear ma'am," cried Fenella. "What is this? You are ill?"

"Sick to death," said Cooper, succinctly, and inaccurately.

"I'll be all right in a moment," whispered Lady Dorton, and denied her statement by a lengthy moan. "I cannot go——"

"Of course you cannot," said Fenella stoutly. "I shall send word at once to Lady Tregwyn."

She hesitated, uncertain in the face of this unexpected *contretemps,* and pressed Lady Dorton's hand. "Don't worry, ma'am," she said softly, "I shall not leave you."

A tap at the door interrupted them. Blake, the butler, informed them that Lady Tregwyn's carriage, in fact, awaited them. "Oh, Blake, tell them——" began Fenella.

"Go, Fenella. You must not be denied just because I have a spasm of revolt of the digestion. Now," she insisted over Fenella's protests, "I wish you to go. It is not quite the thing, perhaps, but Lady Tregwyn will take care of you, and with her daughter and nephew, there could be no way for you to—" She broke off then, not quite saying, "get into trouble," but her thought was as clear as though she had shouted it.

Fenella glanced at Cooper, standing Gorgon-like over her hapless mistress, and knew well that Lady Dorton was right. Cooper would not allow Fenella within arm's length of the patient. Fenella thought darkly that it would be just like the dragon maid to bolt the door against her.

"Well, if you're sure—" Fenella said doubtfully.

Lady Dorton waved a hand vaguely. "Just go, my child. Quickly. I fear I shall be disgracefully sick in a moment."

Fenella, bowing both to circumstance and to her own strong desire for a gala evening, hurried to pick up her dark green domino and matching mask. Blake stood in the hall waiting to see her off. He watched her come down the stairs, her feet seeming hardly to touch the steps, and thought again, like thistledown, as you might say. Aloud he said, "Best not to worry, Miss Fenella. My lady will be all right in the morning. She's had attacks like this before, and not serious at all. Young folk should enjoy things, while they can."

Then, as though he feared he had said too much, he stood back stiffly.

"Thank you, Blake," she said, flashing the smile that could warm the hardest heart, and set afire a heart that was softer. She paused before the girandole mirror, and settled her domino to her satisfaction around her slim shoulders. The enveloping garment served the purpose both of protection against inclement weather, and also, since it was unadorned and of a plain color, as disguise for the wearer. The little mask in her hand would successfully keep her features from the rude gaze of the populace, and she would put it on before they reached the Gardens.

She stopped just before leaving the house. "Blake," she said, worried, "will she be all right? Should I stay and call the doctor?"

"Not at all, Miss," Blake said kindly. Then, looking at a spot just above Fenella's head, he added, "My lady did not wish to partake of this evening's expedition, I gathered?"

The dimple in her right cheek appeared momentarily. She

would not agree with Blake, for such confidence between them would derange his sense of propriety, but she understood him well enough. She contented herself with saying, demurely, "I do not know what time I shall return."

He bowed, and she left the house.

Lady Tregwyn's brougham was comfortable indeed. The footman closed the door smartly and swung up behind on the box as the coachman whipped up the horses.

Fenella sank back against the excessively comfortable squabs of Lady Tregwyn's brougham. Sophy, the lumpish Miss Tregwyn, was dispossessed of her seat beside her mother, and was forced to ride backward, along with her young cousin Ned.

They had hardly left the square when Fenella had second thoughts about the evening. Sophy bore a clear resentment at the fate—in the person of Fenella—which had placed her on the backward facing seat.

She said simply, but with foreboding, "I shall doubtless be ill," and then lapsed into determined silence.

The fourth occupant of the coach also was silent, but in Ned's case, he was simply too shy, at fourteen, for any kind of speech.

Fenella said to him, "I imagine you will not like to return to Dorset right away, will you?"

He ground out something that sounded like a lone syllable, without others to make into a word, and crouched in the corner of the seat. It was kinder, thought Fenella, to ignore him totally.

Fortunately, Lady Tregwyn made up for them all. "Too bad Lady Dorton is ill," she said, in a conventional sop to courtesy, "but then we should have been crowded during the ride, shouldn't we?" Her hand stroked the velvet cushion. "I should not have liked to arrive with my gown crumpled. So shabby, I always think. But then, I'm not like some who care not for appearances," she added, in a clear reference to Caro Lamb, Fenella realized, for she added, "But then, she's gone to the country, you know. To Brocket, and I shall not envy anyone who must be charged with keeping her there!"

Fenella, fortunately, was not required to respond, for Lady Tregwyn's voice flowed constantly on, with hardly a ripple to snare the attention. Fenella joined the others in silence, understanding why Sophy could be so uncommunicative. There was never a chance to speak, even if Sophy had something to say, a possibility that Fenella considered, and discarded.

The ride to Vauxhall was at last coming to a close. The coach took them as far as the carriageway went. They all alighted, and Fenella was gratified to note the cool breeze on the portion of her face not covered by the mask.

Nor, to Lady Tregwyn's outspoken pleasure, were their gowns rumpled, even though, as Fenella pointed out, their dominoes would cover whatever sins the ride had perpetrated on their garments.

Ned was moved to speech, a monosyllable directed at his aunt. Fenella did not perfectly hear it, but Lady Tregwyn was capable of interpreting it. "He's hungry," she announced, "so shall we go directly to our box?"

As flighty as she appeared, Lady Tregwyn knew the art of producing those items she wished for. It was a very short time to wait before the waiters came to receive their orders.

While they waited for supper, Lady Tregwyn spoke constantly to passersby, and once in a while one of her acquaintances leaned over the railing of the box to visit at more length.

Sophy was so far drawn out of herself as to leave the box and move tentatively in the direction of some strolling musicians that caught her attention, and Ned was completely enthralled by the night enchantment of the Gardens.

Fenella was content to let her thoughts run as they would. Not run, she thought, more like drift. There was no urgency to her thoughts—they ran along like beads on a thread, Aunt Kitty, Lady Dorton, Cooper's frown, Caro's blazing love for Byron, a daunting cavalier whose arrogance surpassed everything.

A passion like Caro's was frowned upon by all of society. It was as though they preferred to ignore any emotions of the more human kind, as though the propagation of the species took place in an atmosphere reminiscent of deedboxes and accounts, of ledgers and entailments. When an honest passion blazed, like a comet out of control, showering sparks upon all who were nearby, it was totally misunderstood—so thought Fenella—and considered as though it were a dangerous brush fire.

It was the way of the world, she decided, and could not be changed. But she sighed in an obscure feeling of regret that such a comet was doomed to extinction, and turned her mind to other things.

She enjoyed the mingling of smells, like no place else on earth. If she were set down, blindfolded, years hence, and told to guess where she was, she would take a deep breath and cry out, "Vauxhall Gardens!"

She fancied that nowhere else would there be that smell compounded of the scent of dry, sun-warmed turf lingering into the evening, the redolence of hot grease from the kitchens, the perfume of persons crowding the walkways, the explosive odor of fireworks.

And the bright colors! The crowds of ladies in their dominoes, in pretty pastels, the gentlemen in their plainer attire, and the soft sounds of summer laughter——

The crowd billowed and surged before their box, and then in the way of crowds, thinned for a bit before the next surge of people. In one of the moments when there were few people passing, Fenella first became aware of the odd behavior of a slender page at the edge of the walk, almost into the trees.

The page was staring strangely at her, she realized with a touch of alarm. Apparently, the page came from an affluent house, dressed as he was in scarlet with silver facings. But why did he scowl, unwinkingly, like a crimson owl, at her?

Well, she would put him out of countenance! She stared back, as unwinkingly as he. But he did not turn away, as she expected. Instead, as though he had been seeking her attention and had now obtained it, the page lifted a scarlet-clad arm and beckoned, unmistakably, demandingly, to Fenella.

2

Gervase Wakeford, Earl of Huntley, newly returned to England from the Peninsular Wars, settled his new coat by Weston on his broad shoulders, looked appraisingly at his neckcloth, tied with military precision and neatness, if not with *flair*. He wiped nonexistent dust from his new Hoby boots—and recognized with something of a start that he was once again a civilian.

Also with a sense of unreality, he realized that he was, for the first time, master of his own affairs. He was now at the age of thirty, the year in which the trusteeship of his affairs expired. Paston, the family legal adviser, was also the man entrusted by the late Earl with the affairs of his Countess, and his two sons, Gervase the elder and heir, and Hereward.

Because of Paston's clear preference for following the expressed wishes, no matter how unreasonable, of the Dowager Countess, Gervase had prevailed upon his mother to buy his commission, and set off for five years on the Peninsula.

He had exchanged one master for another, for Wellington was no easy taskmaster, but Gervase persevered and won for himself a place at the general's right hand and the esteem of his fellows.

Now, the trusteeship having expired, Gervase had come home to take up his responsibilities. He had come through the years of constant warfare unscathed, a blessing he was devoutly aware of.

"Not like poor Tom," he said to his reflection. He'd been sent off to the wars long before Gervase had gone—some petticoat involvement, Gervase remembered—and would be coming home with his left arm all but useless.

Civilian Gervase was at loose ends, this night. Newly attired in the fashion, without friends, he descended the stairs and took counsel of Crocker, the factotum who held the town house staff, meager as it was, in readiness for any member of the family who took the whim of traveling to London.

"Crocker."

"My lord?"

"What do you do of an evening?"

"M—me, my lord?" Crocker paled.

"Never mind. But—"

Manfully, Crocker strove to understand his lord's need. Not gambling, nor—possibly a woman? Crocker thought not—at any rate the women that Crocker knew best. At last, a happy thought inspired him.

"The Gardens!"

His lordship's eyebrow shot up. "At this hour, Crocker?"

"No, no, my lord. That is, I mean. Well, it's the Gardens

across the river, my lord. Vauxhall, they call it. It's a fine place, my lord, especially at night."

Gervase thought a long moment. Then, with an almost imperceptible sigh, he assented. "Why not? Even a garden would, I should think, be equipped with fresh air, and a bit of room. I confess that I find the city unbearably oppressive."

"Crowded, like," agreed Crocker. "I'll order the coach."

As Gervase entered his coach, a new one, yet unmarked with his heraldic bearings on the panels, he murmured to the coachman, "I suppose you know the direction? Yes, of course, you do."

He noted without comment that besides the coachman there were two footmen behind him on the box. He had been accustomed to moving about the lines of battle nearly alone, and here in the heart of the capital, he required a driver and two attendants. Amusing! He would not have been surprised to notice that they carried obtrusive weapons—which in fact they did.

It would take some getting used to, he thought, as the coach rumbled over cobbled streets toward the river, to pick up the ongoing affairs of a man of substance in a peaceable kingdom. He reflected, not with pleasure, upon his mother, the Dowager Countess. Clearly preferring her younger son, Hereward, she had spoiled him past recognition, and Gervase could not now remember that his mother had ever spoken with affection to her older son. Well, it couldn't be helped, he decided. Nor could he expect brotherly love from Hereward, who allowed his resentment of the heir to become palpable.

These, he sighed, were problems enough. But they were tomorrow's problems. Now he would allow himself to be diverted by the attractions of London's amusements. He toyed with the mask that Crocker had found somewhere. "All the crack, my lord, to go masked," he said.

Vauxhall Gardens burst upon Gervase like the onset of fairyland. He could not believe what he saw. The same smells that had struck Fenella an hour earlier now assailed Gervase. Far from the smells of mud, of men dying, of the unutterable filth of war—yet why did he see in his mind's eye that faraway scene so vividly?

He stopped short, unaware that Sam coachman had not yet driven away, but instead watched his lord with misgiving.

"Nickles!" said Sam in a commanding low voice. "Look yonder. His lordship—"

"Aye, daft he looks, don't he?"

There would have been no question about Sam's next move, had it been Mr. Hereward there, or even her ladyship the Dowager. Sam held no affection for either, and followed orders stolidly, even as foolish ones as her ladyship could think up, which was, according to Sam, as silly as a baby's. But the Earl, now—that was different. Sam was succumbing to the same sweet charm that had brought Gervase the blind loyalty of his men, not so long past.

"Nickles, go with him."

"But," objected the footman, thunderstruck, "he dint say so."

"_I_ say so, you silly, go after him. He's not a Bartholomew baby, that's the truth of it, but what his lordship is used to in the wars is _honest_ killing."

"What if he sees me?"

"He's not supposed to see you," snarled Sam, "but he's a trusting man. He'll get into trouble one way or another, you'll see. Hop to it."

Nickles hopped. Nothing loth, he was eager enough not to stay with the coach, listening to Sam, who thought he knew it all, and hearing Keeling's ragged snores, until reprieved by his lordship's summons.

He had lost time arguing with Sam, and now his lordship was nearly lost to view in the crowds. Nickles hastened after him, uncomfortably aware of the heavy pistol thrust into his belt, and fearing the rough edge of Sam's tongue if the master came to grief.

Unaware of his servant thrusting through the crowds behind him, Gervase strolled through the byways of Vauxhall Gardens. He had forgotten that places like this still existed.

The soft summer twilight, more deceptive than true darkness, blurred all sharpness, all clear definitions, blending everything it touched into one soft enveloping dream.

Lights twinkled in the branches of the trees, like stars captured by the reaching arms, and from somewhere came the strains of a violin. He thought he would never weary of watching the groups of pretty women, masked—how did he know they were pretty? he wondered, but he _knew_—flittering like sandpipers. The men's voices added bottom to the muted music of speech—

He moved aimlessly, easy to follow now, thought Nickles. But what was he thinking?

Even Gervase himself would have been hard put to shape his thoughts into words. But he was grateful to Crocker for sending him here. It was the most efficient way of "returning" him to England. The soft air, the muted voices, the *gentleness* of England—paler than Spain, almost faded, but this was where he belonged, not in the strong contrasts of the Peninsula.

Above all, he was entranced by the sounds of laughter. Struck by the realization that he had not heard such sweet, amused sounds since he had left England, he thought tolerantly of the world. The one word to describe all this—he stood in the path, searching his mind—was *kindly.*

Laughter, in Spain, was cruel and mocking. Even the word for laughter sounded harsh and crackling—*carcajada.* There was no way to say it that didn't set up jangling echoes.

He started forward again. Then he realized why he was thinking so strongly of battles, of his struggling, fighting men. The fireworks had begun, and the faint smell of gunpowder came to him on the breeze.

Enough of that! He turned away from the open fireworks ground, and came to the area near the pavilion. Here the aroma of suppers routed any memory of gunpowder. And there was laughter—one silvery laugh in particular that struck his fancy. He traced the sound to its source, a slim graceful girl in a green domino, her features masked of course, but the very tilt of her head bearing a suggestion of grace and delicacy.

I'm in danger of falling in love with a laugh! he told himself, and made to move on.

He longed to know the owner of such a laugh, but he saw no way to accomplish his goal. He had been sentimental in his return to England, seeing himself in his country home, a serene laughing wife, at some future time, his children around him—the dream of every Englishman. But suddenly he was conscious that his plans were altering almost as he watched them. He would find out who that young lady was—if she were betrothed, he would deal with it——

But if she were already married?

"Huntley! Is it really you?" The voice jarred his dream, shattering it.

"Lady Jersey, is it?" he said tentatively. "It has been such a long time, you must forgive me——"

"I should not have known you, I confess, had it not been for your striking resemblance to your father."

"I have been told I favor him. I consider it an honor, of course."

"Much better than the Talbots, I assure you! Although it's a great indiscretion to speak so of your mother's family. But forgive me? Your father would have done so!"

Gervase made a reply he considered adequate, but realized in a moment that Lady Jersey would not have heard whatever he said. She laid a hand on his sleeve, and said in a confidential tone, "Do you know that Byron is here tonight?" Seeing his mystified expression, she laughed softly. "Oh, my dear, you are so far out of tune with the times that it would take me a week to explain! But just this—Lord Byron is a naughty man, a poet, and Caroline Lamb has thrown her cap over the windmill for him! But then she's been rusticated—by force they do say—and he is here enjoying himself madly! That's the way of men——"

Gervase urgently sought a means to escape from this rattle-pated woman, considering some excuses that would not do in polite society.

"Watch out for highwaymen," she warned him. "All the roads are plagued with them. I cannot think why the government doesn't do something with them—all these idle veterans back from the wars. We've got to think of something to do with them."

Gervase said with a civility he did not feel, "I am sure most of us veterans will be happy to take up our former lives, Lady Jersey. If we are able to do so. I myself—"

For once, the lady blushed. "Huntley, I am so sorry——"

He bowed stiffly, and watched her leave, as though fleeing a burning city, without regret. His own company, while melancholy, was better than any he had found here tonight.

He had been immobilized by the lady for so long that Nickles allowed his vigilance to falter. His lordship might stand there talking the night away, and Nickles succumbed to temptation. Never before had he been to the Gardens, and his senses were besieged by too many sights and sounds to sort out.

How cunning the lights were in the trees—like as if the leaves themselves were bits of the stars. He heard the music that seemed to come up out of the very earth, and marveled even at the people who passed, many of them looking just alike in their voluminous coats, like—what did they call them, dominoes?

A flock of giggling girls swept past him, and he looked after them with joyous surprise. One of them, prone to mischief, pulled the girls, arms linked, back to surround poor Nickles.

"Come on, come along with us! Ready for a romp in the fields? Let's find a place—"

Giggling as they swept him away, and finding him nothing loth, his captors took him stumbling away with them, until a bit down the road, he remembered——"I've got to get back," he told them in rising alarm; "for all I know this is a trick!"

"Poor game at best!" cried one of the girls. "Let him go! We'll find a livelier one!"

They twirled him around, five pairs of hands snatching at his coat and pulling, and left him reeling. He was alone on the walk. Where was his lordship? And worse yet, which was the way the girls had taken him? He moved back along his trail, almost sobbing in his fright. Suppose this had all been a trick? A means to lure his lordship away from his protector?

The clearing where the tiers of boxes rose, aglitter with flickering lamps and twittering with voices, opened up in front of Nickles, to his vast relief. But his alarm returned at once, when he could find no sign of his lordship.

Nickles allowed his frantic fears to guide him. He searched masked faces, receiving more than one menacing growl from gentlemen he discommoded. And then he saw Gervase.

Literally bumping into him, too late he remembered Sam's orders to remain unnoticed. Nickles bounced off his lordship's stocky figure like a caroming billiard ball. He had done it all wrong! This night would live forever in his thoughts, if not his nightmares—

At a safe distance, he paused to catch his breath and look back. His lordship had not moved. He was standing half concealed in the shadows, looking toward the tier of boxes. Nickles worked out what must be the magnet that drew Lord Huntley—a miss in a green domino in the first box.

And Green Domino was staring back! Nickles smirked—his lordship wasn't wasting any time! But then, he noted that the lady was not aware of his lordship in the shadows. She was staring, true enough, but at someone else.

Nickles subsided. The ways of the nobs were unfathomable as the sea, but one thing I know. I'll not lose his lordship again this night. He gave token thanks to the Providence that had enabled him to find Lord Huntley again, and no harm done.

No harm done was perhaps the opinion of Nickles alone. Gervase's sentimental mood was evaporating. He could have fancied himself drawn by Green Domino and her silvery laugh. But the night was turning sour, and he blamed, quite rightly, his encounter with his father's onetime friend. How friendly had that relationship been? He did not remember his father well, but would never blame him if he had sought solace in other arms than the redoubtable Lady Huntley's.

Now he noted that the lady of his fancies had allowed her attention to be drawn to his vicinity. Involuntarily he drew back in the shadows. Already common sense was assuming command—better to leave the night's attractions, all of them, still in the vague ambience of dreams, rather than have them turn to ashes at close hand.

But the lady was not looking at him. Instead, he discerned that her gaze was fastened upon a figure a few yards away at his right hand—a page! It was true that the page was an object to attract the eye—scarlet livery, faced with silver. A neat figure, thought Gervase, no more than a boy by his appearance. Was it still unusual for a lady to fix her interest in a page boy? If this were an ordinary trend, then Gervase had been away too long, or not long enough.

He was surprised to find how high was the structure he had built of fancies, based upon a laugh that caught his ear. Best go home, now, and sleep away the disillusion. And leave tomorrow, he decided, for his newly inherited manor in Essex, his grandfather's home.

Then he stopped short. A prickle of uneasiness touched him, stirring the hairs on the back of his neck. It was a feeling he had had before, one he knew well. Six months ago, he would have known that French soldiers were near, creeping toward him with their guns primed and loaded.

Now—hundreds of miles from the nearest French soldier—he was convinced that his instincts still served him. He must be wary, for there was danger nearby.

But there was no indication in this peaceful scene, of Londoners taking the evening air and enjoying themselves and each other, that the slightest possibility of trouble might arise.

And yet he stiffened—and watched.

3

Fenella had eyes only for the elegantly clad page. She must be mistaken—the page could not by any conceivable means be acquainted with Fenella. Nor could there be any excuse for his impertinence.

She glared at him, facing him down. But then, surprisingly, the page again raised a scarlet-sleeved arm, in an imperious gesture, sorting strangely with the livery of subservience—and queerly feminine.

Fenella knew that page—who was no page at all. Caro Lamb! But Caro was at Brocket, closely, if affectionately, guarded by her long-suffering husband William! She was reported to be devastated by Byron's indifference, said to have taken to her bed in howling pique.

But it was more than clear that Caro Lamb was not at Brocket, no matter what her watchful family might think. She was here at Vauxhall, garbed in the scarlet and silver page's livery that fitted her boyish figure like a second skin. And she was insistently beckoning to Fenella.

A multitude of thoughts scampered hurriedly through Fenella's mind. Her godmother would be horrified if she yielded to Caro's demands. Lady Tregwyn would tell her that she risked her reputation unequivocally, were she to be seen with Caro the Scandalous. But Caro was such an ill-starred, lonely creature—

Fenella could not be sure that Caro beckoned to her. She considered snubbing Caro, but then the scarlet patch of color moved in the darkness, and she knew that Caro was perfectly capable—not from mischief but merely from an inability to see herself as others saw her—of coming after Fenella and pulling her out of the box. Hastily, Fenella raised her eyebrows and pointed to herself in inquiry. Caro nodded vigorously.

Fenella found some excuse for Sophy, who had returned. She did not at that moment know what she said, nor could she afterward remember—her thoughts were focused toward preventing Caro from making a scene here before many she knew.

Fenella slipped out of the side door of the bowfronted supper box, and stood for a moment in the shadows. She could hear Sophy's voice raised in a petulant whine behind her, and knew that Lady Tregwyn would be apprised of her absence within moments. A group of revelers passing gave her the opportunity she wished for to slip across the open space between the box she had just left, and scarlet Caro.

She spared a thought to wondering how Caro had escaped her guardians, and whether she was still deep in the throes of her bitter disillusionment with Byron. Fenella had not quite liked him from the beginning, but certainly it was beyond enough that he would brazenly cast off an earl's daughter, even though she was married, and raise a scandal the like of which had not titillated fashionable London for a decade.

She reached Caro's side, and together they withdrew into the shadows, ignoring a stocky gentleman of military carriage not far away.

"What are you doing here?" demanded Fenella in a whisper. "You're at Brocket."

"My dear, I could not abide Brocket, not while there was a chance of seeing Byron. I'd follow him forever, you know. Wherever he may go. I'd live in a cave with him—"

Practical-minded, Fenella said, "I should imagine that you would find it too damp."

Caro ignored her. "I broke the chains they bound me with at Brocket—"

"Chains?"

"The chains of Love, my dear, so much stronger than Iron."

"Caro, be sensible. You can't win Byron back—" She broke off. She had gone too far. Caro's eyes took on the flat glitter that betokened trouble.

"I should not imagine you capable of understanding the nature of a love like Byron's and mine. It is a consuming fire, you know, that will bring me in the end to a small pile of ashes." Caro considered the words she had just spoken, and apparently fancied them, for she added, "A small pile of ashes, no more than a handful that one could fling into the breeze—and there's an end of poor Caro Lamb." Swiftly altering, chameleonlike, she turned as practical as Fenella could have wished. Unfortunately, her goal was as outrageous as ever.

"Byron is here, you know. I have found out that he is still in London. He told me he was sailing at midnight last week for the Mediterranean. But he didn't. Poor fool, he was so anxious to spare me, you know."

Fenella could have put her own interpretation upon Byron's reasons, but wisely held her tongue.

"I'll be your page, Fenella. Let us go and find Byron. I wish to surprise him—"

She pulled with determination at Fenella's sleeve—"Most unpagelike, Caro!"—and together they left the clearing, turning onto one of the paths that forked off and disappeared, winding through clumps of shrubs in a way designed to furnish small stretches of privacy along the way.

"Caro—" Fenella protested once, but her companion tugged all the fiercer at her sleeve.

"Quiet! Don't let him know we're coming!"

This evening, Fenella thought, might well live in the history of London society. Already Caro's mad suicide attempt had taken on the permanence of legend. She vowed that, no matter what lay just ahead, she would cling to her anonymity and trust that she could steal away, unnoticed, unsung, and most of all, unnamed.

"We must find him before the fireworks!" whispered Caro straining ahead.

There would be a vigorous and noisy display of fireworks to end the evening, even though small spurts of explosives had spasmodically punctuated the night.

"I should hope so," rejoined Fenella. "I must be back in Lady Tregwyn's box long before then. In fact, Caro, I should go now."

She could well have elicited more response from a post than from Caro. They passed strolling groups, safe in the disguise of masks and dominoes. Neither of them noticed the sturdy gentleman following them. Nor, to do Nickles justice, did the Earl of Huntley notice his footman trailing him.

"How did you get away from Brocket?" Fenella demanded finally.

"Slipped away. The servants are all my friends, you know," she said airily. "There he is!"

There indeed, Fenella noted, was Byron. His companions, she thought thankfully, were all masculine, so there would not be any need for Caro to scratch cheeks or tear garments in a jealous rage.

They were just ahead, Byron and his friends. His limp was unmistakable, even from the rear. Caro, clearly oblivious to anyone but her quarry, cried out, "Byron!" and rushed forward to him.

After that initial cry, Fenella found that events transpired too swiftly for her to remember them with any clarity. Caro ran to Byron's side, and the lame man turned swiftly to confront her. Whether his awkward foot threw him off balance so that he fell against Caro, or whether he swung his arm out to ward her off, was uncertain. Caro cried out, falling to the ground.

Fenella screamed and ran to the fallen girl. "You beast!" she said, forgetting caution for once and allowing her true feelings to emerge. "She hadn't hurt you!"

Byron's companions, a seedy lot, muttered among themselves, "Get out of this, friend!"

Seeing them about to escape, leaving Caro helpless on the ground, Fenella threw herself on the nearest of them. "Wait!" she cried.

An arm swung, fetching a stunning blow on the side of her head and knocking her mask half awry. She fell to her knees, hearing a ringing in her ears that muffled the cries around her.

"Now you've done it, mate!"

They moved swiftly. Grabbing Byron by the arms, they all but lifted the frail, cursing figure off the ground and rushed him away from a situation that could only worsen.

Caro came to life and leaped apparently unhurt to her feet. Ignoring the companion she had suborned, she screeched and ran after her absconding lover. The pursued and the pursuing vanished around a bend, out of sight.

Fenella lay where she had fallen. Her half-open mouth tasted of wet earth, and a stinging sensation arose in the neighborhood of her left cheekbone. She would get up, she promised herself, in a moment. In the interval, she knew that someone came and knelt beside her, placing a tentative hand on her arm, as though to search for broken bones. A moan escaped her, and was answered by a muttered profanity.

Other footsteps came, responding to the shrillness of Caro's screams, and Gervase, kneeling beside Fenella, his hand on her wrist, thought quickly. He was determined to guard the girl in the green domino against any sort of trouble.

"Look you," he said, raising his voice, "the thieves went that way, around the bushes. You may be able to catch them."

After a moment, he chuckled. "Now, then, miss, they've gone. Let me help you. Can you sit up? How badly are you hurt?"

"I'm an idiot," said Fenella in a surprisingly strong voice. "I should never have let her know I saw her."

"I don't quite understand. Who were they? More importantly, who are you?"

The question brought Fenella back to a realization of her position. Lying on the ground in an undignified position, alone with a man she did not know and whose mask seemed to muffle his voice, she knew she could not return, however armed with excuse, to Lady Tregwyn, but what else could she do?

She said, "How will I ever get out of this?"

Her rescuer suggested, "Back to your box. I shall come with you, of course, and you'll be safe."

"Strangely, I do feel safe with you."

"Then, let me help you to your feet."

She swayed a bit, standing, but there were no bones broken. Her mask still hung from one string, and for the first time Gervase saw the features of the lady in the green domino. They satisfied him. He noted the pert nose, the wide, mobile mouth. He could not discover the color of her eyes, for it was dark, and moreover she refused to look up at him. But he saw the sweep of dark lashes on cream-skinned cheek, and knew that the color of the eyes made no difference.

"Can you walk?" he said at last. "Back this way?"

"No, no," she cried in sudden agitation. "I could not go back. Don't you see? Oh, it's such a coil!"

"If you won't go back to your party," began Gervase. He turned impatiently as though in search of inspiration, and found it.

"Nickles," he said with resignation.

"My lord?" Nickles responded with commendable poise, even though he had allowed Lord Huntley to discover that he had followed him as though he were a green one just up from the country.

"I suppose I should be grateful to Sam," Gervase began.

But a plan came full-blown at that moment, and Gervase was not inclined to cavil at the ways of Providence. Giving instructions to his man, Gervase turned to his charge. "I am going to send you home in my own coach," he told her.

"I couldn't put you to so much trouble," she said shakily.

"On the other hand, if you will not return to your friends, then I have no choice."

They made their way, following Nickles' instructions, toward an exit from the Gardens, where the coach was waiting for them. Sam was gratified, not that his lordship had run into trouble, but that he had been foresighted enough to send Nickles after him.

Fenella noticed that there was no crest on the panel. She glanced at her rescuer in alarm. "Who are you?" she asked. "For I shall wish to thank you——"

"And be assured that you are not being kidnapped at the same moment?" said Gervase. "You need not fear. At least, you will be better off than lying on the ground under a bush."

"Oh!" She climbed into the coach. He made to follow her, but saw her stiffen, and stopped on the step. "I shall instruct my coachman to follow your directions. You will be safe enough with him."

He dropped to the ground and shut the door. In a voice clear enough for her to hear, he instructed Sam as he had promised. "I'll take a hackney back, so you need not return here."

He watched the coach trundle off. She'd be safe with Sam, he thought, but to his great surprise he was conscious of a strong wish to be with her, at her side, defending her against all enemies, and chasing that forlorn look from the sweet face of the girl, revealed for the few moments that her mask had slipped.

Ruefully, he recalled his wish to throttle the breath out of the ruffian who had knocked his enigmatic miss to the ground. Almost as though, he realized, the brute were an infamous Frenchman!

Gervase returned to his surroundings to see, with some dismay, the anxious face of his footman who was standing a respectable distance away, watching him like an overanxious retriever.

"Well, Nickles, let us see how to find our way back to our beds. I have lost my taste for this place."

While his fancies revolved around Fenella, the lady herself found her thoughts a-riot. She had certainly never intended to fall into such a coil. An evening of the utmost respectability—that was what her godmother intended, and that was all she expected. But events had conspired against her.

She sank back against the comfortable squabs and tried to set her thoughts in order. She had certainly not expected that scarlet-clad page to be in truth Caro Lamb. The Lady Caroline, according to what the world of London knew for a fact, was at Brocket, sequestered out of sight, and, hopefully, out of mind.

But she had somehow turned up here at Vauxhall Gardens, in pursuit once more of the brute Byron. And what a truly frightful and terrifying sequence—

She closed her eyes against the real terror that had enveloped her. She could still be lying, forsaken and dying, if not dead, on the hard ground, had it not been for her rescuer. It was proof of her restored equilibrium that she could reflect on the fact that Caro had longed for the wildest romance, but it was Fenella who was rescued from an uncertain fate by a masked nobleman.

How did she know he was gently born? This coach, for one thing. It was a costly affair, even though it had no clue to his identity on the panels. Nor had she been able to catch a glimpse of his features. He wore a mask, of course. Beyond that, she had not been able to look into his face. She was so intent upon keeping her own identity secret that she kept her head down, her gaze on the ground, muffling her features in the broad collar of her domino.

How she wished she could thank him for his care of her—his rescue, his extreme consideration when he did not attempt to follow her into the coach, his—She could not think sufficiently kindly of him to give him his just due. He was a paragon—

And she did not know his name.

Nor, to her chargrin, had he insisted on hers, proof that she was simply a nameless damsel in distress, and would be forgotten by morning. Well, she thought, at least he would not be able to trace her, even if he wanted to. For she would not allow this great coach to rumble up in front of her godmother's door, so that all the square could see her alight, alone, from a closed carriage.

"Set me down, coachman," she called as they emerged into

the late-hour traffic in Piccadilly, where the Regent now lived, "near Berkeley, if you please."

She would make the rest of her way on foot, she decided.

The traffic was nearly at a standstill. Devonshire House was ablaze—dear Georgiana, Caro's aunt, must be entertaining the entire *ton* tonight.

But at last they edged past the worst of the crowd, and Fenella descended from the coach.

"Thank you," she called, her voice distorted by her mask. Sam saluted her, and watched her as she wove through the crowd of lackeys and footmen, grooms and coachmen, waiting for their lords and ladies outside Devonshire House.

Sam scratched his head, and then patted his tall hat back on his head. "I'll just see what that young lady is up to. Maybe she's no better than a light woman!"

It was wide of the mark, he was sure, but he knew that his lord would wish to hear that the miss got home safely. His virtuous decision was greatly enhanced by a lively curiosity. He threw his reins to Keeling, and stepped with majesty to the ground.

"Mind you walk them horses. Be back in a jiff, I've no doubt."

Sam the coachman disappeared in the crowd.

4

"There is simply no *reason* for this!"

Lady Dorton's *malaise* that had kept her from accompanying Fenella to the Gardens, had departed sometime in the night. But now, she thought wildly, all the ills of the world would be on her head before her nuncheon. "What have I done that I should deserve this—this ingratitude?"

"I'm sorry, ma'am," said Fenella in the meekest voice she could summon.

Lady Dorton had been in a laudanum-heavy sleep when Fenella slipped quietly into the house, unaware of the burly figure following her some distance behind. Mercifully, thought she, she would be spared any recriminations. It must have been Cooper, the jealous abigail, who had informed her ladyship that her scapegrace charge had come home unescorted and alone.

"Outside of enough!" cried Lady Dorton. "One might think you were a Paphian!"

Fenella bit her lip. She had been innocent, indeed. Preserved from harm by the kindest of men—and then to be accused so unjustly! Her eyes brimmed. She did not trust her voice sufficiently to defend herself.

"If it had not been that Lady Tregwyn sent around this morning to ascertain whether you had arrived home safely—"

Fenella suddenly found her voice. "This morning? One might have expected her—if she were as worried as she pretends to be—to have called last night. I have told you, ma'am, that I felt ill and came home."

"Without mentioning the fact to Lady Tregwyn?" Lady Dorton cried in heavy disapproval.

Fenella gave up. No use to explain, she decided, something that was indeed quite unexplainable, especially to someone who would not believe a word of it. "I'm sorry, ma'am," she repeated, and vowed to say not a word more.

Her rescuer would have had a hard time getting her out of *this* scrape!

Lady Dorton continued to mention the ungratefulness of Providence throughout the whole of that day, mollified only slightly by a note from Lady Tregwyn promising not to say anything at all to anybody about Fenella's mischancy headache.

"At least, your shabby behavior will not be trumpeted all over London!" said Lady Dorton grudgingly.

Fenella forbore to make comment. So far at least, Lady Dorton knew nothing of the very real danger which had lurked in the remote darkness of the pleasure gardens. Fenella was conscious of a strong longing to find her rescuer, and thank him once more.

But even more was she anxious to learn his identity. He was no one she knew, she was quite sure. His build, stocky yet possessed of competent grace, did not fit any of her acquaintance. There was an unusual aura about him—his coat, his equipage, all seemed new-minted. To her sorrow, there was no one she dared ask about him.

But perhaps she might see him around London. Surely he

would have entry to any house in town—his bearing told her this. Her heart lifted a bit. She would find him——

"Just to thank him," she said, alone in her room. "He is doubtless betrothed, or wed, or ugly—I'll forget him. After I thank him."

But there was no opportunity. Lady Dorton was taking no more chances with her wayward charge. All invitations were scrutinized at breakfast, and turned down.

"I do not care to go out into society yet," she said evasively. "I am not very well."

But Fenella was convinced that she was to be kept prisoner, at least until Lady Dorton's indignation had ceased to boil. In her own resentment, the figure of her rescuer ceased to intrigue, and by the end of the week, his existence had been all but forgotten.

If I were Caro Lamb, thought Fenella, I would find a way to leave Dorton House—but her practical sense asked, What would you do then?

Fenella's feelings were only slightly relieved by throwing Byron's *Childe Harold* across the room.

Fenella's forced retirement from the social scene lasted one full week. Lady Dorton improved the idle hours by dwelling at length upon Fenella's base ingratitude by causing her godmother to lose all scrap of decent reputation, varied by a theme in point-counterpoint that only Lady Dorton's impeccable name had kept Fenella from a series of dreadful *snubs*.

It was almost a relief when, at the end of a seemingly interminable week, Fenella found herself in her grandmother's mammoth traveling coach on her way back to Morland Manor. The carriage, unostentatious but, to the discerning eye, in prosperous good taste, lumbered through London at an early hour.

"Berkeley Square," Fenella identified notable places to her Aunt Kitty, sent by Lady Cleviss to fetch Fenella home. "We must turn left on Regent—"

"My dear Fenella," chided Aunt Kitty, amused, "do not forget that I had two Seasons in London."

"Dear aunt, of course I hadn't forgotten," said Fenella, not quite truthfully. "But you must observe many changes?"

"It was not so long ago as that," commented Kitty drily. It had been a waste of time, though, for Kitty nourished a *tendre* for a man no longer eligible. She never spoke of Tom anymore, and assured herself that another ten years of forgetting could banish his dear face from her dreams entirely. She concentrated now on reciting names of streets like a litany.

"Old Tyburn Road. How many tragic journeys have been made along this street! Clerkenwell——Shoreditch——we'll soon be on the high road, and leave this dirty city behind us. I hope we shall encounter no delays. I long to be at home by nightfall."

Fenella had scarcely listened. Now she said, in a small voice, "Was Grandmama *very* piqued with me?"

Kitty considered. "Not exactly *piqued*, I should say. More disappointed than angry." She laughed briefly. "You see, Lady Stover had learned—you know what an impossible *gossip* she is, not at all kind—of some of the, to put it bluntly, *escapades* of Lady Caroline Lamb. And Mama took her to task—for you may imagine that Lady Stover shared her information with a wealth of innuendoes—and said that Fenella knew far too well what was due herself and her family and would not fall into that somewhat seamy—or do I mean *steamy?*—clique—"

"Oh, dear," said Fenella, her voice muffled in her collar.

"And then came Lady Dorton's letter."

"My godmother exaggerates inordinately," Fenella pointed out. "Aunt Kitty, I am distressed that everyone puts such dreadful interpretations upon poor Caro's actions. She is in love!"

"Not the first woman in the world to feel that emotion, I think? But most keep their emotions decently hidden."

Deceitful, thought Fenella, burning with the borrowed heat of Caro Lamb's unbridled passion. She lapsed into silence, broken only by the rumble of wheels, the rhythmic hoofbeats of the four gray horses, and, infrequently, the indistinct voices of the coachman and groom on the box.

The day wore on. They made good progress, skirting Epping Forest near midday, and Kitty visibly relaxed. "We're safe now," she said. "The highwayman would never dare to stop us on such a traveled road."

"Nor in daylight," Fenella added.

"There are such terrible stories about the highwayman—he is so daring!" Kitty sighed. "They say he is a gentleman, newly turned outlaw. In only a month, he had held up *twenty* people!"

"A romantic tale," scoffed Fenella. Aunt Kitty might not

accept Caro's romance, but she was willing to believe in gentlemen outlaws!

"We shall not reach home by day, but at least we shall not be stranded in the forest." A quirk of amusement touched her. "Like babes in the woods!" Kitty, now that her fear of imminent murder was past, was able to turn her thoughts to more prosaic subjects.

"Old Lord Huntley—you remember him?"

"Of course. The invalid at Wakeford Hall. He died."

"I do not know the new Lord Huntley, at least not well. He came down to see his grandfather when he was a young lad, but then he went to the Peninsula. His mother is a Talbot. An unpleasant family as a whole."

"Well," said Fenella comfortably, "no need to disturb ourselves about them. In town we might see them often, but here, in all likelihood, we'll not see anybody at all."

"Will you regret leaving London?"

Fenella could not speak for a moment. She would regret it as though her heart were torn from her bosom—but then she remembered she had heard Caro speak so extravagantly, and smiled. She patted Kitty's hand in reassurance. "Of course. But I'll manage."

After a few miles, Kitty returned to the subject uppermost in her mind. "Lord Huntley—Gervase Wakeford, you know—or his younger brother. I do not know them at all." She added, in an altered tone, "I knew their cousin, Thomas Prentice."

Something in her voice caught Fenella's attention, but when she glanced at her aunt, she saw that Kitty was much the same as usual. A mass of fair hair, usually escaping into soft tendrils around her cheeks, crowned the soft serenity of Kitty's incomparable complexion, her kind blue eyes. Rarely was there a twinkle in the eyes, and Fenella wondered often what her aunt had been like as a girl. Was she always as faded, as gently perfumed, as though she were last year's lavender sachet?

"Hereward, I think they called him. Lord Huntley's younger brother, I mean. I remember we thought it amusing—one son with a Norman name, and the other pure Saxon. I never suspected their mother of having a sense of humor—none of the Talbots does, you know—but I do recall my dear governess telling the great deeds of Hereward the Wake—and then to learn of Hereward Wakeford! My dear, it was nearly my undoing, I promise you!"

The journey passed pleasantly enough, in drowsing, in small conversation. They passed Chelmsford in the last of the light. The full summer moon hung at their right hand, rising as it seemed directly out of a band of trees skirting the road.

"Not far to Witham now," pronounced Kitty with satisfaction. "We'll be home soon."

Just then, to put the lie to her words, the coach faltered and came to a hard stop. Fenella called out of the window. "What is it, Grimsby?"

"Naught but a bit of brush fallen across the road, miss. We'll be on our way in two jerks."

Kitty quavered, "I haven't seen a soul since we left Chelmsford."

"Grimsby says it's only brush. They'll have it cleared away in no time," Fenella said, more stoutly than she felt. Kitty's uneasiness was contagious.

How could there be brush, lying undisturbed, across a well-traveled highway? But, she recalled, this was a time of day when most folk were neatly within their houses. The full moon would likely bring out travelers taking advantage of the strong light, but just now, at dusk, there was no one on the road.

But how came the brush there? There was no wind.

Kitty shrank into her corner. Her eyes were fearful, and it was clear that she expected this hour to be her last.

"Don't be afraid, Aunt Kitty—" Fenella said futilely, but her words fell on deaf ears. Such were the rewards of a peaceful life, she thought—to be incapable of bearing the least discommoding event. Fenella would take good care not to allow such lethargy to overtake *her!*

She leaned to look again from the window. The road seemed clear now. Grimsby and the footman Wall had dragged the obstruction to the side of the road. She could make out the deeper shadow that was the mound of broken branches. But where were Grimsby and Wall? They should have returned by now.

But they did not reappear. Time stretched out. The silence around the coach suddenly seemed ominous. With a muffled word to Kitty, she opened the coach door and slipped quietly to the ground. The coach lamps scarcely illuminated the road. She moved cautiously to the front of the coach.

Suppose the servants had freakishly lost their minds—and vanished, leaving her and her aunt alone? Fenella lifted her chin. In that case, she vowed, I shall simply mount the box and drive us home!

The horses stamped impatiently. The groom Cates was holding their heads, and spoke soothingly to the animals, but the turn of his head as he peered into the darkness beyond the faint glow of the lamps was eloquent of alarm.

The shadows shifted, and Fenella caught her breath. But it was only the shadow of a tree caught up in a passing fitful breeze.

Cates heard her step and stiffened. "Oh," he said in gusty relief, "it's only you, miss. Gave me a start, you did. Best get back inside, miss. Grimsby'll be here. I hear him coming now."

His tongue, loosened by uneasiness, suddenly clove to the roof of his mouth. He uttered a strangled cry of warning to Fenella, but it was too late.

Into the faint light around the coach stepped a man who was on second look clearly not Grimsby. The coachman did not usually wear a mask, Fenella thought wildly, nor carry a gun, whereas the newcomer held in each hand a long-barreled pistol, looking as huge as one of Wellington's cannons.

He could not be a highwayman!

"A highwayman!" she squeaked. She hoped Aunt Kitty had not heard her, but her hope was vain. Within the coach could be heard the unmistakable sounds of incipient hysterics.

"Ah, a fair lady!" said the highwayman in mocking tones. But his voice was clearly that of a gentleman. Fenella was somewhat reassured. "More than I hoped for!"

"Who are you?"

A lazy laugh answered her. She could not see his face, but strangely she was not alarmed. This was such a farce! she thought. She had seen much the same story on the stage, one night. She could not remember the details, but she knew it ended happily.

"I am the new owner of all your jewels and coin," explained the masked man. "I regret that I don't have a free hand to relieve you of your baubles—especially that gold chain around your pretty neck—but I'll be satisfied if you drop them all in a scarf."

"You are not a true highwayman!" she objected, pleased to hear her voice steady. "You did not say 'Stand and Deliver!' "

"But you were already standing," pointed out the outlaw. "I suppose I could say, appropriately, 'Deliver.' But you will do that without argument."

She said, "I really can't take this seriously—"

The outlaw lifted the gun, so that the barrel's enormous eye looked directly at her. "Best believe me, lady. I am in deadly earnest."

Without another word she plucked off her bracelet, the gold chain around her neck—hurriedly, so that he would not be tempted to remove it himself—and put them into a scarf, along with what Aunt Kitty gave her with shaking hands.

The outlaw had to shove one gun into his belt, in order to open the scarf and peer, frowning, at the contents. "Not much here!"

"It's all we have!" Fenella was recovering her courage. "Where is our coachman? What have you done with him? And the footman?"

"Safely in the bushes," he informed her. "They will be restored to you in time."

The scarf and its contents disappeared inside his coat. But he seemed strangely reluctant to leave. He stepped to one side, so that he could see Fenella better. "I must apologize for the unavoidable delay in your journey. I trust you are not going far."

Fenella for the first time felt a touch of real fear. When the gun had been pointed at her, she reacted simply to the circumstance. But now, there was a more distinct chill in the air, and she thought, This is truly serious.

From the coach Aunt Kitty's moans came distressingly loud, forming an antiphonal chorus to her own thoughts. "Do not harm the servants," said Fenella swiftly.

"Where are you going?" repeated the highwayman.

"It is truly not your affair," she said stoutly. "Let Grimsby go, and we will soon be out of sight."

"But not out of mind," the outlaw responded gallantly. "In my dreams—"

"Nonsense!" she said, her voice sharpened by fear.

"You," said the outlaw to Cates. "Where are you going?"

When the groom found his voice, he told the truth, to Fenella's vexation.

Morland Manor! thought the highwayman. I made a mistake this time. But—danger is the point, after all!

At that moment, Grimsby, recovered from the slight tap on the head that had immobilized him, staggered onto the road from the shadows.

With a guttural cry, he lunged at the highwayman. But the thief had ears like a cat. Swiftly he moved. Before she knew his intention, he had taken her around the waist and swung her in front of him like a shield.

Grimsby's praiseworthy, but inept, attempt at rescue failed.

"You'll stand where you are," ordered the outlaw in a sharp voice, "else your mistress will pay the price!"

He backed away from the coach, pulling Fenella before him, backward into the shadows beyond the road. Only when the coach was hidden from their view did his arm relax, and she could catch her breath.

"Don't scream!" he said. "I mean business, you know. I have no wish to swing by the neck until dead. One word of this, one word that gets me caught, and—"

He set her on her feet. "By the stars above," he breathed in a different tone, "if I do swing for it——"

He cupped her chin in his hand, and tilted her face to look up at him. She closed her eyes lest he read her fear in them. He kissed her then, slowly, gently, his lips lingering on hers.

She could feel a response rising in her, and her eyes flew open. "Remember me," said the outlaw.

She gasped, seeking for words that would flay him. She was angry and frightened, indignant and tremulous, but before she could say a fraction of what she thought, he had vanished.

She turned back toward the road. Lifting her skirts, she knew she must run to get help, get the authorities to seek him out, and cut him down like the dog he was——

But for a reason she did not understand, she waited until she heard the clatter of hooves behind her, before she cried out to summon her servants to her aid.

5

In London, the week following Gervase Wakeford's visit to Vauxhall Gardens was a busy one. He moved in society, with a purposeful eye glancing at all young ladies of small stature and graceful ways, but he could not find his lady of the green domino.

He expected that his interest in her would wane, if he could not see her again at once, but to his surprise her pert features and her silvery laugh would not vanish. He made up his mind midway along that week—the same week when Fenella was sequestered sternly by her godmother—that find her he would.

He held in his hands faint clues, for Sam coachman had followed the lady home. But when Gervase approached the square where Sam had seen the girl safely inside, he could not make out which door had opened to her and closed behind her.

He took his problem, with some misgivings, to Paston, who had managed the Wakeford affairs for many years. He had many other affairs to deal with Paston on, and managed to insert his question in a casual fashion.

"I cannot say, my lord," said Paston with regret, "for you know I do not go much into society, but I have certain ways—yes, I may say I have certain ways to inquire. I suppose your lordship does not wish to appear in the matter?"

"There is no need to mention my name," said Gervase with some alarm. He was becoming convinced that Paston's discretion was as tight as a sieve.

"I see," said Paston with a wise nod of his head. "Very well, my lord, I shall do my best. The Wakefords, I might say, have never had cause to complain of my zeal on their behalf."

"Do not let your zeal outrun your wisdom," advised Gervase drily.

Paston saw him downstairs to his coach. "I shall send to your lordship all I find out on that certain matter," he promised. For one horrible moment Gervase thought the man was going to *wink* at him. If he does, Gervase thought, I may forget myself so far as to stretch him on the ground.

The episode left him ruffled. He was making too much of it, he told himself. Only a laugh, and the wide innocence of her eyes when her mask slipped—and he was building a dynasty on them!

He turned his attention to the affairs of his family, now for the first time under his direct control. His trustees relinquished their charge when Gervase reached his thirtieth birthday, six months ago. Now, possessed of substantial holdings in more than half a dozen counties, he undertook the formidable task of mastering the financial statements and understanding the scope of his responsibilities both to the family and to his many tenants.

Not much time to think about those innocent eyes, he concluded, with regret. But Paston was true to his promise, and late in the week brought his information to his master.

"The lady's name I have learned, my lord," he said. Enjoying the sensation that he was about to produce, he lingered on the details. "She was orphaned a few years ago, and went to live with her grandmother. And, I believe, an aunt. An impeccably well-bred lady. Not that I should have suspected your lordship of anything else. But she has been a member of Society—I should say a delightful member—for this past Season. Not a breath of scandal—but then—if there were, I should not be the one who was informed of it—" He caught Gervase's grim eye upon him, and interrupted himself. "In short, the lady's name is Miss Fenella Morland." He had saved the best till last. "She lives at Morland Manor, an estate that borders your own Wakeford Hall in Essex."

Gervase took a moment to digest this news. "And where is she staying in London?"

"Actually, nowhere, my lord."

"What!"

"She *was* staying with her godmother, Lady Dorton, but she has left for the country. I have been told—not that I believe it for a moment—nor do I wish to pass on gossip, especially concerning a lady who——" He tacked sharply to make his point. "Lady Dorton kept the young lady at home this past week. *And* Lady Cleviss's coach came to fetch her granddaughter home."

Paston finished in a blaze of triumph. Given a delicate mission to carry out, he had succeeded. Beyond that, the impact of his news upon his lordship had been gratifying. Surely Lord Huntley was the next thing to stunned.

Gervase had forgotten Paston's presence. He was in truth astounded by learning that his lady of the Gardens was a near neighbor, and he would have every chance to make her further acquaintance.

Paston interrupted, as gently as though he were only a reflection of Gervase's thoughts, "The lady is not betrothed."

Paston had meant to reassure Gervase on the subject. If Gervase were indeed interested in marrying the girl, what could be more vital to his plans than knowing that there was no impediment to his pursuit?

But instead of the information having a relaxing effect upon Gervase, it had quite the contrary. Suddenly Gervase gave Paston an arrested look, indicative of furious thought. If, according to Paston, the lady were not betrothed, then why would her grandmother summon her home so abruptly?

It was clear enough, to Gervase, that somehow the godmother had gotten wind of that episode in the Gardens. Suppose he approached Lady Dorton with the truth of the incident? That he, Gervase Wakeford, Earl of Huntley, had been in the girl's company—but then, it would be likely that he would be sent off with a warning not to call again. His own behavior, while innocent enough, yet was capable of the meanest interpretations.

If he were to recall himself to Miss Morland's acquaintance, would she fall at his feet in gratitude?

He could not decide which course to follow. It seemed to him, after reflection, that she did not recognize him. He had been masked, and his voice distorted. Even his coach had no markings to give him away.

A smile quivered on his lips, and then grew. Was it possible that she would not know him again? It was more than likely. And if so, he might well court her on his own terms, as a suitor of wealth and breeding, a near neighbor.

Suddenly he did not want her to look upon him with favor born of gratitude for his timely appearance at a crisis. His parents' marriage had been a disastrous one. From observation of it, he had wished for a wife who would love him, and to whom he could give all the devotion of which he was capable.

No—he decided abruptly. I shall not lean upon an appeal

to her undoubted gratitude. I shall simply pursue her with the single-mindedness of any man deeply in love—and he realized that he spoke true.

"Paston, well done," he said. "I'm obliged to you."

Paston spent a few moments gathering up the papers he had brought, some of which Gervase had signed, and others he had questioned and set aside for further information. He made his way to the door, and turned to say his farewell.

Gervase was staring into the fire, a slight smile hovering about his lips. "Paston," he said, "send word to Wakeford Hall to make ready for me. I shall go down in two days."

Later that day, Gervase wrote a letter to his mother. She was in Bath, he had learned, and although he had expected her to come to London to greet him after five year's absence, she had simply written a short note to tell him where she was.

"Oakbury is too isolated, and Wiltshire bores me."

Her refusal to come to London was no more than he should have expected, he knew. The note had come to him several days after his return from the war. He had read it, balled it up and flung it into the fire.

Hereward had always been her favorite. Gervase had learned that fact early, and had grown accustomed, if not resigned, to it. He himself was too much like his late father, and his mother could not forgive him for the resemblance.

Fortunately, his father had not had to endure the marriage long, for he had died in a hunting accident when Gervase was fourteen. Not for the first time did Gervase wonder about the accident. It was the only time that his father had gone hunting without inviting Gervase along——but speculation was fruitless now.

He would not make an issue of his mother's lack of welcome. But his plans required her presence at Wakeford Hall, and he couched his letter in terms that conveyed his strong wish that she join him in Essex.

"I shall hope to see my younger brother at the Hall also," he wrote, "for there are certain family matters that must soon be settled."

He also wrote to Lady Cleviss, as a near neighbor. "I shall be coming down to Wakeford Hall within a few days," he finished, "and at that time I shall take the liberty of asking if I may call upon you." He paused, pen in air. Should he mention Kitty? He faintly remembered her, but he fancied that his cousin Tom remembered her more clearly. But if he mentioned Kitty, should he also reveal that he was aware of Miss Fenella's existence? Wary of tipping his hand too soon, he closed his letter with the usual compliments, and sent it off. He had mentioned neither.

The two letters sent, he turned his mind to other matters. He had two days to spend in town before he dared descend upon his new household at Wakeford Hall.

Meanwhile, the letters were provoking, at a distance, differing responses. The letter to the Dowager Lady Huntley found her at the house she had taken in Bath. Hereward arrived, just as she was perusing her elder son's missive.

"I expected you yesterday," she said sharply.

He raised his eyebrows. "I had no idea that you were counting the days. Are the baths palling on you? You can always divert yourself by going to London."

"Never!"

"Oh, yes, I should have realized that you will not rush to London while dear Gervase is there."

"Nonsense. I shall hope I am not avoiding my son. Why should I? He knows what is due his mother at all times."

"Somehow, my dear Mama, your protest doesn't ring true. Is there any coffee in that urn?"

Lady Huntley, usually most attentive to Hereward's needs, waved a hand. "Ring for it."

Hereward, poised on the brink of a sharp question, thought better of it and retreated. He rang for the coffee. Not until he was sipping a fresh cup did he venture to ask, "What is in the letter?"

"You may well ask."

"I just did, Mama. Pray, is it a note from Paston saying you are outrageously overdrawn?"

"Worse. It is an impertinent letter from your brother."

"Impertinent? One might have thought that our illustrious general would have eradicated arrogance from Gervase's character."

"Don't talk nonsense, Hereward," said his mother, testily. "Gervase never had an ounce of arrogance."

Hereward reached for another muffin. "Do you mean to keep me in suspense, ma'am, or am I to know the contents of the letter that has ruffled your even temper?"

"He has summoned me. Not to London, but to that place in Essex where your grandfather lived."

Hereward's hand paused in the act of buttering his muffin. "Wakeford Hall?"

"Of course. And he wishes you to come too."

"That may pose a problem, ma'am. Why, after five years away, does he command our presence in Essex? I assume it is a command?"

"Read it yourself," said his fond mama. "One might have expected him to post down here to see me. After all—"

"After all," interrupted Hereward, setting down the letter, "one might have expected him to have the decency to get killed in battle."

"It would have been best," she agreed. "Even though I must sound like an unnatural mother, yet it is a constant source of aggravation to see you, my dear Hereward, scraping along as a younger brother when you are much more fit than he to be the heir."

"Mama, I do very well. And I am in no state to wish I were the heir. I should not like to fiddle around with farmers all the day long. I should not make a proper heir at all. Just give me my allowance—which I know you and Paston have made a generous one—and helped by one or two endeavors I have in hand, and I shall do fine."

But Lady Huntley was not entirely mollified. "You are more like my family than the Wakefords, thank goodness. I have never understood Gervase. So like his father—and I didn't like him either."

"Gervase does have an excruciating sense of duty, ma'am. He will take good care of the family holdings, so that you and I may enjoy the prosperity he will insure for us. Such a sense of duty, I thank God, is missing in my makeup."

His mother told him fondly, "You are more of a man than he is."

"Or perhaps more of a devil!" he retorted.

She laughed indulgently. "Now, Hereward. But that does settle it. I shall not go to Essex. Gervase needs to learn a lesson—his mother is not at his beck and call whenever he chooses to send for her."

Hereward frowned, his mouth drawn down in disapproval.

"What is it? I think I may safely deal with Gervase."

"Your normal good sense, ma'am," began Hereward, basely flattering her, "must be asleep. I think it might be well to respond to this." He tapped the letter lightly.

"What on earth for? I shall not enjoy Wakeford Hall above half, I assure you."

"But what has Gervase in his mind? That is what I am sure will occur to you. I think we need to find out what he wants."

"What could he want? Surely he can come here to tell me his wishes. Not that they would make any difference, you know."

"I've heard some things, ma'am. Rodney—you remember him—told me that my esteemed brother is considered a most formidable officer. He's not a boy anymore, begging your pardon, ma'am."

"Rodney is a rackety idiot."

"But he knows many army people. I think we must not underestimate Gervase, much as I would like to forget him altogether. He has the whip hand of us, you know, for the control of all the family fortunes is solely in his grasp."

"Not entirely, Hereward. I am still his mother, and he will not, I think, order me as he might one of his subalterns!"

Hereward paused. It was far from his wish to go to Essex, for there were certain of his activities there which would not bear the light of day. He still remembered a certain kiss from a reluctant lady who had no choice but to submit. Even though her groom had blurted out her destination, he still believed that he was in no danger of having been recognized.

But his plan had been not to return to Essex right away, at least. Now his plans were awry, thanks to his detestable brother! But although prudence dictated a long absence from the Essex roads where he was likely to come a-cropper, he could not ignore Gervase's wishes. Best he be on the scene, to keep an eye on Gervase, if nothing else.

Besides, what fun it would be to play at being the heir's devilish brother, and hug his own secret to his chest!

He looked up to see his mother's fondly anxious gaze on him. He burst out in genuine amusement. He knew just the proper word to bring his mother around to his way of thinking.

"Suppose old Gervase is getting married?"

Lady Huntley was offended. "I hope I shall know how to deal with any bride of Gervase's. In truth, I imagine Gervase himself will be more amenable if he has an innocent bride to protect!"

"Ma'am, forgive me if I say you are a true Talbot, through

and through. I shall not bring any bride of mine home to you, I assure you!"

"Now, Hereward," said his mother.

"I wonder," said Hereward, glancing quickly at her, "if there might be——No, I shall not trouble you."

"With what?"

"The worst thing that can happen," said Hereward, playing her as an angler plays a good-sized trout. "But you are well aware of that."

"Hereward, I beg of you, tell me."

"Suppose Gervase takes the bit in his teeth. He would be within his rights to leave you with only your dower."

Lady Huntley swelled with indignation. "He wouldn't dare!"

Hereward thought, but did not say, A man who has faced Napoleon's cannon for five years might well dare anything!

"I shall never allow that. I shall expect him to give me Oakbury at the least; and an increased allowance——"

Hereward, alarmed, feared he had gone too far. "Now, mama, I did not say he was getting married. We don't know. Don't antagonize him, ma'am, if you will be guided by me. Let us go down and see what he is talking about. I confess, I do not quite like the sound of that 'family matters to deal with.' We would be well advised to find out what he thinks, and then, dear ma'am, I shall leave it to you to adjust his thinking more appropriately."

Not only Hereward's own allowance was at stake, he knew, but also the generous gifts from his mother, were she to fall into straitened circumstances.

He excused himself, and left his mother to her increasingly gloomy meditations. She knew he was right, and yet she could not conceive of the plain truths that he told her. It was true that of her own she had only the small house in Yorkshire where she had lived as a girl, and an income sufficient to live comfortably in it.

She had tried to force Gervase's father to settle at least one of the substantial houses on her, and guarantee an income she might consider ample. But he had not done so, and that unfortunate hunting accident had put an end to her hopes.

She had managed to do well by cajoling Paston to advance funds as she requested, and she had become accustomed to the arrangement so that she could not readily admit the possibility of any other.

Now the best she could hope for—if Hereward were right in thinking that Gervase might be a changed man—would be a dower house and a sufficient income. Conscious of her claims on her older son, but also aware of a cold curl of doubt set in motion by Hereward, she made up her mind.

"I will go at once to Wakeford Hall. Gervase is not going to make a fool of me!"

Once again, although she did not realize it, Hereward had managed to lead her in the direction he wished.

The other letter written by Gervase in London reached Lady Cleviss, a far shrewder person than Lady Huntley. Lady Cleviss was well aware of the ways of the world. If Lord Huntley made formal notice of a call on her, one could be sure that he wanted something of her.

Not Kitty—surely Huntley was not asking for the hand of Kitty Morland. Kitty was getting past it, after all, and besides, she still mooned around about that fellow, the grandson of old Lord Huntley—what was his name, Tom Prentice? Old Prentice was a martinet from the beginning, and pulled Tom out of a growing affection for Kitty and sent him off to war. A sad affair, but done with now.

No, reflected Lady Cleviss, Huntley doesn't want Kitty. Then—

How could he want Fenella? For aught she had heard, the child had never met him. She had prattled about all her new friends and parties and routs and rides in the country until Lady Cleviss wondered that Fenella had had time in her months in London even to sleep.

But never in all the artless, innocent confidences that Fenella had made in the two days since she had returned to Morland Manor, had the name of Gervase Wakeford, Lord Huntley, come up.

None the less, Lady Cleviss promised herself one thing—if Lord Huntley wanted Fenella as his bride, then as sure as Lady Cleviss sat at her breakfast table with his letter in her hand, he would have her!

6

Morland Manor was a comfortable country residence, home of the Morlands for a number of generations, seat of the barons of Cleviss for a hundred years.

The estate had satisfied the needs of the family, and provided more than sufficient leisure for each member to follow any inborn bent that attracted them.

But it failed to have answers to questions that Fenella, during her first week at home, turned over constantly in her mind. There was little to do, and in truth she had no wish to lapse into what now seemed a dull, uneventful stream of days that stretched into an unlimited future.

The nature of the questions that plagued her most was such that she could not make inquiry for the answers. What had happened—to take one question—to Caro after Byron and his friends carried her off, shrieking? It was apparent that Caro's body had not been found on the heath, lifeless and violated, for news such as that would have penetrated even Lady Dorton's close guard.

Probably, Fenella answered her own question, Caro's family had found out that she was not at Brocket Hall, and had searched until they found her.

Fenella had a strong affection for Caro, even though the latter's behavior was mostly shocking and in all cases extreme. By a natural process, her thoughts moved on to the masked stranger who had rescued her. How kind he was! she thought in retrospect. How considerate of him to send her home in the coach, and not force his own presence on her!

Had she thanked him sufficiently? She could not recall a word that she had spoken. Her emotions had been in such turmoil—too late she had recognized the real danger in which she had been. Never before had a hand been raised to her, even in discipline by her father. Certainly she had never herself been the victim of violence before!

What would have happened had the stranger not come

along as timely as he did? Or—she shuddered—if he had been a different kind of stranger?

She would have done all differently, if it were to do again. Now he did not know who she was, nor how he could even make inquiries about her, if he wished to meet her again. She had been so clever in making the coachman set her down a short distance from her home, and she had a clear recollection now that when she had slipped into Lady Dorton's door, there had been no coach in the square. She had not been followed, she was sure.

She must needs, then, forget him. She promised herself she would, just as soon as the masked stranger removed himself from her dreams!

She picked up the new *Lady's Magazine*, and fluttered the pages idly. She tossed it on the table.

"What good are new fashions?" she asked of the air, "when I shall never again go anywhere?"

Her maid Agnes spoke from the doorway. "Best go downstairs, Miss Fenella, as soon as may be, for her ladyship is asking for you."

"What does she want?" wondered Fenella, in a mixture of curiosity and a certain dread lest rumor of her last night in Vauxhall Gardens had at last run as far as Morland Hall.

Agnes, too dignified to answer, simply held the door open, and waited.

A lively feeling in the pit of Fenella's stomach set her heart to pounding. She had little doubt that it was a guilty conscience that prodded at her, and she could only hope that the truth was not written on her forehead.

She thought with determination of other things—not the masked stranger, not Caro Lamb, nor even the unspeakable Byron. Unbidden, the highwayman slid into her thoughts.

He was not subject to summonses from his grandmama! Nor, if Fenella were not so bound by her upbringing, and so unfortunately a woman, would she be!

The naughty thought came to her as she reached the lower hall. If I were Caro Lamb, I'd be out robbing stages myself!

Lady Cleviss was waiting in the buttercup-yellow morning room. She sat in her favorite bergère chair, of mahogany, the back and seat fashioned of spiral reeding. Fenella had once ventured—when her grandmother was in town—to sit in it, but it was vastly uncomfortable. Lady Cleviss maintained that it kept one's posture properly erect.

She looked up when she saw Fenella at the door. "Come in, child," she said, pleased that her voice gave no hint of the melting love that filled her for her only grandchild.

"Good morning, Grandmama."

"I trust you are beginning to feel at home again? One cannot, you know, live on a high peak of social activity forever."

"No, Grandmama, I did not expect such a whirl to go on."

"But," said Lady Cleviss shrewdly, "you did expect it to continue through the Little Season? I imagine so, for London in the autumn is most exhilarating. Perhaps another year."

Fenella did not reply. In truth, there seemed to be nothing to say. She was aware of a faint resentment against her elders, even Aunt Kitty, for the circumstances under which she had returned to Morland Manor. It was as though everyone she knew thought the worst of her, and she had done nothing to deserve such frowns.

"Sit down there, child, opposite me. Not on the edge of your chair, Fenella! One might think you feared I might pounce on you!"

"No, Grandmama. But I am curious to learn what you wish me to do."

Lady Cleviss looked down her long aristocratic nose, a mannerism that she thought—vainly—concealed her shortness of sight. Instead, it gave the impression that she disapproved of all that her gaze fell upon, when in truth she saw scarcely half of what lay before her.

"Fenella, my dear, do I understand that you will do whatever I wish you to do?"

"I scarcely know—"

"Of course, you are well advised not to commit yourself blindly. But I have no surprises for you, my dear. All I wish for you is a happy marriage. And one, of course, of impeccable standing."

"But there is no one I shall wish to marry," objected Fenella. "I know I was a failure in London, for I attracted no one—at least no one who attracted me," she finished in a burst of honesty.

"Well, confession, so I understand, is a beneficial exercise for the soul," said Lady Cleviss after a few moments. "But a good marriage is not necessarily made in one Season. Perhaps another year in London might bring a notable success." She looked long at Fenella. The child was pale, she thought, almost as though she were brooding over dreams gone awry. It was too bad to distress her further, but the moment for plain speaking might not come again, and Lady Cleviss was ever one to seize an opportunity even when it appeared on the distant horizon.

"I must tell you, my dear, that this business of Caroline Lamb is the worst possible thing that could have happened."

"You must not believe everything that Lady Dorton told you!"

Lady Cleviss's eyebrows lifted. "You do not know what she told me," she pointed out. "Unless you have a conscience that troubles you?"

Too late, Fenella saw where her outburst had led her. She shook her head. "No, ma'am," she said, truthfully, "I have done nothing of which to be ashamed."

Lady Cleviss waited for further revelations, but none came. "I am glad to hear it," she said at last. "I did not believe that you had behaved with any but the most strict decorum. But rumor does not know you as I do, Fenella. And rumor can—if not quite *tarnish* your reputation—yet can raise questions that might better be left unasked."

"Yes, Grandmama."

Even though her grandmother said she believed in her innocence, Fenella was not convinced. How else could she explain being brought to Morland Manor in such haste? She stirred restlessly.

"All that is beside the point," resumed Lady Cleviss. "I wish to tell you that we may expect a visitor today, and I shall expect you to receive him along with me."

"Him?"

"Our neighbor Lord Huntley has written to say he is coming down to Wakeford Hall and wishes to renew my acquaintance."

"I thought he died." Surely Aunt Kitty had told her that?

"Not the old man," said her grandmother, with irritation. "Young Gervase, who has just succeeded. I think it is possible that he has it in mind to make an offer."

Fenella sat immovable in her chair. Stunned, she opened her lips and closed them again without sound. Finally, she stammered, "Off—offer, for me?"

"Certainly not for me," said Lady Cleviss with a touch of grimness. "What is it? You know him?"

"No, ma'am," said Fenella. "But then, he doesn't know me

either. Why would he want to offer for me, when he has never seen me?"

Lady Cleviss said slowly, "That did occur to me. But then, there is no guarantee that he has an offer in mind. It was only the unexpectedness of his writing to me, I suppose." She laughed shortly. "I expect it is only my own anxiety to get you married, child."

Fenella relaxed. "Are you then so anxious to be rid of me, ma'am?"

"Not at all. But I may as well tell you," said Lady Cleviss more soberly, "that this business of running with the Byron crowd in London is not something I would have wished. Lady Dorton is a fool not to have stopped you before the world had wind of it."

"But Grandmama, I did nothing—I was certainly not in Caro's pocket, as Lady Dorton said—Please, ma'am, don't think so harshly of me—" She threw herself at her grand-mother's knee.

"Now, now, Fenella, I don't think harshly of you at all. Don't cry, my dear. I shall not like you to greet Lord Hunt-ley with puffy eyes. He'll think you a watering pot for certain, and there is nothing that sends a man away with more speed than the merest hint of a lachrymose scene."

"But—"

Lady Cleviss cupped her hand under Fenella's chin. "Look at me, my dear. There, that's better. Believe me, child, I do not think you guilty of anything at all. But it is what the world chooses to think that matters. And I warn you right now, I shall be glad to have you safely married to a man who can defend your name against the world."

"But—" Fenella said again.

"For, Fenella, I know you well, and you are very dear to me. But I would be less than honest if I did not tell you now that you have more spirit than is good for you. Now then, go on upstairs with you and set your face to rights. When Lord Huntley calls, we shall see what is on his mind. But, marriage or not, I shall hope to see you the very model of a proper young lady."

Fenella went to do her grandmother's bidding. She bathed her face in cool water, and wondered whether she dared apply a light touch of rice powder to her cheeks.

She revolved in her mind the possibility of escape—and concluded sadly there was none. She could only wait numbly until her grandmother sent for her, to descend and meet the great Lord Huntley.

Gervase, now settled at Wakeford Hall, would have been appalled had he known that his letter to Lady Cleviss had so easily been deciphered. He had made up his mind to pursue the girl he had rescued, at least as far as meeting her.

He was more than ordinarily cautious, for he had weathered the military storms in the Peninsula through avoidance of the impulsive. He was uncertain, now, whether he and Fenella would suit. For the moment, his purpose went no farther than speculation.

None the less, he dressed with unusual care, and presented himself at Morland Manor. Would Fenella recognize him? He repressed a smile. When Worth ushered him into the Blue Salon, where Lady Cleviss rose to greet him, he was grateful for the training that allowed him to respond civilly, saying the appropriate things, while his thoughts were totally on Fenella.

He had braced himself to meet her, fancying her wide-eyed surprise—or, supposing she did not recognize him, picturing to himself her flustered grace when confronted by a man she did not know.

But all his fancies were in vain, for Fenella was not there. He scarcely knew how he spoke, but he could read in Lady Cleviss's manner that he had at least committed no *gaffe*.

When at last he rose to take his leave, he was rewarded. Lady Cleviss rang for Worth. "Lord Huntley, I should like to make my granddaughter known to you. After all, we are near neighbors, and our families are old friends."

Fenella, unmasked, appeared even prettier than he remembered, and younger. He wondered whether she had not, that night, escaped from her governess.

But on second thought, no school miss could look at him with such a level gaze, such a cool, impeccable aloofness in her manner. He was conscious of a daunting chill, even in the way she held her hand out to him. But as he bowed over her hand, he caught a glimpse of the curiosity leaping in her eyes, and immediately revised his impressions.

She did not recognize him, he was sure. After all, he had worn a mask, too, and his had not slipped. Besides, she had been out of the ordinary at wit's end. There was no need, he realized, for him to promise secrecy on his part about that incident, for the young lady now before him was meeting him as a stranger.

Surely there were depths in Fenella that would reward probing. He took his leave, believing that he had successfully masked his thoughts—all of them. He was nearly home before he was aware that he had come to a shattering thought. He wanted desperately to penetrate past that cool enameled exterior, and find again the appealing, excited, frightened, lovely girl he had rescued.

He had, as certain of his friends might have said, received a leveler. Struck as though by a thunderbolt, he had fallen irrevocably in love. Thank God, he reflected, I gave no hint of my feelings—I shall not wish to frighten away the innocent.

His gratitude was misplaced, for Lady Cleviss had no sooner seen Worth close the door behind her neighbor than she turned to Fenella.

"Now, then, child," she said, "we must be on our guard. Let us forget entirely that business of Caro Lamb."

"But Grandmama, I did not participate—"

"You were there," interrupted Lady Cleviss sharply, "and the world saw you together more than once. Believe me, Fenella, that is sufficient to raise questions, if nothing more."

Fenella sank into a chair and covered her face with her hands. "I swear to you—"

"No need, child," said Lady Cleviss in an altered tone. "I know you are innocent. Believe me, you could never deceive me. I know you too well. But what we must do now, and I assure you that it is in your own best interests, is to make sure that Lord Huntley believes you."

"What has he to do with me? A more dull, stodgy man I never hope to see!"

"But if he offers, Fenella—"

She put her hands in her lap and looked up at her grandmother. She read in Lady Cleviss's unyielding features that appeal was useless. If Lord Huntley wished to marry her, he would certainly have her grandmother's encouragement.

He might not have her own approval—but Fenella's heart quailed. She had not the magnificent intolerance for the ways of the world that she admired so in Caro Lamb.

And yet, she thought as she climbed the stairs to seek a haven in her own room, even Caro Lamb had been married to William, whom she affected now to despise!

So what hope was there for Fenella?

7

The day following Gervase's momentous visit to Morland
Manor, a huge traveling coach, complete with attendants on
the box, coachman handling four black horses with ease, and
three mounted and armed outriders, lumbered heavily up the
newly raked gravel drive, and halted before the doors of
Wakeford Hall.

The Dowager Lady Huntley had arrived.

Gervase emerged on the broad front steps to greet her, followed by Buston, his butler, and joined shortly by his head
groom, Bonner.

Lady Huntley's maid descended and, glancing apolo-
getically at Gervase, for whom she had always had a
fondness, turned to supervise the immense task of assisting
her mistress to alight from the coach.

Lady Huntley's voice came clearly from within the coach.
"I am stiff. Tolland, you should have rubbed my limbs. I
doubt I shall be able to walk in less than three days' time.
Tolland, give me your arm. Where is my son?"

Gervase had been immobilized by the spectacle of what
looked like all the movable goods in England arriving at his
door. He had seen Wellington's army on the march, less en-
cumbered than his mother. Now he sprang to her side.

"Oh, Gervase, it's you." He admitted his identity to her. "I
meant Hereward. Where is he?"

Hereward was at hand. He dismounted, tossed the reins to
a stableboy, and sauntered, without hurry, to his mother's
side.

"Well, Gervase?" he queried. "Back from the wars at last."

And not a moment too soon, thought Gervase. "As you
see," he spoke aloud.

"Well, we'll have a fine family reunion," laughed Hereward, "If, that is, we can get our mother on her feet."

It took some effort. Lady Huntley was indeed stiff from
her long ride. Tolland had been ordered to rub her ladyship's
limbs, and she had performed that duty faithfully, until the

coach approached Chelmsford when Lady Huntley fell asleep.

"I wonder you do not mean to kill me, Gervase," said his mother in a carrying voice, "dragging me all the way from Bath. My ailments grow worse, and I fear will never recover themselves, but you see the enormous sacrifices I am willing to undergo when you so command. I did wonder that you didn't come to Wiltshire, but then—you never were one for consideration of others, especially your poor mother, I vow—"

Gervase felt his cheeks warm in dismay. She had not changed at all. He had been mad to hope that she might at least welcome him back unharmed from the war.

Between them, he and Hereward got her up the broad shallow steps to the entrance. Lady Huntley stopped, before entering, to look around her at the graveled drive, the stretches of near lawn bordered by well-pruned bushes, and gasped, "I have always thought this place shabby above all. And my opinion has not changed."

So saying, she entered the house.

The coolness that Lady Huntley encountered in the hall was due not entirely to the dim interior heavily shaded from the sun. Buston, the butler who had served old Lord Huntley for forty years, had been won over, in a mere couple of days, to his new master. Gervase had a sweetness of disposition which would always command devotion from his soldiers, and from his servants. Buston was as fiercely partisan as any feudal liege man, and he viewed Lady Huntley with prejudiced eye.

His master's mother would receive the civility of the house, vowed Buston, and not a hap'orth more. As for his lord's brother—there was a bad 'un if ever Buston saw one.

Lady Huntley paused before entering the drawing room. "I cannot see any reason which requires my presence here, Gervase. I shall inform you at once that I shall not take on the task of refurbishing this house. These rooms have not been touched in a decade, I wager. No, it is all past me now. I have not the slightest interest in spending months in the midst of painters and upholsterers. I should not even be surprised if there were not traces of rot in the timbers."

Buston was indignant. Lord Huntley—the old lord, that is—had been ailing and feeble, but he was not witless. The house was sound, that it was!

The door closed behind the family, and Buston was at leisure to descend to the servants' hall and carry the direct-witness account of the arrival of the Dowager.

In the drawing room, the Dowager tested several chairs before she found one that held her girth comfortably. Even so, she sat upright in it as though the very touch of the mahogany arms might soil her Indian shawl.

"Now then, I have made a journey that was tedious in the extreme, I assure you, and I demand to know the reason you sent for me in such peremptory tones. Not at all," she told him in a lowering voice, "the manner in which I shall expect you to address me in the future. Have you forgotten that I am your mother?"

Gervase found that all the patience he had acquired, all the tact that dictated a civil answer on his part, was about to be strained to the limit. He was in a curious state—a part of him still curried favor with his parent, but there was within him a new awareness of his own responsibility to himself, as well.

"Not in the least, ma'am, have I forgotten," said Gervase, "even though I might have hoped for a warmer welcome upon my return to England. But I have a specific reason to be glad of your presence here."

She studied him. "Pray, what is that?"

"In due time, ma'am," said Gervase, refusing to be drawn.

Lady Huntley may have wished to bully the answer out of her elder son, but Hereward, standing just to the side, where Gervase could not see his gesture, passed her a warning look that dried the words on her tongue.

"Very well," she said at last. "I shall hope that at least the beds are not damp, but truly I do not expect to be at all comfortable."

"My staff," said Gervase with the slightest of emphasis, "is entirely at your service, ma'am."

Apparently the beds were not damp, for the Dowager, the next morning, showed no signs of a sleepless night. Gervase forbore to ask her how she had rested, for he had determined not to open any opportunities for criticism. His mother would find sufficient occasions with no help from him.

Breakfast passed peaceably enough, until the end. Buston was clearing, when Gervase said, "There will be a guest for luncheon, Buston, and no doubt he will stay overnight."

The Dowager interrupted sharply. "Who is it, Gervase?"

Mildly, he said, "Paston. He has promised me a full accounting of the trusteeship, and I am persuaded I shall not understand all his figures without several days' study on it."

His smile was pleasant, but it brought no reassurance to his mother. She had no guilty conscience, she told herself—she was certainly entitled to all the benefits of the Wakeford estates that she had received during the past five years. The trustee—Paston—had been most accommodating. She was convinced that she had nothing to fear from the most scrupulous attention to the accounting, but yet, she was uneasily aware that Gervase had altered, in small ways. She must make sure that she talked to Paston before he was closeted with Gervase.

She waylaid Paston upon his arrival. He was full of civility, even obsequiousness, but when he disappeared beyond the oaken door of Gervase's study, she realized fretfully that she had abstracted no solid promises of putting her frequent advances from the estate in the best light.

She had truly not expected Gervase to survive the fierce fighting in Spain, and since Hereward would then inherit, she had no compunction about drawing substantial amounts on her own accounting, and turning the funds over to her adored younger son.

Hereward came upon her unexpectedly. "What, ma'am? Not blue deviled so early in the morning, I shall hope?"

"Paston's in there," she told him without ceremony. "With the estate accounting."

"So? Surely this does not chill you to the bone? I had not suspected you might have a guilty conscience, ma'am?"

"Not at all," she retorted stoutly. "But I am uneasy, and I confess I know not why." She straightened in her chair. "But then, I can manage Gervase."

Hereward did not reply.

Unaware of the doubts engendered in his mother's bosom, Gervase at this moment was already poring over the accountants' sheets covered with columns of small figures. He would have a headache this night, he was sure.

Paston was at pains to justify his trusteeship. He was no fool, and while he realized that Lady Huntley had been within her rights, yet he had frowned—in private, naturally—upon certain of her demands, which he deemed excessive, but not exorbitant.

"Your instructions, my lord, if I may remind you—"

"You may."

"Were that Lady Huntley was not to be stinted in her style of living."

Did I say that? wondered Gervase. Of course I did—one last attempt to buy her affection. That is past now. But he did not convince himself. Her presence was too large, too overpowering, for him simply to divorce himself from their relationship. She had always cowed him, and perhaps she always would.

He set himself to studying the reports, asking questions as they occurred to him, and getting a good grasp on the Wakeford affairs.

"This small holding, my lord, here at Wakeford Hall does not appear in the accounting. You are aware, of course," prosed Paston, "that your grandfather kept it in his hands. He said he did not want to be turned out by the heir."

"He said that?" Gervase was hurt. "I should never have troubled him."

"Ah, but," pointed out Paston, "there was, if your lordship will forgive me, every chance that you would not survive the war, and then, of course, your younger brother would inherit the whole."

There was no more said on that subject, for both understood that Hereward would have been a mischancy heir. Even more reason, thought Gervase privately, to wed at once, and provide heirs of his own.

It was mid-afternoon before Paston and Gervase emerged from their conference, in time for their dinner engagement at the Vicar's in Witham.

Mrs. Watling, the Vicar's devoted wife, was well born. She had turned down several eligible matches in order to marry her beloved Francis—the younger son of a mere baronet—who had entered the Church. They were supremely happy, and Mrs. Watling did not dwell on the past. But she did consider herself socially qualified to invite even Lord Huntley and his party to her table.

The only other guests were Sir Edmund and Lady Stover, the squire and his wife. Sir Edmund was stout and tightly corseted, putting Gervase much in mind of the Prince Regent himself. His lady, however, bore no resemblance to the billowing females fancied by the Regent. She was thin to the point of emaciation, with a sharp nose and an attitude of distinct awe in the presence of the Dowager Lady Huntley.

Thin as she was, she put away an enormous amount of food, Gervase noted. The conversation swirled around her head, as she applied herself with single-minded concentration to the repast—three removes, with prawns, crayfish, and asparagus as well.

Gervase too was bemused, but not by the well-dressed beef à la Mantua. He scarcely touched his food. He had a strange feeling of being at once at Mrs. Watling's table, surrounded by his own family, and at the same time looking at them through the wrong end of a telescope. A telescope put—perhaps like Lord Nelson's—to his blind eye. For he suspected that he had been blind for long, and now was about to recover his vision.

He did not think he would like what he would discover.

The Watlings seemed unusually well informed. Lady Hester Stanhope had left Jerusalem with Michael Bruce, traveling with at least ten camels and four asses, friends, servants, and asses. Lady Hester slept in an enormous tent, gaudy against the dun mountains of Syria, and there seemed no question that she did not sleep alone.

It was here that Lady Stover made her single contribution to the conversation. "All Whigs are notoriously immoral." No one answered.

Later, as the party broke up, and the Wakeford coach was trundling up to the vicarage door, Gervase drew the Vicar aside. "I shall give myself the pleasure of calling upon you in a few days, when perhaps you will be able to tell me how I can best help your church."

"Lord Huntley," said the Vicar, from a full heart, "I shall anticipate your visit with the utmost gratitude."

Gervase smiled and joined his mother for the homeward ride. Thankfully, he thought, the good food and generous serving of wines had been sufficient to send Lady Huntley into a drowse, and they arrived home in silence.

Long after Paston had gone to the bedroom prepared for him, and after the house had at last settled into somnolent silence, Gervase sat in his study. He had much to think about.

It was clear that his mother had drawn her allowance with regularity, as had Hereward. But there were far too many informal withdrawings to his mother's account to make sense. The estate paid all the expenses of the house in Wiltshire where she lived, and the town house was at her disposal as well.

There was no escaping it—Gervase came to the conclusion that Hereward's allowance had been augmented by the sums their mother had demanded. Paston, he knew, would not have honored Hereward's requests for money, but Lady Huntley could—and clearly did—obtain the money for him.

There were more questions that arose on the subject of Hereward than Gervase wished to consider, at least now. The figures showed that Hereward had been made the wealthier by at least ten thousand pounds a year for the five years that Gervase had been away.

Fifty thousand pounds—almost a nabob's treasure. Fortunately, the estate could sustain such a drain. There was no possibility that he would find himself in River Tick.

The fire had died to embers, and still he sat. It was an insult—his mother's deceit, drawing the money in clear violation of the wishes of the heir. He had said his mother's needs—not Hereward's.

It was clear that she considered him of no account. The grim lines set in his face as he brooded.

All that his mother had of her own—that was not predicated on Gervase's good nature—was the small manor in Yorkshire, north of Scarborough, where she had grown up. There was also settled on her by his father at the time of their marriage, an income competent to enable her to live comfortably. All else—the house in Wiltshire, the sojourn in Bath, the London house—all else was Gervase's alone.

And he must decide what was best for those under his roof.

What would his father have done? There was no answer to that question.

There was a rocky road ahead. He hoped he would have the perseverance to win through to some kind of happiness at the end. He leaned back in his chair, closed his eyes, and the sweet innocent face of Fenella Morland smiled upon him in his dreams.

8

Although in Lady Cleviss's thoughts, guided more by wish than fact, Lord Huntley intended to offer formally for Fenella, the same conviction did not reside in her granddaughter's mind.

Fenella was in a curious state. Her weeks in London had culminated in a mammoth misunderstanding, and there was no way to set it right. She had truly been innocent of all the charges levied against Caro and her circle, but no amount of denial would convince anyone. It was true Grandmama proclaimed her belief in her innocence, yet she was moving with what could only be called indecent haste to rivet Fenella to the stodgy Lord Huntley.

Wooed by attorneys, betrothed by contract—but there was never a mention of love.

She glanced out of the corner of her eyes at Aunt Kitty. They were driving in the small chaise to the vicarage in Witham. Aunt Kitty had a light, sure touch on the reins, and a small smile touched her lips.

"You like to drive," said Fenella.

"Of course. It is one thing I do well, and there are few enough of those so that I cherish the small skills I have." She negotiated a blind turn with ease, the wheels coming no more than a foot to the hidden milepost. "But don't begin to feel sorry for me, Fenella. You will have the chance that I didn't, and it would be wrong not to grasp the opportunity to marry and set up your own household."

"But it's so—so crass!" cried Fenella. "If you mean Lord Huntley, how does he know we would suit? I swear we shall not. A duller, more uninteresting man I have not met."

"Fenella," her aunt laughed, "I am persuaded that is not the case. Do not tell me you never met Lord Alvey? Or Percy North? There is *ennui* in person!"

Fenella smiled. "I had forgotten them indeed. But then," she added, "neither of them has come to call on Grandmama."

They had reached the outskirts of Witham before Kitty took up the conversation again. "Mind, Fenella, I am not desirous of preaching to you. Mama will give you all the sermons you require. But don't let prejudice stand in your way. Don't let foolish desire for affection ruin your life. Even a humdrum marriage is better than none at all, for you will not have to bear the pity of your friends."

The tone of her voice was not bitter, but contained the ashes of bitterness overcome. Fenella could not find words to answer with, and they drove up to the vicarage gate in silence.

Mrs. Watling appeared on the front step to welcome them.

"My goodness, Miss Morland, and Fenella too! What a pleasant surprise! I've got the kettle on the boil, isn't that fortunate, and a new order of jasmine tea, quite fragrant but refreshing for a change. Do come in, and I'll just tell Annie—"

The tea, hot and delicious, provided a steaming accompaniment to the conversation. "Miss Morland has been so faithful, so helpful," Mrs. Watling told Fenella, "and many an infant in this parish sleeps warmly thanks to her kindness. But doubtless you feel, Fenella, that helping in the parish work is for old women like me. Believe me, there is need for all of us, even though Witham is not a poor parish. I thank God every night on my knees that we have not been called to a slum church. I fear I could not abide such a life. London is not all excitement, but I suppose you saw nothing of that side of the city?"

For a moment a dark memory of shrubbery, of hands raised in anger against her, of falling to the ground, assailed her. She shook herself mentally.

"There was a good deal of pleasure, as I am sure you know," said Fenella, choosing her words.

"The excitement," broke in her aunt, "was on the road down from London."

Mrs. Watling's intense interest left Fenella, to her relief, and focused on Kitty. The vicar's wife, although unquestioningly loyal to her husband, was more than frequently weary of the endless round of parish activities. She would never have confessed it to a soul, but once in a while, she dreamed of being taken captive by the Turks in the Mediterranean——

"We were robbed," said Kitty.

The effect was all she could have wished.

"Robbed!" shrieked Mrs. Watling. "Not—not truly—and by that handsome gentleman-outlaw? Tell me all about it!"

"Well, I thought we would be safe enough, for you must know that I have heard too about the latest threat to our safety. But Lady Stover had said that the outlaw had taken the outskirts of Epping Forest as his—what do they call it, beat?—and I believed that when we left Chelmsford we were safely home."

"Don't stop! Please go on," begged the Vicar's wife.

"Then it happened." Kitty, for once the unquestioned center of attention, expanded. "There was brush across the road——"

A most unwelcome intervention occurred. The Vicar himself appeared in the open doorway.

"My dear, I am so sorry to interrupt your little gossip, but I wish—"

Mrs. Watling suppressed her obvious retort with an effort. Little gossip, indeed, when the question was one of law and order in the land! She said, more mildly than she felt, "Miss Morland was telling us about her unfortunate experience with the outlaw."

The Vicar traveled his own road. "Lord Huntley has been kind enough to come to inquire about what his grandfather had done for our little church here. Unfortunately, in recent years, his health had failed so that he quite forgot the church. Quite understandable, I am sure, but then——" Understanding struck him. "Outlaw? Did I hear correctly? Miss Morland, surely you were not so insulted as to have to confront our newest threat to life and limb—"

"Miss Morland was telling us, Frances," said his lady, oppressively. Then she caught sight of the tall gentleman standing behind the Vicar. It was only, she thought vagrantly, when one saw Lord Huntley in conjunction with others that one realized how tall he was. His great breadth of shoulder gave him a stocky look which was more than a little deceptive.

"I should hate to cut Miss Morland's conversation short," observed Gervase mildly. "Pray, continue."

"A most exciting tale," Mrs. Watling remarked, irrepressibly. "You were saying, Miss Morland, that there was brush across the road?"

Thus encouraged, Kitty had no choice but to go on. She could find no fault with her audience, who listened raptly.

"Yes," she said, "the brush. Coachman pulled up, and he and one of the servants began to clear it away—"

She told her story haltingly, divesting it of all the fear and trembling she had experienced, overlooking her moaning within the coach, but dwelling heavily on Fenella's courage in facing down the outlaw.

"How brave!" cried Mrs. Watling, clasping her hands in an excess of emotion. "Fenella, my dear, how could you refrain from absolute screaming in terror? I vow I could not have done aught but hide my head under the cushions!"

Fenella did not reply. Gervase, who had been watching her during her aunt's narrative, was faintly uneasy. He could not forget her innocence at Vauxhall Gardens, a naïveté that had taken her down a garden path, alone but for that luridly garbed page—and he could not now credit her with the wisdom that was the better part of valor. Had she gotten into more trouble than was apparent from her aunt's bald story? He longed to know, to straighten out her perplexities for her, but he saw no easy way to learn the truth.

The Vicar's voice broke in on his thoughts. "You must know, Lord Huntley, that our district is beset by a bold new bandit, one whose face has not been seen, at least clearly enough for his features to be recognized."

"Masked, I suppose?"

"Of course. I should hope that we have sufficient law in these parts so that no highwayman would dare expose his features in blatant daring!"

"But we did not report this robbery," objected Kitty. "All we wished for was to reach the Manor in safety."

"You feared for your lives!" breathed Mrs. Watling, as excited as though she sat in a box at Drury Lane.

Fenella spoke for the first time. "He seemed most courteous."

"Courteous!" exploded the Vicar. "I suppose you might even call him gallant?"

Fenella, feeling chided, stared at her folded hands in her lap. Gervase was diverted for the moment noting the delicate heart shape of her face, the rounded chin, just now trembling.

"Oh, no," cried Kitty. "Not gallant. For how can he be considered so, when Grimsby was attacked, and he held poor Fenella as a hostage, don't you know?"

"*Grimsby* did?" cried Mrs. Watling.

"No, no, the outlaw did. He dragged Fenella away, and left her in the woods."

Her words produced profound silence. Then Gervase, suddenly seeming larger than before, said, "Fenella, were you hurt?" It was a symptom of his distress of mind that he called her by her first name, but no one seemed to notice.

Fenella raised her eyes to look directly at him. "I am quite all right, Lord Huntley. The outlaw only wished the servants not to shoot at him. I was in more danger from Cates than from the outlaw," she explained.

It was reasonable enough, thought Gervase, and yet he did not feel fully convinced. By the Lord Harry, if he ever got his hands on the ruffian who dared to touch his Fenella, he would—

The excess of his reaction came to him, and he subsided. Clearly the girl was not hurt. His Fenella! He had no right to think of her so, but he vowed that before he was much older, he would gain that right, in her eyes as well as the world's.

"A new man on the road?" he said to the Vicar, pleased that his voice gave no hint of the strain he felt.

"So they say. Two months ago, I think, was the first we heard of this man. Rides a horse with two white forefeet. An ease of manner that makes his victims consider him a gentleman. Though what the times are coming to when gentlemen are outlaws and highwaymen are gentlemen, I cannot say."

Gervase and the ladies took their leave at the same time. Kitty lingered behind to speak to Mrs. Watling, so that Gervase and Fenella strolled together toward the waiting chaise.

In a low voice, he asked, "Have I said aught amiss?"

She glanced quickly up at him, her green eyes wide. "Oh, no, sir. How could you?"

"It must have been a most distressing experience for you." When she did not answer, he blurted out, entirely against his will, "How I wish I could have saved you from it!"

Irresistibly, she remembered her rescuer at the Gardens. He might have spoken in just such a fashion. But he was no more to her now than a fairy prince might have been. He had saved her when she was in dire need, and then vanished out of her life. She smiled at her odd fancy—he had probably, by now, turned back into a frog!

Gervase was reassured. She had not been hurt. It was now his mission to prevent such occurrences in the future.

"Essex," he said, "is not a beehive of excitement, it is true.

Not in the least like London. But it is too bad that the only incident of moment should have been such a frightening one."

"I quite agree, sir. Essex is not like London."

He detected a kind of desolate note in her voice. He wished he were as smoothly gallant as, say, his brother Hereward. *He* would have no difficulty in indulging in a light flirtatious exchange, which meant nothing. That was the difference. Gervase was entirely serious, and flirtation was as alien to him as, for example, speaking in the Red Indian tongue.

"I should like—that is to say," fumbled Gervase, "if there is no excitement here, then we must provide our own gaiety. Perhaps we could plan—an outing?"

Fenella had not truly thought of Gervase himself—only her grandmother's conviction that he would be an entirely acceptable husband. Now she looked at him squarely. She saw a face that was set in serious lines, unaccustomed to laughter. But instinctively she also knew that he was kind. He was trying to please her, and she responded with courtesy.

"I should like that," she said simply.

"You will undoubtedly be able to inform me as to the most interesting sites to visit, for you know I am mostly a stranger to Essex."

"I too, for I did not come to live with my grandmother until only four years ago."

"Well then," he said, with a sudden smile that utterly altered his expression, "we shall explore the countryside together."

If she had it in mind to protest, she was prevented by the arrival of her aunt.

"My dear Fenella," she said hurriedly, "we have stayed much too long here. Mama will be wondering where we are."

"Miss Morland," said Gervase, "I have suggested an outing, perhaps next week if the weather continues fine. You and Miss Fenella, and we at Wakeford Hall. A day away from routine tasks will be diverting, don't you agree?"

Kitty, flustered, stammered something that he took as agreement. "Well, then, I shall send to Lady Cleviss to fix a date."

A sudden eruption of noise a little way down the street, in front of the inn, claimed their attention.

"I didn't never!" was the clearest word they could hear.

The fracas resolved itself into a creature of small stature, covered by dirt as though he had slept with pigs, and possessed of a frenzied desire to regain his liberty. He struggled with violent futility in the hands of an enormous bailiff, who held him by the arms, and was fully occupied in dodging the vicious kicks his captive favored him with.

Sir Edmund Stover, the squire, and therefore the portly representative of the King in the district, stood watching them. He glanced up when Gervase approached. "The highwayman, Lord Huntley. My man caught him in a lie-by down the road toward Chelmsford."

"A fairly unsavory lie-by," observed Gervase, wrinkling his nose. "Is he the new terror of the roads, do you think?"

Fenella and Kitty had been handed up into their chaise by the Vicar, and now had joined the two men on foot. Sir George was expansive. "Caught him for you, Miss Morland," he boomed to Kitty. "You'll not be troubled on the road again, I warrant you!"

Kitty frowned. "This man? Not our highwayman, I am sure of that." She turned to Fenella. "You don't think—"

Fenella turned away. "Sir Edmund must know—"

Gervase was filled with misgivings. Fenella's actions did not march well with her clear innocence. Clearly there was something of a mystery here, a puzzle that he must solve, whether he liked the answer or not.

"Leave it to Sir Edmund," advised Gervase. "He will see justice done, Miss Morland."

After reminding her of the outing to come, he watched the chaise move briskly down the street and turn on the road to Morland Manor. Then he turned to the squire.

Gervase made some searching inquiries of the prisoner, and when he was through, he exchanged a long look with Sir Edmund. The latter nodded. "Right you are, Lord Huntley. This one's not the one. Though, mind you, I am sure he's done something illegal, and if I knew what, he'd be in gaol sooner'n Christmas, if not for worse." He looked at his prisoner sourly. "If he's not gallows bait, I never saw one. Ah well, I hope I know my duty to the King's justice. Let him go."

The bailiff, reluctantly, released his grip on the dirty creature. Gervase thought he'd be gone like a shot, out of reach and out of sight, before Justice changed her mind.

But he lingered, hesitating, and then blurted out to Gervase, "You're a real gent, you are. So I'll tell you this—word is, a real high-toned nob has moved in on the territory. Nobuddy asked him, and he ain't what yer'd call welcome, but he's not that easy to say get out and be damned to." He spat to leeward, just missing the bailiff's boots. "He jist showed up and did a few, but now nobuddy's seen aught of him for a week. Ain't missed none, I'll say that. He's mean, your ludship, real mean."

Gervase had much to think about as he rode toward Wakeford Hall. He set his mount to a slow lope, a gait he found conducive to serious thought. By the time he turned into the drive leading to his own front entrance, he had sorted out certain goals in order of their urgency. His future just ahead might contain some rocky terrain to cover, but light over the ground would bring him through.

He tossed the reins to a stable boy, and entered his house. Of all the manors at his disposal, he was learning to like Wakeford Hall best. No wonder his grandfather had held on to this small estate when he turned the remainder of Wakeford lands over to Gervase's trustee.

The house was small in comparison to Oakley in Wiltshire, or the town house, or the ancient seat of his grandmother's family, now part of the Wakeford holdings, a magnificent old mansion whose foundations were laid in the time of Henry the Seventh, and whose additions sprawled over several acres just outside West Wycombe with a splendid view of the Chiltern Hills.

Wakeford Hall was comfortable, with large, airy, sun-filled rooms. He hoped Fenella would grow as fond of it as he was.

His thoughts of Fenella were rudely jostled as he paused on the threshold of the best parlor. Lady Huntley was enthroned on the sofa, one maid carrying a tray filled with teapot, cup, and plates of assorted comfits. Another maid was arranging a rug across the Dowager's knees, to an accompaniment of complaints, and Buston, stiffly aloof, supervised the activity.

"Oh, there you are, Gervase. I cannot think what you can find to do in this forsaken place that takes you away for hours. I no longer wonder at your neglect of your mother, Gervase, for I assure you I have long since become accustomed to your lack of filial duty. But I do not complain, you know. Just a trifle more tea, if it's hot, for I do dislike a dish of cold tea."

This last remark was made to the servant. Gervase glanced at Buston, and read there the traces of incipient mutiny. Clearly his intervention was called for.

"Buston, I shall be much obliged to you if you would send someone to fetch Warrod to me." Buston bowed and went out, clearly delivered from a hated prison.

"Trust old Gervase," said Hereward from the far corner of the room, "to put duty before pleasure."

"Hereward, I did not see you at first. I assure you that duty is ever uppermost in my mind."

"Of course. I find this atmosphere stifling, Brother, and wonder how you can abide it. No cannons, no martial music? Just sheep." His voice was heavy with mockery.

"Not everyone defines duty the same," said Gervase mildly. "But I do not intend to discuss the finer points of philosophy with you."

"You surprise me," said Hereward drily. "In that case, you will not object if I leave Wakeford?"

"Leave? I shall hope to have your company again soon," said Gervase, "as soon, in fact, as three days hence."

"Is that an order?"

Gervase looked levelly at him, and did not like what he saw. His brother had long been cosseted by their mother, and the soft indulgence had done him no good. He was truly a wastrel and a rake—gambling and women were two of his more harmless diversions, he had learned from certain inquiries set afoot in London—and Gervase could expect no good of him. He might well have to deal with his brother eventually, but he had too much else to do first.

"Let us say," he said with a tight smile, "a strong request. For we have much business yet to discuss."

Hereward reflected for a moment. Defiance was his nature, but a certain element, not of prudence, but of caution, entered into his consideration. Gervase had the power of the purse strings, and this was no time for quixotic rebellion. "I will return, dear Brother, set your mind at ease on that point."

Gervase bowed in acknowledgment.

Might as well do the thing handsomely, thought Hereward. "I'll just go over to Cambridge for a couple of days. By the way, Brother, I've sent for my yacht to come to anchor at Cogges Cove. My skipper will send word here, when he arrives."

"Yacht? A new acquisition, I assume."

Hereward assured him, "I paid for it, don't worry."

Mildly, Gervase said, "I have no intention of worrying about you."

He left the parlor, leaving Hereward to decipher whatever meaning he might find in the equivocal words. "Do you think, Mama, that he will not worry whether I eat or not? Does this mean—and I fear well it might—that my allowance is to be cut?" His eyes narrowed as he looked after his older brother. "I shall not like that above half."

Lady Huntley had dismissed the servants. "In the greatest confidence, Hereward, I will assure you that nothing will go awry. I shall see that Gervase does not forget his duty to you."

"Yes, Mama, but do you know, I wonder whether Gervase has not changed more than we think?"

"Nonsense," said Lady Huntley. "A mother always knows her own children. Pray hand me another of those macaroons."

Gervase, in the study, had all but forgotten Hereward. His mother was on his mind, to the exclusion of all else for the moment. He needed her here, for the purposes of adding her approval in the conventions of his courtship of Fenella. It would be shabby in the extreme if Lady Huntley refused to take her traditional role in the marriage festivities. Suppose she were to retire in anger to Bath?

He had no great trust in her compliance. He would have to make sure that his wishes were carried out.

She and Hereward were his only relatives, except for his cousin Tom Prentice and his sister. He had seen Tom briefly before his own departure for England. Tom had been grievously wounded, by the French, and was in hospital in Lisbon. His cousin's attitude had been disturbing—almost as though he didn't care whether he lived or not. Surely it was not the almost total uselessness of his left arm as a result of his wounds that had caused him such despondency?

Tom was to have returned to England the week after Gervase. He was doubtless now at home, in the dubious care of his sister Amelia, who was a positive antidote! Tom would be a pleasant companion, and much better off here than at home.

Gervase drew pen and paper to him, and began to write. He tapped the pen against his teeth, just before he came to the end of his invitation. Should he mention his own hopes of taking a bride?

The odd memory came to him—Tom had once wished to marry, but his odious father had come between them and sent Tom off to the war. Even though that had been the better part of fifteen years ago, Gervase was too kind to mention his own expectations of happiness.

Besides, he wanted his betrothal *settled*. Lady Cleviss had given him to understand that his offer would be welcome, and this afternoon Fenella had not seemed to hold him in adversion.

He signed the letter to Tom.

His prospects had never looked brighter.

9

Lady Huntley was entirely satisfied with her life. She was not overly perceptive, rarely saw a viewpoint other than her own, and therefore did not suffer the qualms of self-doubt.

She had always been a figure of authority, she deemed, and especially so to Gervase. So much like his father he was, she thought, that she might well disregard his wishes as she had her late husband's.

She had not come, of course, to Wakeford Hall out of consideration for Gervase's position. She did not trouble herself to make even a token submission to his expressed wishes. Instead, she informed him, at the beginning, that she had come simply out of curiosity.

She recalled, however, Hereward's doubts about his elder brother. Had the Peninsular Wars changed Gervase as much as Hereward would have her believe? She could not countenance any alteration in the current status. She was Huntley's mother, and she would exact from him the respect and docility he owed her.

She passed a sleepless night. Hereward's hints, like unseen thorns in the shoe, rubbed against her peace of mind, and she could not help but remember that Hereward spoke only the truth when he pointed out that she was entirely dependent on

Gervase for the lavish funds she had become accustomed to. All that was her own was a small cottage of no more than fifteen rooms in Yorkshire, a cold and damp country that she had left behind with heartfelt gratitude on the occasion of her marriage more than thirty years before.

It would be as well to obtain from Gervase certain assurances as to her future financial comfort, in legal form, of course, without possibility of alteration.

By the time she fell asleep, toward morning, she promised herself to see that Gervase fulfilled his duty toward her at once. Never one to rely on defense of a position, however impregnable, she resolved to go on the offensive, at her first opportunity.

At breakfast the next morning, since the opportunity did not clearly present itself, she ignored the lack.

Gervase rose from the breakfast table. He rarely spoke at breakfast, and in truth found it most difficult to carry on a conversation with his mother at any time. It seemed to him that the two of them had no point of common interest—not even the small change of gossip, for he knew none of the people who filled her life, and she cared naught for his friends.

This morning, she stopped him before he reached the door. "Gervase, I suppose you are about to go out for the day, and leave me entirely alone?" He half turned, his hand on the latch, and waited. "I hope I have not come away from Bath only to sit in this forsaken house with no company, and no entertainment in prospect?"

"No, ma'am," said Gervase. "Not only for that."

"My intellect has never been called defective, and I imagine I can comprehend as well as the next, but I confess that the reason for my being here at Wakeford Hall—a house, I must point out, that was never my favorite, and indeed I made no objection when your grandfather decided to keep it out of the estate until his demise—the reason, I say, completely escapes me."

He turned over a number of possible answers, but decided—coward that I am, he thought—on equivocation.

"One might imagine, ma'am, that you could divert yourself in the midst of your family?"

She laughed, a short sound without amusement. "One son left to amuse himself elsewhere, and the other—you, Gervase—off on your own affairs from dawn to dusk."

"I should not have to remind you," he said meekly, "that my own affairs, as you call them, provide the prosperity with which we are all blessed."

If there was a barb in his remark, she chose not to recognize it. "I shall not wish to stay overlong away from Bath."

With real curiosity, he came back and sat at the table, asking, "What would you do in Bath, or in fact, at Oakley?"

"I shall not hope to make you understand the delight I take in my visits to drink the waters in the Pump Room, the strolls on the Promenade, meeting my friends—all manner of things. I vow we laugh all day long."

And shred reputations by the coachload, he thought, and wisely did not say.

"But here, I cannot pretend I am happy. There is nothing to do!"

"On the contrary," said her elder son. "I wish you to call on Lady Cleviss, my near neighbor at Morland Hall."

"I do not know her."

"That is the purpose of your calling, ma'am. Tomorrow afternoon at three would be a suitable time."

Musing, she said, "I suppose one should call. I should not like her to feel that I scorned to make her acquaintance."

He warned, "I hope you will not succumb to an expression of scorn, for Lady Cleviss's grandfather was a duke, and was well known for his ability to put people in their places. I have heard that Lady Cleviss resembles him greatly."

His mother pursed her lips. "On second thought, I shall not trouble myself to begin an acquaintance with her—or anyone else, for that matter. For I shall not remain here long enough to undertake an entire social involvement."

Gervase said nothing at first. He had expected to postpone a confrontation with his mother until he was better prepared, but she had precipitated this discussion, and he must make the best of it.

After a moment he smiled. Unwilling to disclose his underlying purpose, he simply said, "I'm sorry." He regretted causing his mother unhappiness in being from home, and for putting her to the trouble of making the call that was necessary to his courtship of Fenella.

She did not answer him, and he rose to leave. The subject was clearly closed, and his mother changed the tenor of her remarks. "Where has Hereward gone, I wonder? I hope he shall return in a day or two. I wish him to escort me to Bath."

Although Gervase did not know it, her sprightly prattle was evidence of her firm conviction that she had succeeded in putting Gervase in his place. He had apologized—so she interpreted his remark—for bothering her even to think about calling on Lady Cleviss. She had no intention now of succumbing to any small diversion proffered as a sop. "If only Hereward doesn't decide to go off in his little boat."

Gervase left her, a sour taste suddenly in his mouth. He could never get along with his mother. She would not change, and he had changed too much. He entered his study to find Warrod waiting for him. For the moment he had forgotten the affairs that lay on his desk, ready to discuss with his factor.

Warrod rose, a hulk of a man with a beefy, red face from years of exposure to all weathers, and a slowness of manner that was exceedingly deceptive. He had a countryman's born shrewdness, and a burning curiosity to experiment with some of the new ways of farming that he had heard about. The old Lord Huntley, bless his soul, had been too old and too ill to trouble himself, but Warrod had done his best to keep the Essex farms in good order. Now, he thanked God, the new earl seemed willing to give him full rein. Warrod was ready.

"Morning, my lord. I may be a bit early on the job, here, but I worked out all this last night and thought to show it to you just as soon as I could get here."

Receiving Gervase's nod, he spread out some papers on the desk, sheets covered in a fair round hand. "Here's the diagram of the upper fields I made out. Likely they're not drawn like you'd be used to, my lord, but you can see plain what it is—"

He had plans for winter feeding—"I asked around, and over Thaxted way there's a pure strain of Southdown for sale. Might have to go as far as Saffron Walden if we get the half-breeds we mentioned. Part Norfolk, you know. Half again as many lambs."

His voice trailed away as he perceived that his audience was not listening. His features showed no trace of the disappointment he felt. He had had high hopes of the new master, for his own hopes and dreams for the farms had been drawn from him with skill, and Gervase had expressed sympathy with him. He had worked half the night, nearly aquiver with enthusiasm, and his reception was daunting in the extreme.

Gervase looked up. "Warrod, my apologies," he said quickly. "My mind is not on this very fine work you've done."

Mollified, Warrod relaxed, and began to gather up his plans.

"No, Warrod, leave the papers with me. I'll look them over a bit later. Just now I wonder what you can tell me about Cogges Cove. A small boat is supposed to anchor there, and I confess I'm curious about it."

He wondered whether he should give a reason to Warrod for his interest. A fictitious reason of course, but he could think of none. An excuse was not needed, as it happened. He caught Warrod's eye, and read comprehension therein. Warrod was no fool.

"Just find out about the little boat, if you please. Is it a yacht, or what?"

Warrod nodded. He wondered whether it lay within his duties to inform Lord Huntley that his younger brother had been seen traveling the roads at night. It would seem to Warrod that, since Hereward's arrival a few days before, he had not spent a single night decently in his bed. For the moment, Warrod decided to hold his peace.

"Aye, my lord, 'tis less than an hour's ride to the Cove, and I'll just ask around a bit."

The next day at nuncheon, Gervase expressed surprise. "Ma'am," he said to his mother, "how is it I see you are not dressed for calling?"

"Calling?" Lady Huntley was aghast. She had informed him that she would not call on Lady Cleviss, and had thought the subject closed. Was it all to do again?

"I told you," she said oppressively, "that I would not call on your neighbor. I am going to Bath, as I said—"

To her total astonishment, her son, for perhaps the first time in his life, interrupted her. "I have no objection, ma'am, to your removal to Bath. After my marriage."

"Marriage! This is the first I have heard of any marriage! I must say I cannot approve of any marriage made on such short notice. I truly cannot approve——" A horrid thought struck her. "Good God, Gervase, you are not marrying Lady Cleviss?"

"Not at all. I hope I am not such a fool as you think me. I intend to marry Miss Fenella Morland."

Lady Huntley then, losing her wits from the shock of her son's news, made a serious mistake. "Without asking *me?*" She saw her error at once. Gervase's gray eyes took on the bleakness of the North Sea in winter. "Well, of course, I know my duty, Gervase, but you cannot have perfectly understood. You have been away for some time—"

"Five years," said Gervase.

"Yes, of course. Five years. And you are out of touch with the world. How many beautiful, wealthy, eligible young ladies there are! And you cannot have become acquainted with any of them. Gervase, I wonder what maggot is in your brain now? For I tell you at once, I do not like this hasty arrangement. It seems most ramshackle to me."

He had set his fork down. The mouthful he had swallowed stuck now in his throat. This was worse than his darkest imaginings, worse than anything he remembered of his mother's opposing him.

His lack of response led her to believe that she was making headway in persuading him to her point of view. She modified her tone. "Let us forget this unfortunate incident," she said, less harshly. "Let us plan to be in London in September. The Little Season will give you a good look at what you have missed by this—this action I can only call foolish. I'll give parties, we'll open the town house—"

She was interrupted by a voice from the doorway.

"What a happy prospect!" drawled Hereward.

"You're back!" cried his mother.

"As you see. Gervase, you are not pleased to see me? And I thought you were most urgent about my prompt return. So here I am, you see, well before my time."

"Just in time," cried Lady Huntley, "for you must know the great shock Gervase has given me. He is to be married!"

"Truly?"

"He wishes to marry the Morland girl. But I insist that we must do our duty by him, Hereward. We shall go to London in six weeks, and begin to renew our acquaintance with the *ton*. I confess I have been out of society for some time, content in my own small circle, but I will make every sacrifice for the sake of the family—"

While she was speaking, Gervase, thoroughly miserable, rose from the table and moved toward the door. He stopped in the doorway and waited. Hereward eyed him shrewdly, and gestured to the Dowager.

"I've ordered the carriage, ma'am, for three o'clock," said Gervase.

Lady Huntley stared at him. "So soon? I must have more time, Gervase. Even to return to Bath, I shall not be able to leave until tomorrow, and that will rush me sadly. Not time enough, Gervase. I should not have expected any consideration from you, but this is beyond enough."

"Time, ma'am?" Gervase raised an eyebrow. "It requires only a quarter of an hour to Morland Manor."

He was gone, leaving silence behind.

Hereward was the first to move. He sat down at the table, and surveyed the broken dishes. "Isn't there any food to eat?" he complained.

They were silent until Buston had brought replenishments and departed.

The Dowager demanded, "Where were you?"

"Don't you know a lady should never display curiosity about a gentleman's whereabouts? So vulgar."

"Pray do not insult me, Hereward. I have had all the shocks my delicate nerves can support. Some village girl, I suppose?"

He smiled, letting her think so. The loot from the night's activity rested in his saddlebag for the moment, and his thoughts turned to a safer repository.

"What _is_ all this?" he asked eventually. "At odds with old Gervase already?"

"I cannot think what has come over him," she began, and continued with a litany of her lacerated feelings.

Hereward, mentally, counted up the total of his illegal enterprise's profits to date. With satisfaction he reviewed his plans, and realized that he was more than three-quarters of the way toward his goal, a sum that would give him total independence were he to remove to the Mediterranean. He had grown inexpressibly weary of England, an emotion that was reciprocated by most of his former friends. There was no place in England for him, he believed, and he would show this country a clean pair of heels——

"You are not listening, Hereward," his mother accused.

"Of course I was," he said falsely. "What you truly mean is that Gervase is going to marry, and the prospect is dreary in the extreme. The town house will no longer be available to you, the stone cottage in West Wycombe—"

"Stone cottage? Beech Grove has more than twenty bedrooms!"

Hereward warmed to his fancy. "You will probably have to take rooms in London—"

"Hereward, your sense of humor is out of hand," his mother scolded, not seriously. "Well, I promise you that Gervase will recover from this brainstorm. I have noticed that young men back from the war take time to settle down."

"Truly? I would have said just the opposite of Gervase. He has settled down with a vengeance, already all but betrothed. I suppose I am correct in assuming that the notice has not yet been sent?"

"Nor will be," promised the Dowager with a frown.

"I should not venture to advise you, ma'am," advised Hereward, "but I am sure it has occurred to you that it may be best to see exactly the extent of my dear brother's expectations? It would not do, you know, to live in daily expectation of another shocking revelation. We should never know when we might consider the danger past, should we?"

Lady Huntley smiled fondly on her younger son. "How wise you are, Hereward! I vow I shall never know how to go on without you. If you will go with me, this afternoon, I shall make the call on Lady Cleviss. And Gervase must be brought to admit his error."

Hereward lifted an eyebrow. "Stop the marriage? I cannot see how you may accomplish that!"

"Not at all," said Lady Huntley, once more serene. "I shall merely endeavor to bring dear Gervase to his senses. I promise you, he will not wed the Morland girl."

10

Fenella, apprised of the imminent visit of the Dowager Countess, felt as though iron doors were clanging shut behind her.

Accustomed only to kind affection from her grandmother,

who had welcomed the bereft orphan four years before, she was now shocked, and indeed deeply hurt, to discover another facet of Lady Cleviss's character, an aspect she could not like.

Fenella received the news of the approaching visit from her grandmother, seated at her white French desk in the morning room, recently redecorated in a soft rose shade most becoming to aging beauty. The cheerful hue did not invade Fenella's thoughts.

"Lord Huntley has sent word, my child, that his mother is calling upon us this afternoon." Lady Cleviss referred to the creamy letterpaper in her hand. "Yes, at three o'clock. I shall wish you to be dressed in a suitable manner, Fenella."

"B—but Lady Huntley is calling on you, Grandmama?"

"Upon both of us," emphasized her grandmother, with a distinct air of triumph. "You see that I was right. Huntley does intend to offer for you."

"A mere afternoon call—"

"Means much, under the circumstances. Lady Huntley is newly here in residence, and she should expect us to call on her in the first instance. The fact that the Countess comes to see us has distinct overtones—" She broke off abruptly. "How can I ever teach you all there is to learn about the ways of society? I vow it is impossible! One simply has to observe." She leaned forward. "Observe, Fenella! And think about what you see. That is the way to learn. I shall be most happy when your future is settled satisfactorily."

"You think that I shall be happy with Lord Huntley?" protested Fenella in a small voice.

"It's up to you," said Lady Cleviss surprisingly. "Your marriage will be happy or not, as you choose to make it. After all, the wife is half of a household, you know, and if your household is managed so as to make all under your roof content, then you must needs be so, as well."

Fenella was not convinced. "But suppose—"

"Suppose nothing, Fenella. I confess I am much surprised at your reluctance. Huntley has wealth beyond counting, an excellent reputation, an elegant manner. What more could you wish for?"

"I do not think we shall suit at all," Fenella replied stubbornly.

Lady Cleviss said, in a minatory tone, "Then what *do* you wish for?"

Fenella took the bit in her teeth. "I have no wish to marry at all."

"I suppose," said Lady Cleviss after an ominous silence, "that you wish to finish your days like Kitty? Love, she said it was when she developed a most unfortunate attachment to old Wakeford's grandson, the Prentice boy. His father put a stop to any pretensions there, and now my dear girl is drying up with heartbreak. You prefer that to a productive and happy marriage? If you do, you've the brains of a peahen!"

Fenella made one last gallant defense. "I cannot like him. He is too austere, too unsmiling."

"Too dull, I suppose you mean." Lady Cleviss drummed her fingers on the desk. "This is precisely why you will accept him. If he offers, that is. You cannot like Huntley? I must tell you that I cannot like what I have heard from Lady Dorton." She pointed to a thick letter, clearly just received, on the corner of the desk. "All of London, she says, is in an uproar over that idiot Lamb woman. Your foolish seeking after meretricious excitement in London—Fenella, I shudder when I think of your foolishness."

"Ma'am, I have done nothing wrong, I swear to you!"

"I believe you," said Lady Cleviss slowly. "But I am not the world, my child. Even the Lambs cannot keep William's wife respectable, for old Lord Melbourne is under the cat's-foot himself—"

"And Lady Melbourne hates Caro!" Fenella cried with some resentment.

Lady Cleviss pondered for a moment. Should she reveal to Fenella the appalling revelations made to her in Lady Dorton's letter? She dreaded to see the wounded expression that would surely leap into Fenella's face, but then, she loved the girl too much to deceive her. "Lady Dorton tells me that you stole into the house, late at night, with no sign of escort, and no word to your hostess that you were going home—Fenella, I have never been so shocked at such loose behavior! And to think, my own granddaughter!"

Fenella stared at her hands, folded in her lap so tightly that the knuckles showed white. How could she ever establish her innocence? On the one hand, her grandmother professed to believe her, and on the other hand her actions indicated no such trust. How she wished that she had stayed home that night, instead of seeking relief from the dullness of an evening alone in Lady Dorton's parlor!

"You see why I wish you respectably settled, Fenella. That wayward streak you received from your mother's family will lead you into more trouble than I wish to contemplate."

"B–but—"

"No buts, child. I do believe that your reputation is as yet untarnished, but you will not return to London, you know. Lady Dorton will not accept you again, nor will I trust her. Now, child," said Lady Cleviss, adopting a coaxing note, "no need to be blue deviled at all. I simply ask you to receive the Dowager with me, and mind your manners. Surely that is not too much to ask?"

Fenella was not proof against the love and gratitude she bore her grandmother. "No, ma'am, of course not."

"That's my dear girl. Now run along, and make yourself presentable." As Fenella reached the doorway, Lady Cleviss stopped her. She said, almost as though reading Fenella's mind, "Now, child, I know there is no wildness in you. You must not think I spoke unkindly of your mother. She was a delightful creature, but most impulsive, thoughtless of consequences. I see no waywardness in you, I thank God."

"Thank you, Grandmama."

"I simply wish to see you settled while I am still here to arrange it. I shall not be comfortable until I know that you are provided for. Now, my dear, run along."

Obediently, Fenella climbed the stairs and donned a suitable gown, a pale green, round gown with a tiny, dark green fern leaf embroidered in a random pattern in the fabric. But her thoughts were heavy with the image of withering Aunt Kitty. She herself had said more than once that marriage should be a cherished goal. Was she speaking from her own conviction, or simply to augment Grandmama's opinions?

The alternatives were equally unattractive. Either to fade as Aunt Kitty had, doing good deeds and running errands for Lady Cleviss, or to put her life into the keeping of an oppressively dull husband.

There was little to choose between. But by the time Grandmama sent for her to greet Lady Huntley in the drawing room, Fenella had remembered Caro Lamb. She had not been hampered by her marriage. And besides, thought Fenella in a burst of unwarranted optimism, perhaps dull, stiff, proper Gervase Wakeford, Lord Huntley, had no intention of offering for her at all.

Lady Huntley, Fenella thought, was quite the most formidable woman she had ever met. She was of ponderous figure, with skin like a tortoise due to years of catering to her own desires. Her eyes were fine, but sadly hidden in folds of fat. However, Fenella saw, the eyes were not concealed sufficiently to hide the active dislike that glittered in them at Fenella's approach.

Lady Huntley's younger son was of a different style. If one looked at him with a critical eye, as Lady Cleviss did, one might detect an incipient resemblance to his mother. A Talbot through and through, thought his hostess sourly. But young Hereward had eyes only for Fenella.

He had come prepared for a strained encounter with Fenella. She had been close enough—close enough! he remembered—to him to recognize him again. Except for the mask, he had made no attempt at disguise, for he had been operating in a territory where he believed himself unknown. But Fenella had not fainted dead away, as one might expect a delicately nurtured female to do. Instead she had roused him to a most indiscreet embrace in the shadows. Would she know him now? His eyes danced with the stimulation of danger.

He bowed over her hand, and then looked up into her eyes. There was no sign of recognition. He was both relieved and disappointed. Surely he must have made *some* impression upon her?

He had a good deal of time to speculate, for tea was brought in, and his loquacious mother commanded the attention of the company.

He listened only intermittently, wearing a deceptive air of rapt attention which concealed his frequent glances at Fenella. Lady Huntley prosed on. "You have quite a pleasant little prospect from your drawing room windows, Lady Cleviss. You must find it very agreeable, I am sure. I myself should not like my view obstructed by that line of trees there, but I suppose there is no harm in it."

Hereward watched Fenella gracefully handing the teacups around. When she came to him, he endeavored, successfully, to touch her fingers with his, preventing her from withdrawing her hand. Startled, and not pleased, she raised her eyes to meet his.

How green they were! he thought. In the night he had not been able to discern the color, but they were indeed green, of a clarity that gave one the immediate impression of looking into a fathomless pool. She dropped her long lashes at once, and without apparent effort withdrew her hand. The whole incident had taken only a moment, and had escaped the notice of the older ladies engaged in their genteel dueling. Hereward was persuaded that she did not remember him, but he vowed that he would make such an impression on her that she would never forget him.

"The trees then, Lady Cleviss," Lady Huntley was saying, "are the boundary of Morland Manor? Then the land beyond, of course, belongs to our family, is that right? I like to know precisely where I am, you see. I have the name—among my own friends, of course—of never being puzzled as to my whereabouts. I have often been able to set coachman right on the way to go."

Lady Cleviss seemed to have little to say. In truth, there was no need to respond, for Lady Huntley would have ignored her. "I like to rest my eyes upon only my own land. The park at Oakley, in Wiltshire, you know, where I spend much of my time, is quite a bit larger than yours. Wherever I look from the window, I see nothing but Wakeford land. It is a great satisfaction to me. I do not like close neighbors."

While Lady Huntley's remarks flowed inexorably on, Hereward's thoughts frolicked about Fenella. His impulsive kiss, the night of the robbery, had risen from an obscure attraction that he did not understand. Now, close at hand, he could see that his instincts had not misled him. Fenella Morland was slim and delicate, perfectly well behaved, but he detected what he thought was incipient rebellion held under tight rein.

There was more to this miss than met the eye at first glance.

It might well be, Hereward decided, that he could do them all a favor.

Lady Huntley would be grateful indeed if old Gervase cried off and decided not to marry this girl. Fenella herself would be the better—in Hereward's judgment—for a little escapade.

And, best of all, Gervase would be done out of a bride, a lady he fancied, and his disappointment would be the keener since it was Hereward who would bring about the ruin of his hopes.

The visit, which had seemed, to some of the principals at least, an endless affliction, came to a merciful close. Lady

Cleviss stood on the steps, seeing her visitors off. Discontent in her voice, she said, "I hope that Huntley can dispose of her, quite properly of course, but in a way so that I shall not be obliged to be civil to her."

As the Huntley coach moved down the drive, the occupants found themselves in mutual accord.

Lady Huntley said, "That is not at all the kind of chatelaine I should like to see at Wakeford Hall, to say nothing of the great house at West Wycombe."

"Or anywhere else?" said Hereward with a broad grin. "I quite agree, ma'am. My dear brother must be preserved from marrying Miss Fenella." He spoke from a different wellspring. Malice and envy of his brother were the main guideposts in his journey through life. Gleefully, he thought, "If Gervase wants her, I'll make a cake of him! There's never been a young lady in the world I couldn't bring around my finger!"

The next morning, Gervase determined to make his future with Fenella secure. He had sent his mother for the desired call of courtesy upon the family of his future betrothed, and he was anxious to receive Fenella's acceptance.

Not the least of the sources of his wish for expedition of his marriage was the continued abrasive presence of his mother and his younger brother. With Fenella as his officially betrothed, he might well send Lady Huntley and Hereward back to Bath, or wherever they wished to go. Their presence here at Wakeford Hall would no longer be desirable.

The Dowager had, surprisingly, said little about her visit to Morland Manor, and he, in his burgeoning wisdom, forbore to inquire. He was not prepared to admit to anyone the depth of his feeling for Fenella.

The first appealing glimpse of her had intrigued him. Now, each time he saw her intensified his determination to claim her for his bride. There was no reason to delay further, he judged, discarding the fourth cravat in a rumpled pile on the floor. His fingers would not do his bidding. At last he achieved a sort of success with his neckcloth, and, without a word of his intentions, proceeded to the Manor.

He found his solitary thoughts poor company. He could not picture his future with Fenella in any detail that would clarify his hopes. But he could not, on the other hand, imagine a future without her. What if she turned him down? What if she had, contrary to any report he had heard, already given her heart to some dandy in London?

If she turned him down, there was always Wellington. Gervase was sure of a place with the great general. But he could not easily cast aside the responsibilities incumbent upon a holder of great estates and honors.

Hardly knowing how he went, he passed the line of trees marking the boundary between Morland and Wakeford. The first Morland had unfortunately built his residence at the north end of his holdings. Lady Huntley might have been undeceived as to the prosperity of the Morlands had she asked her son, for he knew that Morland land stretched far to the South, even though their north prospect was short.

His interview, behind closed doors, with Lady Cleviss was short and highly satisfactory to both participants. When Lady Cleviss emerged, and sent for Fenella, she was conscious only of accomplishment. Gervase had come up to the mark handsomely, and she had no doubt that Fenella would do as she was bid.

Receiving her grandmother's summons, Fenella could hardly hear for the noisy riot of her thoughts. She had no illusions now that Gervase was simply a friendly neighbor. Even Lady Huntley's call yesterday had made no mention of a closer connection between their families. She had allowed herself to hope that her grandmother was mistaken in her convictions. Now that hope was destroyed.

She did not remember going down the stairs. Just so might a sleepwalker proceed, but her training stood her in good stead now. Her civility was ingrained in her, and no matter what her thoughts told her, her tongue would speak pleasantly and well.

She stopped short on the threshold of the drawing room. Gervase's broad shoulders were outlined against the window, where he stared unseeing at the view so maligned by his mother.

He heard Fenella's step, and turned. His breath stopped for a moment. She was so lovely! He managed, at last, to find his tongue. "I have been admiring the prospect from the window." As witty conversation, he thought, his remark did not shine.

Fenella's wits betrayed her. "It may be so, sir, but it must be far better to look always over one's own lands, do you agree?"

"I fear I do not perfectly understand."

"Lady Huntley expressed that opinion yesterday, you know," explained Fenella, truthfully, but not tactfully.

He frowned. It would have been better to inquire of his mother how the visit had gone, he knew now, for there might well be pitfalls ahead, dug by his own close relative.

Fenella saw his frown, and mistook it for disapproval of her revelation of his mother's remark. She turned shy, feeling shamed at the start of what promised to be a very painful interview.

An embarrassing silence fell between them. She longed simply to flee, to run until she could run no more—anything to come to an end of this dreadful scene.

And suddenly, while her mind had wandered fitfully, she became aware that he had in fact made the offer she had not wanted. She did not recall his words—which were in fact far from memorable—but she knew that he was looking at her with undisguised expectancy.

She must answer. She opened her lips to speak, but no sound emerged.

He heard a pounding in his head, as though beset by a multitude of hammers. He had thought this proposal would be simple—a mere asking and a prompt, even if not ecstatic, acceptance. He had faced enemy guns hundreds of times, endured filth and mud and disease and misery more often than not, but—

This was, quite simply, the most agonizing moment of his life.

He was rooted to the floor, looking down into her eyes, set provocatively in her heart-shaped face. The desperate expression of appeal he saw there brought him to life. It was her need he answered.

He crossed the short distance between them and took her hand. Looking into her eyes, with ineffable kindness he said, "I think we will suit very well."

She was torn. All of her screamed, No, no, we would not suit at all. You cannot ask me to deal with that monster your mother. You must not expect——

The faded, forlorn figure of Aunt Kitty rose before her tormented eyes. Even she would urge marriage.

Fenella heard herself stammer aloud, "Yes, Lord Huntley."

He took a deep breath. He pulled her toward a settee and sat down beside her. He longed to put his arm around her and draw her head down onto his shoulder, but he feared to frighten her. Instead, he took her hand. "You have made me happy, you know. And I shall endeavor all my life to make you content." When she did not answer, he continued. "I shall be pleased if you will call me Gervase."

"I shall try," she murmured.

He wavered then. Should he remind her of that night in Vauxhall Gardens? Would the recollection favor his suit with her? He decided the time was not ripe. But his mind ran on London and, for lack of response from her, he began to speak of the city.

"I am sure you have seen much more of London than I have," he said. "Perhaps next year we may open the town house and spend a few months. I shall welcome your instruction on the most interesting sights to see."

London was vivid in her mind, as one looks back upon a happy time never to come again. She could not imagine any gaiety connected with a sober expedition determined to view the sights. If spontaneity were gone, then there was little left of amusement.

"There is much to see—" she answered dutifully. "The loveliest sight, truly—" *Is Vauxhall Gardens by night,* trembled on her lips. She averted disaster. "—must be the marbles that Lord Elgin brought from Greece."

Captive of his own knowledge, Gervase spoke unfortunately. "You will be safe with me, you know, in London."

She jumped to her feet, wringing her hands. Of all things, he must remind her of the scandalous rumors that Lady Dorton had heard. How fortunate she was—she thought he believed—that he would condescend to protect her, to wed her even though her impulsiveness had led her into trouble.

"Wh-what do you mean, sir?"

He pulled her down beside him again. "Pray listen, Fenella. I meant nothing at all, only to reassure you." Her eyes brimmed, obscuring the fire of resentment that flickered momentarily. He said, as he had once before, "Have I said something amiss?"

"No, Lord Huntley," she said, drawing herself up stiffly. "I am sure you are civility itself, and I am much obliged to you."

He was taken aback. "Lord Huntley? Am I not to hear my Christian name on your lips?"

"Gervase, then," she said shortly. Suddenly, she gave him a

sunny smile innocent as a child's. It was truly not his fault that she felt so low in her mind. If she must marry him, she must, and an unpleasant task—so her governess always said—became less so if done with grace. "If you wish it."

"I do wish it."

After an interval, the details of which neither of them could recall later, he went home. She clearly did not remember him, he was convinced. So, he reasoned, her reluctance was entirely due to her maidenly innocence, and not gratitude for his rescue of her.

But the marriage was now satisfactorily arranged, and he was quietly pleased. All would now go forward in the prescribed steps of formal betrothal and wedding, and all would be, as they say, "merry as a marriage bell."

He began to whistle as soon as he was out of sight of the house.

11

The betrothal of two prominent residents of the area was not publicly announced, but it did not pass unnoticed.

Courtesy, though not inclination, demanded a return call by Lady Cleviss, now that the families were to be more closely connected. A date was fixed for two days after Gervase's announcement to his mother that Miss Fenella had indeed accepted him.

"I shall wish the marriage to take place as soon as can be accomplished," he told the Dowager Lady Huntley. "You will be glad of an early return to your own affairs, I am persuaded."

"I hope I know what is expected of me," said Lady Huntley huffily. "I confess I do not like such haste in a matter of grave importance to us all, Gervase. You cannot have known the minx above a month—more likely two weeks—and yet you have thrown yourself at her feet."

Gervase feared to open his lips, lest, like Pandora's box, all manner of things escape. His mother glanced at him. His continued silence struck a note of uneasiness in her. She was prepared for a wrangling kind of argument with him, an encounter in which she possessed the greater armament. It was difficult to perceive how she could overrule the heir on the subject of his marriage. He was of age, and in control of the family finances, and all that was left to her was moral suasion. She was sure it would be sufficient on this occasion, since her influence had always prevailed in the past.

"Then I shall expect to receive Lady Cleviss the next afternoon but one, I suppose," she said, sighing hugely as witness to her sacrifice. "I am sure she will be looking forward to the occasion, for she has little enough to amuse her."

However, Lady Cleviss seemed not to realize the opportunity available to her, for she refused to go with Fenella to Wakeford Hall.

"You will go, Kitty, for we must be civil, at least until the marriage is accomplished," said Lady Cleviss to her daughter, privately. "We dare not place any obstacles in the way of dear Fenella's happiness."

Far from being the fool most of her acquaintances thought her, Kitty was possessed of a lively intelligence and a wispy humor that was revealed only rarely. Now she smiled briefly.

"If aught goes awry, I shall bear the blame, I see."

"Kitty, my dear, I can trust your equable nature to overlook anything that dreadfully common woman says. I cannot bear such insults, and she will press me until I set her right." Lady Cleviss for once was humble. "Do, Kitty, go with Fenella and make my excuses. I truly do feel ill—at least when I think of dealing with That Woman again."

At the appointed hour, Fenella and Kitty climbed into the closed coach. There was the slightest hint of rain, else they might have taken the chaise. "We are going in style," was Fenella's only observation, until they had started down the drive on the short journey to the neighboring Hall.

"It's too bad of Grandmama," said Fenella. "She got me into this, but she does not stay to see it through."

Kitty laughed. "I suppose you would rather see two ladies of dignity come to a complete severance of relations? Mama would be hard pressed not to put Lady Huntley in her place, and what a coil that would be! In Lady Huntley's own home, besides. But of course it is not her own home, but—you understand me," finished Kitty, hopelessly entangled.

"I should not wish a brouhaha," said Fenella, insincerely,

"but I could wish we would never hear again of the Wake-fords. Any of them."

Her aunt sat up straight. "Listen to me, Fenella. You are talking fustian. Lord Huntley is kind, he appears of good intelligence. Surely his manners are thoughtful, and I understand that our great general Wellington valued him highly. To think that you have gained such an advantageous match! My dear, your gratitude should be unbounded!"

Fenella's retort was kept safely in silence. Reason told her that Kitty was perfectly in the right, but still, she herself could not precisely agree. Gratitude was a small enough stone to serve as foundation for a lifelong connection. But she had no choice. Caro, of course, was not bound by her marriage—but Fenella could not quite bring herself to contemplate infidelity unmoved.

Lady Huntley, far from being dismayed by the absence of Lady Cleviss, whom she considered her enemy, was pleased when Kitty made her excuses. A small smirk of triumph touched the Dowager's full lips. Clearly, she thought, she had routed the old lady, even if she were a granddaughter of a duke.

Kitty, in only a few moments, was profoundly grateful that her mother had chosen not to come. For Lady Huntley seemed determined to be as obnoxious as she could—an exercise in which she was a past mistress.

"I have asked Buston to serve us tea," she said, when they were all seated. "I do not have things quite as I should like them, yet, but in due course—as long as Gervase wishes to stay here—I shall endeavor to bring the household staff to the standards I am accustomed to."

Kitty gasped inwardly. Was Fenella then to live under this woman's thumb? She was sure Mama would not accept such a ramshackle arrangement. She was not alone in her dismay. Buston, for nearly the first time in his life, rattled the cups as he placed them on the small saucers. He had already taken the measure of both his lord's mother and his younger brother, and was at this moment turning over in his mind alternative places of employment.

"Can you imagine?" said Lady Huntley, "the staff had laid out the Wedgwood service for tea. I cannot like the earthenware at all."

Lady Huntley had prevailed, at least on the tea service, for Kitty recognized a fine collection of Worcester porcelain.

Gervase was angry. He had directed his mother to invite the Morland ladies to tea—it was expected of her. But he should have known that his mother, being opposed to his marriage as too hasty, would endeavor by any means at her hand to alter his arrangements.

He was aware that she prosed on, but he deliberately ceased to listen, and diverted himself with fantasies wherein Fenella trustingly put her hand in his, and they set in motion plans to make of Wakeford Hall an Eden in Essex.

His gaze lingered on Fenella. She was clearly embarrassed and revolted by his mother. He could not blame her. He had been away too long, or he would have realized that his mother's unpleasant qualities had been augmented by five years of indulgence and wilfulness. He wished with all his heart that he had not sent for her. But he had, and there's an end to it, he thought.

Kitty, while carrying out her conversational duties—requiring merely syllables of agreement infrequently, was clearly counting the moments until it was proper to leave.

Fenella glanced up suddenly, and caught Gervase's gaze on her. She looked away quickly. How dreadfully stiff he was, and cold! It was obvious to her that he cared naught for the havoc his mother wreaked.

Warrod appeared in the doorway, and Gervase answered his summons. Carefully closing the salon door behind him, Gervase led Warrod into the study, and closed that door as well.

"My brother's yacht?"

"I've gone to Cogges Cove, just as you said, my lord. No sign of a boat. Except, of course, an old rowboat drawn up above the shingle. Some local's Sunday outing boat, likely."

"It hasn't arrived at Cogges Cove yet, then."

"Begging your pardon, I went on beyond, seeking word of the boat. While I was there, you know. Saved another trip, in case." He waited until Gervase nodded impatiently. "Nobody never heard of the boat."

"Nobody?"

"I didn't go as far as Brightlingsea, not having the time to spare, without your orders, my lord. But no one knew aught about the boat."

Hereward's little boat—he said it would be coming in to Cogges Cove. But if no one along the coast knew the boat, then that meant the boat was not ordinarily at anchor in the vicinity. Gervase had a high regard for the sharp observations of countrymen.

"No one heard of it," he repeated, almost to himself.

"Well, my lord, barring one or two. They *said* they didn't know of any boat, like you said to ask about, but then, I don't know as I'd believe what *they* said, not even if they swore to it."

Gervase was thoughtful. There was something very queer in Hereward's story. If the boat were not anchored in Cogges Cove, nor had any one any knowledge of it, perhaps the yacht did not exist. But then why did Hereward make such a point of its prospective arrival? There must be a reason, but Gervase could not understand it.

He dismissed Warrod. "You've done a good job on this. I should be obliged if you said nothing about my inquiry."

His factor was hurt. "My lord——"

"I know you won't," said Gervase, with his rare smile. "By the way, I've looked over the figures you left with me. A very clear explanation, too. I agree, we should look into the new hybrid strain. One day next week, I should like to go with you."

Warrod departed blissfully. The new lord was a right'un, all right.

Gervase returned to the drawing room. The yacht still on his mind, he frowned. Fenella, noticing, folded her hands in her lap. She had been much in bad graces recently, been overwhelmed by lectures from Lady Dorton and sermons from Grandmama, and she took Gervase's obvious disapproval as a personal matter.

Gervase's attention was riveted upon his return by his mother's monotonous voice. The matter of her conversation had moved on and arrived at the subject of unsuitable marriages.

"A Wakeford habit," she said, pursing her lips in disapproval. "An example is Gervase's aunt, my late husband's sister. She married Waldo Prentice, a dreadful mistake. I might have told her, but the damage was done before I came into the family. A foolish woman!"

No one pointed out that Lady Huntley herself was a prime example of Wakeford bad judgment. But Gervase decided that enough was enough. "My aunt was a delightful woman," he observed. "It was unfortunate that she did not live long enough to be of help to Tom when he needed her."

"Tom was an idiot!"

None of the Wakefords was sufficiently cognizant of the details of that long-ago affair of Tom's to realize that Kitty was the central figure, if not the pivot, of it. Gervase saw only that his guests were uncomfortable, that Miss Morland had turned wooden-faced and silent. He must, since he could not silence his mother, see that Fenella and Kitty were extricated at once.

Lady Huntley, anxious to regain control of the situation, sniffed. "Some petticoat involvement, I recall. A good thing that his father took charge. Bad judgment, you see—a romantic fancy which, if indulged, would have ruined his life."

Silently, Gervase reflected that a useless left arm, legacy of the remedy for the romantic fancy, was equally ruinous.

Kitty, forestalling Gervase, stood up. Her face flushed unbecomingly under her fair hair, but her voice was firm. "We must go. Fenella, you don't look at all well."

Fenella was startled. She felt as fine as she could, and her aunt had not looked in her direction. She opened her lips to protest, but stopped. Any excuse, no matter how inaccurate, would serve to remove them from this—this horrible afternoon!

The carriage was brought hastily to the door. Kitty, who had not said another word, leaving Fenella to provide the civilities required, climbed into the vehicle. Not until they were moving down the long drive from Wakeford Hall did she make a sound—the sound of dry, retching, horrible sobs.

Fenella was frightened. Never had she seen Kitty so overset. It was as though the foundations of her own world had tottered. She put her arm around her aunt and held her, feeling convulsive shudders pass from Kitty's to her own body.

"How could she!" came Kitty's words, muffled, choked, but giving hope that she would soon be herself again. "That dreadful woman!"

"I quite agree," said Fenella vaguely, but soothingly.

"We were truly in love," claimed her aunt, startling Fenella. "We were too young to know our minds. That's what his father said. It was wicked to tear Tom away and put him in the army! Wicked, wicked!"

"And your Tom—that was *their* Tom?"

Kitty nodded. Her hair was escaping, tendril by tendril,

from the close cap she wore, giving her a vaguely disreputable appearance. Neither noticed.

"That evil old man must have been right, for I never heard from Tom again. Not a word."

Kitty gulped twice and sat up. She patted Fenella's hand and said, "Thank you, my dear. I am all right now. I must apologize for being so foolish. But you see I don't even know if he's alive. There were so many casualties, and I read the lists most carefully, you know. But—I never heard."

Judiciously, Fenella said, "They didn't speak of him as though he were—not alive."

Kitty burst out in a renewed fit of anger. "That's worse! If he's alive and still doesn't want to come to me—his father's dead, you know—I simply cannot bear it!"

The coach, having left the Wakeford gates behind and traveled a short distance on the road, now turned between Morland gates. The fine raked gravel made a different sound beneath the wheels.

Fenella remarked, "That dreadful woman! Aunt Kitty, they surely didn't know—"

Kitty interrupted. "It makes no difference now. I can't believe that Lord Huntley would be unkind, but it's all past now. You know, I just realized, I have never cried over Tom, not even at the very first. Not until now."

Fenella, indignant both on Kitty's account and on her own, exclaimed, "I can't think how I shall *endure* her!"

By the time the carriage stopped before the broad steps of the Morland Manor entrance, Kitty's emotions were under control.

"One thing," Kitty pointed out, "we shall not have to return there again."

Fenella forbore to remind her that there was every likelihood that communications between the two families would increase rather than come to a conclusion. She had accepted Lord Huntley—today she could not speak his Christian name—and she was bound by her promise. But she need not be misguided into believing that she would ever be happy again.

When Fenella, following more slowly, arrived in the foyer, Aunt Kitty was disappearing at the top of the stairs. Worth was bright-eyed with curiosity. Miss Morland had indeed been in a taking, was his thought, and he'd give odds that it was that old woman at the Hall was behind it all.

Lady Cleviss was waiting for their return. Fenella dutifully entered her grandmother's favorite rose-hued sitting room, and sank unbidden into a chair. "Grandmama, it was dreadful!" she burst out.

"You don't surprise me," said Lady Cleviss. "Tell me, child."

Fenella gave a rapid résumé of their entertainment. "You know she had the Worcester porcelain out, a full set. I should not have been surprised had she brought in the sideboard covered with asparagus trays and turtle pans!"

"Nor I," said her grandmother. "But you have not told me the whole, Fenella."

"No more have I," admitted Fenella. "But that dreadful old woman—I shall *never* like her—talked about unwise marriages, and called Tom Prentice an idiot—and I can't remember all she said. But Aunt Kitty was most distressed!"

Lady Cleviss seemed suddenly old. "I wonder whether I have made a mistake," she said slowly. After a moment, she straightened, and added, more briskly, "No, of course I haven't. Lord Huntley is a Wakeford, takes after his father's people. No trace of Talbot."

Fenella said softly, "I shall not be able to go on with her."

Lady Cleviss was herself again. "No need to worry. Once you are wed, I promise you, I shall dispose of Lady Huntley. But I shall hope that Huntley himself will see to it that you are not bothered."

She looked lovingly at Fenella. She had no qualms about the coming marriage, except for the formidable Dowager, but the granddaughter of a duke would be able to deal with her! But Fenella did not brighten, as she hoped.

"Grandmama, I cannot think that Lord Huntley—that is, Gervase—entirely likes me."

"Nonsense! He does not need to like you at first. That will come." She spoke bracingly, firmly closing the lid on doubts. "Now, my dear, a word of advice. We must go on, and not make too fine a point of this—unfortunate conversation. We must gloss over the woman's excessively bad manners, and be grateful that Huntley resembles her not at all. And we shall not call again on her."

This resolve, while scrupulously kept, did not mean that the two families would be preserved in isolation. Aside from the necessary notice taken of the betrothal by the families involved, wider notice of the intended nuptials was taken by notables of the region.

Sir Edmund and Lady Stover, already planning a dinner and ball in honor of Gervase's accession to the title and his safe return from the Peninsula, enlarged their design to take on the aspect of an informal celebration of the proposed happy union.

Kitty refused to make one of the Morland party, and, blessedly, Lady Cleviss did not insist. She only said, mildly enough, "There are few occasions for entertainment, and you could find people to talk to. You would not be obliged to do aught but speak to That Woman."

Kitty wailed, "Mama, you don't know how *insulting* she was!"

"I can well imagine. But she will not stay long here, and there is no need for you to fret about the future. I shall take care of it, in due time."

Neither of those listening doubted in the least her ability to dole out the events of the future as would best suit her. Fenella's spirits rose, as they entered the coach for the hour's drive to Stover Lodge.

12

Sir Edmund and Lady Stover did not entertain often, but when the occasion demanded, they did not stint of their efforts.

Stover Hall was a comfortable residence, even if small compared even to Wakeford Hall. Lady Huntley's assessment of her host's home was unequivocal. "Not grand, of course, but I should deem the rooms comfortable. I myself should not like to be so cramped."

By fortunate chance, Lady Stover had arranged the seating at the dinner as though she were entertaining the Montagues and the Capulets. Gervase was placed next to Fenella. The Wakefords, mother and younger son, were arranged next to Sir Edmund, and Lady Cleviss, outranked, sat a distance down the table.

Fenella scarcely knew what she ate. Sitting next to Gervase, inhaling the pleasantly clean aroma of his shaving soap, she was too aware of him. As course followed course, the soup, fish, cutlets, fricasee of chicken, she swallowed a few mouthfuls and barely touched the wines that followed in bewildering succession. After dinner, the ball guests began arriving. There was much company.

The Watlings, the Vicar and his brightly curious lady, dressed in an assortment—so it seemed—of shawls. With her inbred air of elegance, she managed to carry it off, Fenella noticed.

The Plamondons from Colchester. Gervase knew they were sheep raisers, for Warrod's memoranda had explained as much. Gervase, standing beside Fenella in an informal receiving line, wondered whether she had noticed that Plamondon himself resembled nothing on earth as much as a short-sighted ram, white-faced and supercilious. He longed to explore her reflections on the crowds of people, but he dared not. But if—he would have said—Plamondon were ovine, then his wife was surely equine.

The Dunmows, Mr. and Mrs. and a coltish son named—Samuel? Fenella could not remember, nor did she try longer than it took to pass the Dunmows on to the next outstretched hand.

A veritable press, it was, and Fenella began to enjoy the evening, in spite of herself.

Beyond the door she could see the sparkling lights of welcome, the promising strains of music coming from the parlor turned ballroom, behind her, and the warm evening air, heavy with the perfume of night-scented stocks.

Through the open door she could see the awestruck stable boys and grooms, taking the horses away, moving the carriages. All the scene needed, she thought, to remind her of Vauxhall Gardens at night, was the sound and sights of fireworks.

With the recollection of Vauxhall, of course, by inevitable progression came the strong image of Caro Lamb, and that frightening, shameful night.

And beside her, not sharing her thoughts—nor could he ever, she believed—stood her betrothed, Gervase. Bound to him by a promise she would not break of her own volition, she felt her elation vanish and she came down to earth with a thud.

At length—shortly after the Thacksteads arrived with their three giggling daughters, improbably named Iris, Pansy, and Rose—Fenella and Gervase led off the dancing.

She was naturally light and lissome, and the intricate steps of many of the newer dances were simple for her. But this was not Almack's. The dances were simple and the music lively, and soon she lost herself in the simple pleasure of movement.

Gervase apologized. "I fear you will find me sadly out of the fashion, but you must know that I have been long away from dancing."

"They do not dance in Spain?"

"The Spanish seem content to dance alone, or in couples." He glanced around him briefly at the sedate pairs marching down the floor. "Much different," he summed up. The bright swirling dancers he remembered, overtones of the Moorish occupation in costumes and music, bore no resemblance to the fair lads and lasses in Stover Lodge.

He would remember, he thought, but not regret, the past. His future would be brighter than he could imagine.

She was sorry to change partners, for Gervase danced neatly, if not with *panache*. But others clamored for her hand, and soon she was partnered with Hereward, then awkward and blushing Samuel, Hereward again. She could not remember how many dances had passed before she faced Gervase again. He said little, and suddenly Fenella's spirits drooped. There was a lack of lightness in his countenance, and—accustomed to looking within her for fault—she at once blamed herself for his mood. She missed a step, and at once Gervase tightened his grip on her fingers.

"Too tired?"

His words were kind, and he drew her from the floor. "No need to exhaust yourself," he told her. The chairs ranking the dance floor were nearly full, and he stood beside her.

She had danced twice with Hereward, and enjoyed herself immensely. He was light and lithe, an excellent dancer. She had the impression that everything he did would be done to perfection—the first time—else he would never again try it. There was no persistence, no determination to try again and again, in his character. Now she sat, the broad figure of Gervase standing beside her, watching the dancers. Her eyes followed Hereward, taking pleasure in his graceful movements. He caught her eye momentarily. His eyebrows rose in mock despair, and she nearly giggled. He was footing it with one of the Thackstead girls, who was nearly incapacitated by her uncontrollable laughter.

She thought she heard a choked sound of amusement from the man beside her, but when she glanced up no ripple disturbed his massive calm. Too bad—she thought—how I would cherish someone who could laugh at such absurdities with me!

People came by and spoke to her, and before long Gervase had moved away. Hereward materialized before her. "Well, Sister," he began, laughing, "are you enjoying yourself?"

"Except for the oppressive heat," she said. The breeze had died down and no longer brought its coolness into the overheated room.

"I know the elixir for that," he said. He stretched his hand to help her up, and drew her unobtrusively onto the terrace.

The darkness, soft as velvet, was refreshing and cool. The lights burned along the entrance, out of sight around the corner of the building, but the faint effulgence was visible to their left. The scent of the flowers in the border was strong with the advent of the dew, and she breathed deeply.

Hereward stood apart from her and remained quiet. After a bit, when she did not speak, he broke the silence. "Why are you marrying old Gervase?"

She was shocked. She stammered, "Wh—what?"

"I never thought he would attract somebody like you," said her companion. His face was obscured in the darkness, but she could detect a hint of amusement in his voice.

Somehow the idea that stodgy, stiff Gervase was her ideal of manhood annoyed her. She retorted, "He doesn't."

"Then, they're making you do what they wish, is that it? I wager they did not even ask your wishes. Too bad of them."

His accusation had been too near the mark for comfort, and now he took a step toward her. She was suddenly vibrant with the knowledge of his physical presence. She turned half toward him, her hand out, beseeching him not to press her.

He took her hand in his. He was laughing now, lazily. "You have not the meek look that my dear brother sees. I should not wonder if you lead him a merry chase. Don't you ever fight back? I own I should like to see a spectacle like that—the timid kitten proving that she does have claws after all."

He had shifted his position slightly. Now he was outlined

against the faint glow from the front of the house. Her memory quivered, and filled her with wild surmise. Something in his outline reminded her—but of what?

"You—" she began.

"Here is your shawl, Fenella." It was Gervase, appearing out of the darkness, holding her shawl ready to place around her shoulders. "You were overheated," he said gravely, glancing at Hereward. "I should not like you to take cold."

"Thank you," murmured Fenella. The magic of the soft night was gone. The pleasure had been almost entirely that of the refreshing air after the stifling ballroom. But she was conscious of a small twinge of guilt for she had enjoyed Hereward's company, and Gervase had entirely slipped her mind.

There was something else, something she had been on the verge of saying to Hereward, but now it, too, had slipped away. Perhaps she would recall it later.

Hereward, stiffening at the first approach of his brother, now laughed. "Best we all go in," he suggested, adding blandly, "I for one feel greatly refreshed." And furious at the interruption, he thought, but did not say.

The three returned together through the tall terrace doors to the ballroom. Fenella believed her absence had not been noted and breathed a sigh of relief.

Her confidence was short-lived.

The next morning, the ball was over and lingered only in memory and in the litter and soiled dishes at Stover Lodge. Some of the participants in the festivity woke with the uncomfortable feeling of being stranded on an uninhabited shore with a mouth full of cotton and a monumental headache.

At Morland Manor, however, there was no sign of debilitating after-vapors of strong drink. In truth, Lady Cleviss had never been in finer fettle. Nor, to be precise, had she ever been quite so displeased.

Fenella's arrival at the breakfast table was the signal for the first salvo of her grandmother's anger.

"I trust you enjoyed yourself yestereve?"

A note in her grandmother's voice alerted Fenella, and she looked up, startled. "Yes, 'ma'am."

"The food was passable, I admit, even though Lady Stover has no sense of taste. I have seen her bolt down the most obnoxious dishes."

Fenella poured coffee for herself with a sinking heart.

Grandmama had sent Worth away, offering evidence that the discussion would be unpleasant, at least.

She could offer no response. "I scarcely recall the dishes, ma'am."

"Doubtless," pounced Lady Cleviss. "For your thoughts were outside, in the dark, with young Wakeford!"

"Ma'am!" protested Fenella. "How could you think it of me?"

"I admit it is not easy to face the truth—that one's own granddaughter is a light-o'-love."

With deliberation Fenella set her cup down on the saucer. Some day, a dark imp in her mind jeered, Grandmama would go too far, and the results could be very unpleasant.

"I think you know that is not the truth, ma'am. If you are referring to the few moments when I left the ballroom—which was, beyond all, stifling—"

"Don't tell me there is another incident I could refer to?" Lady Cleviss looked down her nose, the better to see her wayward Fenella.

"No, ma'am. I collect that you saw me leave for a breath of air with Hereward. But if you were watching me that closely, then you also know that I was at all times only a few steps from the door."

"Go on," said Lady Cleviss grimly. "That is an alleviation, though hardly a justification."

"Perhaps you will remember that Gervase came to us almost at once with my shawl?"

Lady Cleviss hesitated. She had not been watching Fenella. Her information came from the prattle of one of the Thackstead girls, not even addressed to her.

Fenella looked shrewdly at her grandmother. "I don't believe you saw me at all," she said slowly. "But you take someone else's word, and consider me guilty of all manner of things."

The girl was justified, thought her grandmother. "But," she insisted, "don't you see that is the worst of it? If your conduct becomes noticed by relative strangers, then it is likely to become distorted as well. As you see it has."

"I hope I know how to behave," said Fenella. "I assure you there was not the least impropriety in my action."

"I believe you, Fenella. But I cannot impress strongly enough upon you that you must not give the slightest opportunity for anyone to breathe scandal against you."

"For two minutes on the terrace!" Fenella was dismayed. "Pray tell me, Grandmama, what could have happened in two minutes?"

Lady Cleviss evaded a direct answer. "I believe you were absent a good deal longer than that. I see it is time for plain speaking. You know that Lady Dorton warned me about certain rumors current in London. I feared, after last evening, that there might be some substance to them."

"Ma'am!"

"You must admit," Lady Cleviss continued with a wry smile, "that there was cause for some doubt in my mind. But I must remind you of this: if I, who know you so well, could think you indiscreet, how easy it would be for others, who have not your welfare at heart, to believe anything to your detriment?"

Fenella exclaimed, "Lady Huntley, of course. Did she tell you where I was, ma'am?"

"No. I do not know that she even noticed your absence, even though you were by way of being a guest of honor. But you do understand my anxiety? I am convinced that Huntley has a sincere regard for you, and surely you cannot expect to wed more successfully."

"I do not think he cares aught for me."

Lady Cleviss thought better of discussing that point. It was Huntley's task, moreover, to assure his betrothed of his affection.

"All I wish you to think about, child, and think about it every moment in the day, is that That Woman not be given the slightest opportunity to poison her son's mind about you."

"If his mind is so easily poisoned," retorted Fenella, "I do not consider him of elevated understanding."

Lady Cleviss rose. "Remember what I say, Fenella." She moved to her own sitting room, leaving her granddaughter thoroughly distraught behind her. The soft rose hues in the room, the deeper tones of the carpet and the brighter woven chair seats, insensibly raised her spirits. This was her most notable success in decorating so far. The colors were unconventional, but they pleased her, and she sought out the comfortable, padded Grecian sofa, and arranged the cushions to suit her.

She was remorseful—at least a little—at having leaped to the conclusion dictated by the overheard remark of that giggling girl—Iris, or Rose? such impossible names!—and accused Fenella wrongly.

But she must guard Fenella's good name and get the girl well married, or she would fail in her duty to the Morland family. She was aware every day of Kitty's fruitless life. If she, Lady Cleviss, had been more forceful at the time, had faced down the tyrant Prentice, perhaps she might have preserved Kitty's happiness.

Lord Cleviss had just been gathered to his Maker, though, at that time, and Lady Cleviss had not yet come to grips with her grief. Little enough excuse for failing Kitty, but at least she had learned that she must exercise all her formidable vigor in behalf of Fenella.

The sofa was most comfortable, and Lady Cleviss lacked for sleep. The night before had been late, and anxiety had kept her company until nearly daybreak. She lifted her feet to the sofa, an unheard-of indulgence in daytime, but she excused herself by the belief that she must give her whole thought to Fenella.

The Lamb business had been bad enough. She had read sufficiently between Lady Dorton's lines to know that Caro Lamb in her pursuit of the foolish poet had irrevocably shocked the London world. Like a cart full of explosives careening down a hill, to explode at the bottom—so was the half-mad Caroline Lamb. And as with explosives, many bystanders were bound to sustain wounds.

Fenella had been much in Caro's company the last few weeks, and, if additional proof than Lady Dorton's letter were required, the fact that not one offer had come Fenella's way provided evidence enough to convince her grandmother.

Now, having gone as far as a betrothal to the Earl of Huntley, Fenella's reputation would be unstained. With the powerful aegis of wealth and position to protect her, Lady Cleviss could safely feel her duty to her granddaughter discharged satisfactorily.

But Huntley must not be given the slightest excuse to cry off. Fenella could not sustain a blow of that nature. Lady Cleviss felt secure enough on the matter of Huntley himself. It was That Woman who would give her qualms until the pair were truly riveted.

No breath of scandal must touch Fenella—no breath of scandal—no breath—

Lady Cleviss's breath came evenly. She was asleep.

At that very moment, Fenella's actions would have appeared to the most tolerant eye suspicious in the extreme.

After her grandmother had left her alone in the morning room, the yellow of the walls and the chairs augmenting the August sunshine, Fenella sat elbow on table, hand supporting chin, and thought.

There was something about last night—somebody who brought a vague recollection to her—she had been about to penetrate a mystery when she had been interrupted. But try now as she might, she could not even recall the moment last night when the fugitive memory teased her.

Her eyes fell now upon the stack of letters still beside her grandmother's place. Knowing full well the rule of the house, that Lady Cleviss sorted and distributed the mail, Fenella tiptoed the few steps around the table, and picked up the letters. Guilt caused her to peer over her shoulder in a most stealthy manner, but no one came to witness her wrongdoing.

She was rewarded. In the stack, clearly not yet scrutinized by Lady Cleviss, was a letter for Fenella. The direction was scrawled in a bold hand, nearly illegible, and franked.

She slipped the missive into her pocket, and strolled so casually, and with such an appearance of innocence, from the morning room as to invite immediate inquiry, had anyone been at hand to notice her.

At last she would learn what had happened to Caro Lamb after the incident in the Gardens.

Feeling the letter burning in her pocket, she forced herself to a rambling pace out of the house, and through the garden until she reached the rose arbor. There, hidden from all eyes, she sat on the marble bench and took out the letter.

She did not open it at once. The teasing memory returned, along with a sense of strong injustice at the ways of the world. She was innocent of all wrongdoing. For while she admired Caro, thought she was incomparably beautiful and dashing, she knew that she was only a spectator in the thrilling drama that Caro Lamb lived every day.

And it had been no fault of Fenella's that Caro had dragged her into the darkness after Byron. Her eyes misted. How close she had come to disaster that night! The memory that lingered just at the edge of recognition caused her to wonder—it was Hereward whose presence last night on the terrace had given her pause to think. She knew him from somewhere—but where?

With Caro's letter in her hands, the obvious solution came
to her. The man who rescued her from the ruffians—could it
have been Hereward?

She closed her eyes, bringing back her mental vision of
that episode—no, it was not Hereward. Not the right build.

Suddenly, she could see Grandmama's point. Were Lady
Huntley to learn about that dreadful night, and Fenella's return home alone, on foot—Fenella shuddered. The consequences might well be the disaster of her life!

13

Caro was alive, if not well, and writing from Brocket Hall.
Her dear Byron was suffering as much as she herself—so ran
the letter—by William's indefensible actions in drawing her
away from London.

"Had I even suspected that I would wed a Dog in the
Manger, I vow to you I should never have consented. Be very
careful my dear friend do not let your husband guide you to
destruction as my darling William has done—"

Fenella suspected that Caro had lost the thread of her
thought, and perhaps even forgotten to whom she was writing. Besides, Caro's aimless scrawl was so difficult to decipher!

"But at least I have experienced the Grand Passion, the
giving up of soul and body to one who scorns me is not what
I would wish, but if I cannot have Byron I shall not have
William. The next you hear from your poor Caro I shall be
no more than a corpse. I shall have William cremate me, a
funeral pyre that will light up the sky that will be a blaze to
tell the world that here perished Love—only ashes remain,
only ashes blowing in the wind, ashes that once could sign
herself your dearest friend Caro."

Grammar and punctuation had, as well, become ashes in
Caro's mind, thought Fenella. She must take good care that
no one ever learned of this letter—

"My dear," said Gervase, "you are troubled?"

"Where did you come—I am sorry, I should not have spoken so—you startled me—" As civilized conversation, Fenella thought, this ranks with Caro's letter.

"I did not intend to steal upon your privacy," said Gervase, rather more stiffly than he intended. "But Worth directed me here."

"I thought I had escaped notice," said Fenella. She did not even take time to straighten out the letter she had been reading before stuffing it out of sight in her pocket.

The clear desire to keep the letter from his eyes did not escape Gervase. Indeed, he was far more disquieted than she could have guessed. The writing, in a bold scrawl, looked distinctly masculine to him.

She gave every appearance of being of troubled mind. Yet the appeal in her face as she made way for him to sit on the bench beside her kept his lips sealed, at least on that subject. She must learn that he could be trusted. He knew of no way to assure her of his real interest except to smooth her way by every means at his command.

He could not ask questions, but he could surely keep his eyes open. If she were pursued against her will by some man—who wrote such an abominable hand!—he could deal with him. But if she had already fixed her affection on him, and were marrying Gervase to please her family, he did not know quite what he would do.

He plunged into the news he brought. "I have had word that my cousin will be coming in a few days to Wakeford Hall. I wished to inform you at once."

"I don't believe I will know him?"

"Tom Prentice," he told her. "He was at one time well acquainted here, when he visited our grandfather. But I am sure you are too young to remember him."

Fenella struggled to overcome her strong emotion. If Tom Prentice were coming—was he the same one that had been Kitty's *amour*? Of course—there could not be two of that name so nearly related.

"I shall look forward to making his acquaintance," she said primly. She added daringly, "And of course his wife."

Gervase was surprised. "Did I give the impression he was married? I did not think I mentioned Amelia, but at any rate, she is his sister, not his wife."

The bees hummed busily in the late roses in the arbor. Far away there was the sound of sheep bleating infrequently, and somewhere nearer at hand a door shut.

"Shall you feel overcome by my relatives? I should like to assure you that you need not fear Tom. He is a most retiring person, and while Amelia is a rattle, she does take particular care of her brother."

"I shall be pleased—" said Fenella vaguely. She scarcely knew what she was saying. She was in a curious state of mind. Gervase was stiff, formal, and spoke as though they were indeed strangers with nothing in common—met by chance in the National Gallery in London, perhaps.

Suppose she were just now meeting him for the first time, as a well-spoken stranger, and not as a future husband. What would she think?

Regular features set in grave lines, eyes the color of the sea, a well-set-up figure—and what was most daunting was the indefinable air of authority that made him seem older than she knew he was. Perhaps it was this appearance of command, of control, that made her quickly review her past actions with a view to concealing the worst.

He was solid, and she felt safe in his company—safe, but far from happy.

While she reflected, he had moved on to the question that had brought him here. "Your favorite jewels," he repeated now.

"Favorite stones?"

"The Wakeford jewels," he said, knowing she had not been listening to him, "will of course be yours when we are married." If, he thought, I can get my mother to relinquish them. "But I should like to give you something of your own. A bracelet perhaps? I should have preferred to order it myself, but I should be far afield in such a matter, not knowing your wishes."

"My favorite bracelet was stolen," she told him. "By the highwayman that night. I should not have been wearing it, for the stones are not suitable for my age, even though the emeralds were quite small."

"I should have expected emeralds would suit you best," he said. "Did the robber take aught else that you cherished?"

"Aunt Kitty was wiser than I, for she was wearing nothing she could not lose without regret. But truthfully, it was not the loss of my possessions that disturbed me. It was the very feeling of helplessness, that he could take what he would and no one would stop him." She stopped then, remembering the one thing he had taken that she could not account for. Her cheeks burned with the recollection of that kiss.

"I'm sorry," said Gervase.

The beckoning of memory held her now. More than the kiss, more than the emerald bracelet, a shape was taking form before her. The bracelet had brought it on, the dark of night, the handsome, gallant outlaw—the tantalizing familiarity of a pair of shoulders. Somewhere she had seen the outlaw again, just recently!

How much of her thoughts had been written on her face for Gervase to read? She glanced hurriedly at him, but he appeared to be watching a lively bird in an overhanging tree.

"I wonder," said Gervase, frowning, "whether there has been any word of the highwayman?"

"I have not heard it, if there has been."

Gervase mulled his thoughts over. "Only the one incident that I have heard of."

Fenella turned on him. "You think I made it all up? There was Aunt Kitty. Ask Grimsby, if you wish!"

"My dear, I spoke my thoughts without heed. I was merely wondering whether the highwayman might be a returned soldier, unable to get along, and turning to the road to make his living. I know this often happens."

"I should not think so in this case."

"Ah, then, you are recalling more about the incident? I would be glad if we could put an end to these crimes."

"I remember nothing!"

Her vehemence shocked him. "I'm sorry," he said in a mollifying way. "I was thinking only in terms of my own duty."

"Duty!" cried Fenella. "A word I have heard overmuch of in recent days! I wish——"

But she was not sure what she wished. That Gervase would not locate the robber, who had not hurt her? That she could remember the vague, worrying identity of the pair of shoulders she knew she had seen, more recently than the night on the road?

He said, casually, "You will like Tom. I cannot promise that you will enjoy knowing Amelia as well, but poor Tom cannot manage the journey alone. He was badly wounded, you know, and seems to have lost his interest in regaining his strength. I shall hope that the bracing air of Essex will restore him, at least somewhat."

They strolled toward the house. The rose-brick chimneys of Morland Manor thrust through the greenery of the great old trees, blending pleasingly with the bluish tint of the slate roof.

"How could a man help but want to live in such a kindly land!" he exclaimed.

"Shall you miss the excitement of the battle?" wondered Fenella. "Will you find it hard to alter your interests?"

"No, not at all. The gentleness of England outweighs all else. I found Spain a harsh land, cruel, with vivid contrasts and little humor. I shall not regret my return home." He paused, and took her hand. "Especially when I have so much happiness to look forward to."

He did not wait for her reply. He kissed her fingers lightly, and said his farewell.

She watched him out of sight, across the lawn and through a small gate that led to a shortcut to the road. It was clear that he did not wish to run the gamut of Lady Cleviss's sharp eyes.

What did Fenella wish? There was no clear answer. She picked up her skirts and ran to the house, as though fleeing. There was an obscure roiling of the waters of her thoughts, her emotions, as though the placid surface that had been her life to this point were troubled by an unknown force, living and breathing below the surface.

She wished she had never heard of Caro Lamb, for one thing.

She gained the side door, hidden in the ivy that covered the south wall of the Manor. Then she remembered.

The highwayman's silhouette in the light from the coach lamps was identical in every detail to that of Hereward Wakeford's, in the faint light from the front of the house, as they stood together on the terrace at Stover Lodge the night before.

Hereward Wakeford!

She gained her room, and latched the door behind her, shooting the bolt home. She must think!

She could not believe that her betrothed's brother was the gallant highwayman. But she must. She went over the details she could remember, and there was no doubt of it. Hereward's own lazy drawl, the look of deviltry in his eyes, the very daring that he carried with him like a powerful aura—all these fit.

And, positive that she knew the outlaw, what should she do about it?

Duty, Gervase had mentioned. Duty was a strong force in her life. And it was her clear duty to give her knowledge to the ear of the law and order, Sir Edmund.

She could not do so. She must first tell Gervase. He would take it amiss were she to carry information to the squire in secret. But were she to tell him, then he must in his position inform Sir Edmund that his brother was so lost to honor as to terrorize women and honest men on the road.

She was not sure of the machinery of the law, but she believed it to be ponderous but irresistible. She dropped into a chair and covered her face with her hands.

There was the other side of the coin—

Her vivid imagination painted the picture for her.

Her identification, strong as it was, could be vouched for by no one else. Hereward could easily show that he had been in Bath at the appropriate time, or sailing on the Channel, or any place but on the Chelmsford Road.

With his denial, Lady Huntley would snort her contempt of the troublemaking minx Fenella, Gervase himself would look at her with censure in his gray eyes, turned cold as the North Sea in winter.

And Grandmama would be sad and sorely grieved at the reprehensible behavior of her only granddaughter.

Fenella did not know how much later she came to the only conclusion she could. She dared not tell what she knew about Hereward. Not for Gervase, not to spare him the shame of his brother's wickedness, not at all!

Only that she loved her grandmother far too dearly to bring grief to her.

14

As Fenella returned to the house, the sun was overtaken by clouds. With the swiftness of change of skies near the sea, the oppressive heat was transformed into misting rain.

She looked through the window streaming with rain, into a

distorted world. But her eyes were fixed on a more sinister scene in her mind, equally distorted. How could it be that the younger brother of a wealthy peer could turn to common thievery?

Every time that the robber cocked his pistol at his victim, he was risking the gallows. Fenella was not overly familiar with the intricacies of the law, but common sense told her that if the penalty for highway robbery was death, then it would be the most practical of decisions to leave nobody alive to point an accusing finger.

No, she told herself, such folly could not be the choice of Hereward Wakeford.

The rain drummed on the window. She hoped that Gervase had arrived home before the worst of the storm, but she doubted he had. The rain had come too swiftly.

She wondered fearfully about Gervase's reaction when he learned that Hereward was the talked-about criminal. She believed Lord Huntley to be stodgy, dull, and devoid of humor. But little as she valued him, she could not find any pleasure in his humiliation.

Agnes rapped on the door. "Miss Fenella? Her ladyship is asking for you."

"All right, Agnes," Fenella answered mechanically.

"Teatime," the maid pointed out before scuttling away.

Fenella quickly set her dress to rights, smoothing her hair. The rustle of paper in her pocket reminded her of Caro's letter, and she hurriedly hid it in a drawer of the dressing table. How remote Caro and her problems were! There were equally serious questions to be answered much nearer than Brocket.

She went down the stairs, still reflecting. She could not reason herself out of the conviction that Hereward and the highway robber were the same man. A shadow was all she had to offer as proof—the shadow of the highwayman in the inadequate light of the carriage lamps, the silhouette of Hereward against the indirect lights on the terrace.

Even at that moment at Sir Edmund's, she remembered, she had had the haunting sense of an incident twice lived through, a time come again.

Every way she turned in her mind, she came to the same conclusion—she was right. But the sheer unbelievability of trying to persuade her grandmother—or anybody—that Hereward had taken to the road must hold her silent.

She paused, her hand on the graceful volute at the termination of the stair railing, as the last argument fell into place. Could she—as the new Lady Huntley—see her brother-in-law hanged?

The argument sufficed. She had held at bay the pleasant memory of the kiss in the shadows behind the carriage, telling herself that the dashing robber doubtless took such shameful advantage of all his female victims. She would not be swayed by such a trick!

She would simply have to make sure that she did not betray her private recognition.

She entered the sitting room where Lady Cleviss and Kitty, the latter resored to her usual serenity, were drinking tea.

"My child, where have you been?" said Lady Cleviss. "Pray don't tell me you were caught in this sudden downpour?"

"No, ma'am. I was—upstairs, and quite forgot the time."

She sat with her tea, and her grandmother continued her conversation with Aunt Kitty. Now that she had successfully solved her own problem of Hereward, to her own satisfaction if not quite in accord with accepted standards of duty, she allowed her thoughts to present to her the news that Gervase had brought. A smothered exclamation escaped her.

Lady Cleviss scolded, "Fenella, you wished to say something? One might expect you to wait until I have finished."

"Yes, ma'am."

But curiosity was a failing that Lady Cleviss battled with constantly, and on this occasion, she lost the skirmish. "What were you going to say?"

"I beg your pardon, Grandmama," said Fenella earnestly, avoiding looking at Kitty. "But Gervase called with a bit of news. There is to be more company at Wakeford Hall."

Lady Cleviss noted that Fenella was ill at ease. "Well, I suppose there is more to come. Although I cannot think what could be more devastating in the way of guests at Wakeford that would be worse than Lady Huntley herself!"

"Grandmama—" Fenella began, "I am sorry, but—"

Belatedly Lady Cleviss realized that Fenella's distress was genuine. "What is it? What's amiss? Not more Talbots, I hope? I shall not call."

"I don't think the guests are of the Talbot connection," said Fenella, skirting around the news she carried. "He said his cousin."

An inarticulate cry broke from Kitty's ashen lips. "C–cousin!"

In a burst, Fenella revealed all. "Tom Prentice, he said."

Lady Cleviss said grimly, "Tom Prentice. I do not like this."

"And his sister. Amelia, I believe."

Fenella was of two minds on the subject of continuing her disclosures. Tom had been cruelly wounded in the fighting, but would it mean more—or less—to Aunt Kitty? Kitty was staring into space, seeing a sight that sorely distressed her. Her hand shook, still holding the Crown Derby cup from which she had been drinking, letting it tilt until the liquid was at the rim.

Fenella rescued the cup and its contents, and set it on the tray. There would be no kindness in revealing Tom's condition, at least now. Nor, she decided, was it particularly relevant, for Kitty found her voice and said, harshly, "I cannot see him ever again." Then she burst into tears and fled the room.

Lady Cleviss said, angrily, "I cannot believe this." Whether she meant Kitty's behavior or Tom's advent upon the scene, was not clear to Fenella, until her grandmother added, "You know about that unfortunate episode?"

"Yes, ma'am. Aunt Kitty was so overset when we returned from Wakeford Hall. Lady Huntley was dreadful, Grandmama. I thought at the time that she did not know the wounds she was dealing, but only by chance hit the mark."

Grandmama scarcely listened. "I suppose Huntley doesn't remember. He was not here that summer, as I recall, and in any event, he would have been too young. That old fool Prentice, Tom's father you know, a tyrant of the first water. I heard that the girl—Amelia, you say?—never wed, and if her father was her example, then I approve entirely."

She set her own cup on the silver tray. "Ring for Worth, my dear, if you please. I have no appetite left." She waited until Worth had cleared away, closing the door behind him. Then she added, "But I shall not receive the young man. He could have written to Kitty."

"Perhaps his papa destroyed the letters," ventured Fenella.

"His pap was destroying no letters the boy could have written in the army," Lady Cleviss pointed out drily. "He's been dead this long time. And now young Tom arrives at Wakeford Hall, fine as you please, and still never a word to Kitty."

"Oh, but he couldn't!" cried Fenella. "He can't write! That is, he was wounded."

Lady Cleviss appeared somewhat mollified. "But he could have asked somebody to write—"

Kitty returned at that moment. "Now," she said brightly, "I ask your pardon, Mama, for my abrupt departure. I am quite all right now. It was just—the shock, you know." She added, falsely, "I haven't thought of him in a dozen years!" Her words deceived neither of her listeners. "But, Fenella, you said, just now—wounded?"

"Gervase tells me he is only now convalescent. It is most doubtful whether he will ever regain the use of his arm."

She could have added Gervase's assessment of Tom's lack of interest in recovery, but decided against further laceration of Kitty's feelings, in the mistaken belief that least said, soonest mended.

Lady Cleviss interposed neatly, "Don't let sympathy lead you into folly, Kitty."

"I shall not, Mama," said Kitty. She had been shaken, dealt a severe blow, but she added stoically, "He hasn't thought of me, I dare say, for ages."

Kitty would have lost any wager she might have placed on that assumption. In the carriage, just now rumbling up from London, Tom Prentice was propped up in a corner of the seat, feeling pain in every jolt of the carriage. His shriveled, useless arm was supported by a bolster, and wrapped against taking a chill in the scarcely healed wound.

He was thankful that he no longer felt the searing thrusts of pain that drove him insensible at the first, and the sharp needlelike jarring was sufficiently intermittent so that he could endure it.

This pain in his arm was comparatively new, only six months old now. The pain in his mind had so long been a part of him that he had learned not to heed it for days, even weeks, at a time. Even so, when it returned, it did so with the same acuteness as the first days after he had been carried away, almost by force, from Wakeford Hall and his beloved Kitty.

"Comfortable?" asked his sister Amelia.

It was fortunate she did not wait for an answer, for Tom could muster only a grunt. He never expected to be comfortable again. But Amelia was a constant prattler, and he had

long since given over the intentions of taking part in her conversations.

Instead, he pursued his own thoughts. The coach was
indeed more comfortable than the narrow board they had
found on which to carry him from the battlefield. But in
truth, he scarcely remembered that journey, where every step
of his stretcher bearers sent an agony through him that
threatened to shatter him. Mercifully he had lapsed into deliri-
ium at that time, so that now all he could recall of that battle
was the sudden realization that he had been hit—the complete disbelief that he had been touched by ball or shot, until
he tried to raise his hand to signal his troops.

Then there were the booming of guns, the shouts of men,
his stretcher bearers grunting close at hand—the one awful
moment when they slipped and he felt himself sliding off
toward the ground—

But the worst part was, now that he was recovering, that
he had received his disabling wound not in a battle whose
name might reverberate around England, but in a skirmish
with a handful of ambushers. It was hardly decent!

A word of Amelia's caught his attention, and he set himself to listen. Any gossip would be better than the gloom of
his own reflections.

"Chelmsford, I said, Tom. I was quite sure you were not
listening to me. Where we stopped at Chelmsford, you recall?
An hour since. All they could talk about there was the highwayman."

Tom forced himself to answer. "Man? Only one? This
looks to be a prosperous road. Room for half a dozen, one
might think!"

"Oh, Tom, your wayward humor! I vow I never know
what you will say next!" She indulged in mock derision, for
she had been at her lowest ebb when she fetched Tom at the
docks when the newest harvest of wounded troops came
home.

He had been so near death, she believed, as made no difference. She had taken him to the town house, cosseted him,
harried the surgeons to do their best, and kept up his spirits
with bracing remarks. Nothing had worked a miracle, however, and she had greeted Gervase's invitation with relief.
Perhaps the country air would succeed where all else had
failed.

Now, to hear him actually joking, even in his dark humor,

was music of angels to her. She might not display her affection, but her feeling for her brother ran deep and true.

"We have naught to fear from any robber," said Tom after a moment. "We will arrive at Wakeford Hall before dark."

"I shall be glad. Although, I must tell you, they say that daylight does not deter him."

"A brave man, then? Or one so desperate as to take rash chances?" He reached, with some effort, to put his hand over hers. "Don't fret, my dear," he added kindly, "I can always faint away. I venture to believe that will so disconcert him that he will fade into the shrubbery."

The effort had for the moment exhausted him, and he lay back and closed his eyes. Chelmsford, Amelia had said. He had hardly noticed the town when they passed through. And yet it brought a myriad of recollections. After Chelmsford would come Witham, and then one turned to the right, toward the sea, and soon—though not soon enough, now!—they would pull up before the broad-stepped entrance of Wakeford Hall.

And where was Kitty now? He had fallen irrevocably in love with the sweet, shy Kitty Morland. After his father had summoned him home, and told him a few home truths— "Miss Morland has sent word that she does not feel you are suited, and wishes to consider the episode closed"—he went off to war. A man's business, war was, and it did no good to think of women, especially a particular woman. But she did have a way of creeping into his thoughts——

At least he did not come home to her, crippled, useless, full of abiding pain and morose of mind. Kitty was spared that. He lay back against the squabs, his mouth tight against the unavoidable jolts of the road, and let Kitty's smiling face come clear to his inner vision.

But the vision was Kitty as she had been. Now, most likely, she was matronly, plump with comfortable living and the production of eight children!

Amelia, almost as though she were reading his mind, said, "Isn't this where it all happened? I had forgot till now. Tom, will you hate coming here? I should never have agreed to come!" She glanced at Tom. His eyes were closed, but she thought he was not asleep. "Papa was wrong to use you so. I always thought so, but you know it would not have done to say so. That ugly heiress he had in mind—Eleanor Chester, you recall—you were quite right to turn her down. *She* wouldn't have stirred herself to take care of you!"

Tom eased his arm on the bolster, unobtrusively, so that she wouldn't notice. Contritely, he said, "I know you've given up much to nurse me. I may not sound so, always, but I am truly grateful."

She exclaimed, "It is nothing, Tom. I would do it a hundred times over. I was not complaining, you know. We have both been badly used. I never wrote to you about Trent, did I? Hugh Trent, the second son of the old baron. But Papa would not allow it."

Tom roused. "I never heard that."

"Well, you had troubles enough. And I was quite overset at the time."

"But now—?"

"You mean because Papa cannot prevent me now. But Hugh is leg-shackled and living in Scotland."

"Not happy, I wager," protested Tom loyally.

"Perhaps not," she agreed, a trifle wistfully. "But then, I was not sorely wounded, as you were, from Papa's tyranny."

"The most grievous wounds, my dear, often do not show."

Amelia looked from the window. She had not thought about Hugh Trent for some time, not really *thought* about him, and she had believed herself satisfied with her life. Not lonely, to be sure, for she was forever on the move, visiting friends in their country houses, but avoiding London whenever she could, lest anyone think she was still hanging out for a husband.

"Forget it," counseled Tom. "What's done is done. There's no way to unshackle him." A wry smile twisted his lips. "Try to think of him as he probably is now. Meek and docile, developing a small paunch, his only conversation yes, my dear, I entirely agree, my dear—"

In spite of herself, Amelia could not entirely smother a small chuckle. Tom was satisfied. He was of some small use, even in such a trivial matter as a moment's beguilement of his sister's loneliness. He set himself to be at least civil, if he could not quite be merry.

"Good of old Gervase to ask us down," he said, and the conversation moved in ordinary channels, until they drew up at the inn in Witham.

Coachman descended and came to Tom's door. "Best ask

about roads, sir, I thought. Been raining here, quite a mort, judging from the puddles, sir."

He turned to the stableboy, panting to be of service, at his left hand. "How far to Wakeford, boy?"

"An hour, less if you spring 'em."

"Roads muddy?"

"Mought be with the rain. Dunno. May not soak in. Land's dry. So they say. Ben't no farmer, my own self."

The head groom approached then. "Come down safely from London?"

The coachman, mindful of the warnings at Chelmsford, said, "So far, safe enough. Not apt to meet any Turpin between here and Wakeford Hall, I don't think."

"Specially," said the head groom, full of importance in his local knowledge, "since he struck again last night."

Amelia squealed faintly.

"Works alone," said the groom, unconsciously pitching his voice a bit higher for the gentry within the coach, "knows somehow when to find a good purse."

Tom joined the conversation. "No doubt he has spies everywhere?"

"Not here in Witham, sir. I'll promise you that!" He glared at the stable boy, who promptly discovered a compelling interest in the weathervane atop the stable roof.

"Mighty well spoken they say. It's a mystery, all right!"

The coach turned onto the road running east from Witham. Tom caught his breath, and Amelia discovered that he was almost helpless with laughter.

"What on earth! Tom, are you mad?"

At length he found his voice. Between spasms of mirth, he managed to explain, "Suppose old Gervase has taken to the road?"

"Gervase?" she echoed.

"Missed all the excitement in Spain, I shouldn't wonder!"

Reluctantly Amelia permitted a small smile to creep across her lips. Her ways had been set by her disappointments, and the shell she had developed served her well. Thwarted in her own desires, her inclinations channeled into narrow, fruitless outlets, she was only dimly aware that she was wasting her life. But with Tom's return, needing her desperately as he did, she was conscious of an alteration in her, even that she was happier. A tragedy that Tom had been so grievously wounded, she thought, but now she was beginning to feel valued.

The small smile developed into a laugh. "Tom, how droll!" she said, in sympathy. Then genuine amusement struck her, and she gurgled, "Imagine Aunt Elizabeth if she were to discover her son a knight of the road!"

In charity with each other, they traveled on. Tom's arm pained even more sorely from the fatigue of the journey, but he minded it less. Laughter was indeed a great physic, worth all the doses of the surgeons.

Gervase hurried out of the door of Wakeford Hall to greet them. Buston was in his element. Stableboys leaped to the heads of the horses. Footmen hurried to assist Amelia to alight from the heavy coach, and others scurried to the boot to unstrap the luggage. Buston and Gervase put themselves at Tom's service.

It was a complicated, delicate business to extricate Tom from the interior without hurting his arm, and supporting him in his weakness. But at last he stood, trembling slightly, and breathed the soft, rain-scented air.

He grinned feebly at Gervase. "I'm glad I came."

15

Mr. Forsyke, the surgeon from Witham, arrived promptly on Tom's arrival, thanks to the foresighted planning of Gervase.

A stout dose of laudanum would make sure that Tom slept the night away, and the doctor descended to Gervase. "Grievous," he said shaking his bald head. "Mending well, though. Yes, yes, mending well."

"You think he'll be all right?"

The bald head nodded up and down vigorously. "All right? Arm'll do. They didn't send him home too soon. One thing they do down in the Peninsula. Don't know why Wellington lets 'em, but they will do it. Send 'em home too soon, and the voyage kills 'em. No, my lord, the wound is well healed. Not much use of that arm, though."

"Will he regain any use at all? You must know that I have not seen the wound myself."

"Aye, of course, you would know did you see it. Quite a bit of experience, I wager, they tell me five years with the army? You've seen it all, then, my lord."

"Not quite all," said Gervase modestly. "But all I require to see."

Mr. Forsyke nodded again. "No use of his arm more 'n he's already got. *Unless* a miracle takes hold. I don't see many of them, tell the truth. But possible, oh, yes, indeed, possible."

Before he left, he paused on the threshold and added, cryptically, "Reminds me of another patient I had once, my lord. Can't seem to believe that there's more to a body than an arm. Could have been his eyes. Could be dead." He frowned ferociously. "Should be grateful!"

By the next day Tom did indeed feel better. Gervase was relieved to see brightness returned to the eyes that were glazed with fatigue the afternoon before. Amelia was well experienced in the conventions of country house hospitality, and already had earned Lady Huntley's gratitude by retailing choice anecdotes that she had on the tip of her tongue.

Gervase was pleased that his mother had taken so quickly to Amelia. At least, Lady Huntley's strictures on behavior had moved from his own to those Amelia told her about. All in all, life would be much easier. But he did want Fenella to meet his cousins and like them, for he wished to see much of Tom over the next years.

Hereward carried the invitation to Morland Manor. He found the company strangely subdued. Even Miss Morland kept her eyes on her embroidery in her lap, her fair hair hiding whatever expression might linger on her features. He noticed, however, that the work was not a stitch forwarder by the time he would leave.

After the swift glance toward Miss Morland, and his manners made to Lady Cleviss, he let his gaze wander to Fenella. Her eyes were fixed on him with an unfathomable expression, which he took to be unadulterated admiration, a reaction he had often experienced.

The thoughts moving secretly behind the green eyes would have astonished him not a little, and alarmed him a bit more. For Fenella was trying to fit the Hereward she saw into the frame of the highwayman she had seen. There was no incontrovertible resemblance, but then, on the other hand, there was nothing which said, This is not possible.

"We shall be pleased to accept Lord Huntley's invitation," said Lady Cleviss formally, for she had little use for Hereward—an engaging rascal, was her private opinion. "Pray give him my compliments, and tell him we shall come." She glanced at Kitty, who did not look up. Well, Kitty might go or not, as she pleased. She had suffered sufficiently already, and Lady Cleviss would not attempt to regulate her behavior.

Before Hereward left, Lady Stover was announced. Too late, thought Hereward, I should have gone before this visitation!

"I am in such a taking!" Lady Stover cried as soon as she had dealt out of hand with formal greetings. "I vow I never thought we would come to such a pass!"

Hereward, feeling the stirrings of interest, said, "A murrain upon the sheep, perhaps?"

He glanced toward Fenella, hoping to see her approval of his wit, but instead caught the quelling eye of Lady Cleviss, and fell silent.

Lady Stover answered, seriously enough, "No, I don't think so. I surely would have heard about it—no, what I mean is the incredible boldness of the highwayman!"

Bold! thought Fenella, remembering his lips on hers.

Bold! thought Lady Cleviss, stopping Morland ladies upon the road, and said, "It takes no boldness to make one's way with a gun, for the victims are not armed."

Hereward said, "But one never knows whether they are or not, does one?"

"Two nights ago," narrated Lady Stover, heedless of the interruptions, "he robbed again. A merchant, of course. Nowadays, women do not venture out after sundown."

"Very wise," approved Lady Cleviss.

"Sir Edmund says it will be stopped. It *must* be."

Hereward, very casually, inquired, "How does he plan to do this?"

"I shall not betray my husband's secrets," said Lady Stover, grandly. He had, indeed, been particularly careful not to share his plans with his lady, from the wisdom of experience.

"The old smugglers' road," Hereward exclaimed. "I am sure there must be one in this region, although I have no knowledge of it."

"Yes, there was a time when the smugglers' road was used,

once a week. But the road has fallen into disuse, and I suppose the old chapel is in ruins."

"Chapel, how very gothic." Hereward grinned.

He was baiting Lady Stover, and enjoying it, thought Fenella. He caught her gaze on him and smiled conspiratorially. No harm in it, his eyes seemed to say, just fun.

"But that reminds me," said Lady Stover, no longer excited but merely troubled. "Some one, was it the Vicar? No, I don't think so. Hunt, our game warden, you know—no, I think it was—" Hopelessly entangled in her uncertainties, she took the only way out. "Anyway, Sir Edmund was told that the last full moon, only last week, you remember, that someone saw a light in the old chapel. What do you think of that, Lady Cleviss?"

Irrepressibly, Hereward suggested, "The Devil himself?"

Lady Cleviss spoke in a voice he had not yet heard from her. "Enough. You are not of this neighborhood, and therefore have little stake in our affairs."

"On the contrary, Lady Cleviss, with all humility. I have a great deal of interest here."

He found an opportunity to speak quietly to Fenella before he left.

"Do not fear, Fenella, for you will soon be under the wing of the law-abiding Wakefords."

"I fear nothing," she said sharply, "for the Morlands are not cowards."

"No smugglers for them? I wonder who led the old-time smugglers? Not Wakefords, for they are full of law and order. Not Morlands, then? I shall give it my thought, and perhaps I can discover the deep secret of the region."

"No need, is there? For Lady Stover insisted that all was past and done with."

"I thought to amuse you," he said, "but you are not easily diverted, are you? I have changed my opinion. Marry Gervase if you insist."

"If *I* insist?" she cried, a bit shocked.

"A life as dull as ever you might wish for," he told her.

She watched him stroll down the drive. Had he turned around and seen her still standing in the door, following his figure with her eyes until he vanished from her view, he would have been excessively pleased. But he would have been entirely mistaken as to her motives, for she was hardly filled with admiration for him. Instead, she was endeavoring to discover some resemblance in him to the highwayman, or to detect some quirk that might prove he was not.

As she turned back into the house, she was convinced that she was mistaken. How foolish to think that he was a criminal! And while the robber had not yet harmed anyone, it was most likely—so Lady Stover had pointed out—that sooner or later the highwayman would find it necessary to fire his pistol, and then the question would not be of a simple thief, but of a murderer.

No Wakeford could murder in cold blood. She must believe that, for she dared not think otherwise. Besides, she told herself, there was no glint of mischief in his eye today. In daylight, there was no resemblance whatever to a figure seen briefly in the shadows.

How fortunate she was not to have made her wild accusation solely on the strength of a shadow in the night!

On the appointed afternoon, Lady Cleviss and Fenella took coach to Wakeford Hall, to meet Gervase's cousins. Kitty pled a headache as an excuse for not accompanying them.

"Mama, I cannot hold my head up, truly," she said, passing a hand over her brow and pushing the damp hair up. "I have not slept. The weather is so oppressive."

"Not just the rain, I think," said Lady Cleviss. "Never mind, child, I shall not insist. You do appear unwell to me, but I promise you that if your headache is not gone by evening, I shall believe it a more serious ailment, and send for Mr. Forsyke."

In an unwonted gesture of affection, she stroked Kitty's hair. "Remember, my child, you have done nothing for which to be ashamed. I shall not like to see you stay in seclusion for very long."

Lady Cleviss greeted Lady Huntley with the wariness of one in close company with a Borgia. She allowed Tom to be presented to her, and made no recognition that she had ever seen him before.

If Tom had girded himself to withstand even the shock of seeing Kitty again, he had no defense against such a direct snub. If Lady Cleviss did not know him, then his road was clear. Surely Kitty was now married, established in her own home, and poor Tom Prentice long forgotten. They would not suit, so Kitty had written his father. It never occurred to him then, or now, to question his father's veracity.

He could not discipline his expression sufficiently to deceive Gervase. Nor, to give her credit, did Fenella mistake his silence for moroseness. Instinctively, she knew he was sorely hurt, and went to sit beside him.

She too was hurt, just now, for Lady Huntley pointedly greeted her as though she were a governess in attendance upon a young lady of quality, rather than her elder son's betrothed.

Fenella was conscious of Gervase's approving eyes on her as she went to Tom. Deliberately putting his own feelings aside, Tom set himself to become acquainted with Gervase's fiancée.

Fenella listened to Tom's praise of Gervase. She agreed that he was kind, and doubtless generous. But she drew the line when Tom spoke of Gervase as a man of humor. Humor? There was none in Gervase!

But Tom had given her a glimpse of her betrothed that she had not seen, nor would she believe him out of hand. For Tom was the recipient of Gervase's thoughtfulness, and therefore prone to believe the best of his cousin.

Those close to him, she considered, should know him best. Hereward called his elder brother stodgy and dull, and surely Lady Huntley held him in low esteem. Fenella did not pause to think that these two had seen no more of Gervase in recent years than had Tom.

In the end, she made up her own mind. Glancing involuntarily toward the object of her thoughts, she saw that he was watching her, gravely, soberly. There was without doubt no humor in him.

She would have been astonished to learn the tenor of his thoughts. He had long since learned to ignore his mother's inexorable flow of conversation, more aptly termed a monologue. Just now his consideration was bent entirely on Fenella. She was surely not the picture of serene happiness, as one might expect from one so soon to be wed.

She sat quietly enough, but a certain restlessness in the fingers of her tightly folded hands betrayed her, and he knew a lively spurt of anxiety on her behalf. She was in trouble, or as near as made no difference, he concluded. The most logical source of affliction, to his knowledge, was a repercussion of some nature from the London business. He must do a bit of investigation, for his most pressing wish was to erase that wistful unhappiness from her innocent features.

Lady Huntley, completely unaware of any cross currents in

the room, was bent on displaying her niece's accomplishments to Lady Cleviss.

"My dear Amelia," said Lady Huntley, "has been beguiling me with the most fascinating tales of society. I vow we laugh all the day about one or another. We in the country, as I have told Gervase more than once, although he does not heed me, feel so cut off from our friends that the slightest *on-dit* refreshes us for a week! Amelia, you know, is so sought after among her friends. My dear, pray tell Lady Cleviss what you told me this morning. The latest escapade of Caroline Lamb, you know."

Amelia was curiously reluctant to embark upon her anecdote. In the ordinary way, she would good-naturedly share the amusing spectacle of unreasonable behavior and illogical vagaries of the *haut monde*, a world in which eccentricity was admired and a whim was never curbed.

But now, to be encouraged in such a fashion by her aunt, was vaguely disquieting. Suddenly she was put in mind of a pony she had seen once. Adorned with a flower collar and made to stand upon his hind legs.

But Lady Huntley's piercing glance was on her, and obediently she began. "You must know, Lady Cleviss, that I did not witness the incident myself. I was staying last month with friends in Derbyshire—"

"You are well out of such society as you speak of, I am persuaded," interrupted her aunt.

Fennella's attention was caught by the interchange, and civilly she listened to an account, exaggerated nearly beyond recognition, of Caro's disastrous and futile suicide attempt at Lady Heathcote's.

Fenella sat, stiff with dread, her eyes focused on a spot near Gervase's knees, waiting for the next revelation. Did Amelia know about the Vauxhall Gardens incident? If so, Fenella had no doubt but that it would come forth, embellished with falsities, and sink her beyond trace.

How horrible to be at the mercy of Amelia Prentice, no more than a heedless society rattle!

In this, she was mistaken. Amelia, while having ample financial resources, was dependent upon others for the solaces of companionship. She had learned that a constant fund of faintly malicious anecdotes about people that everyone knew, tales of the world in which she was at home, was a sure guarantee of invitations.

She had, for want of anything of more value to occupy her days, cultivated this talent, so eagerly welcomed by many ladies of her acquaintance.

Now, suddenly, it was borne in on her—particularly seeing Tom's grave gaze on her—that her achievements, attained by assiduous effort, assumed an appearance meretricious in the extreme. It was a distasteful truth, one she could not swallow at once.

In a hasty, ill-considered effort to alleviate the malice of the tale, she burst out, "But Lady Caroline has such great charm! It is no wonder that she is prone to insist upon her own way."

"Charm!" cried Lady Huntley. "I hope such rackety behavior does not pass for *charm*. I shall be sadly out of it, if that is the way of the world now."

Amelia remained silent, her own guilt-tinged thoughts drumming in her head.

Lady Huntley pursued the expression of her own opinions. "I wonder they can keep her confined at Brocket! I believe the family removed her there?" She scarcely noticed that her companions were silent.

Amelia's cheeks flushed slowly. She had truly not realized how she had appeared, no more than a malicious rattle, a purveyor of gossip no matter how untrue, simply for the fleeting satisfaction of company to fill her empty days. Now, in the presence of Tom, of fearsome Lady Cleviss—Amelia recognized in her the worth of two Lady Huntleys in force of character and impeccable integrity—she had rarely felt lower. Lady Cleviss's nearsighted stare had seemed to Amelia a gaze as from an Olympian goddess.

Gervase felt it was time to intervene. Aware of Amelia's inexplicable discomfiture, and Fenella's mental anguish at the very sound of Lady Caroline's name, he searched with haste for diversion.

Unfortunately, the sole subject that came to his mind was one he had not yet settled in his mind. "I have not spoken," he said with more honesty than tact, "to Fenella, but I am planning some alterations—"

Lady Huntley veered to meet the enemy. "Alterations? Here?"

"You may recall, ma'am, that an older Wakeford saw fit to brick up a door and a window in the room that serves now as dining room. It seems to me that were these bricks removed, we should have a great deal more light, for the wing faces the south—"

He was looking at Fenella. It was Lady Huntley who commented. "I do not think it at all well to open up that room. One never dines by daylight, and I never pass through the room until late in the day. You cannot have thought of the expense, Gervase."

"I shall endeavor to consider it," said Gervase briefly.

"Of course, no gentleman understands the countless details of household management. No matter how fine a staff of servants, and I must say the staff here is not to my liking, it takes the hand of the mistress of the house to think of the small items. The sun, for example, fades draperies and carpets. Gervase has his head in the clouds if he thinks otherwise. There is a very fine Turkey carpet in that room. I shall not like to see the sun destroy it."

"We shall have to move the carpet, then," said Gervase mildly.

"I have always thought that the small parlor at Oakbury would set it off nicely," remarked his mother.

Lady Cleviss had stayed as long as her minimal control of her tongue would allow. She longed to rout Lady Huntley from the neighborhood. If Gervase did not see that Fenella's life was free of his mother's influence, then she would. Now, of course, was not the time.

"I have always wondered," said Lady Cleviss in her clear voice, "at people who prefer personal discomfort rather than allow minor harm to such replaceable objects as furnishings." Her steady gaze at Lady Huntley left her with no doubt of her opinion. "Are you ready, Fenella?"

Fenella rose hastily, clearly thankful that the deadly afternoon was over. She glanced at Lady Huntley, her words of leave-taking on her lips. But she was struck dumb by the malice that glittered in her hostess's eyes. Sheer hatred. But why?

Gervase saw them to their carriage. While they were still in the hall, he said, "Pray give Miss Morland my best wishes for her recovery."

After the coach had started down the drive, he turned. Tom was leaning against the door to the parlor. "Miss Morland? You mean *Kitty*?"

Surprised, Gervase agreed.

"I thought she was—far away."

"Not at all. You'll have many opportunities to get acquainted with her."

"I *am* acquainted."

Too late, Gervase remembered. "It was Miss Morland, then—Tom, I'm sorry. I was thinking too much about Fenella—"

"Don't be sorry," said Tom, brusquely. "All in the past now."

He turned stiffly, and began to climb the stairs, slowly, holding hard to the railing with his good hand. His back was bent with pain—or, thought Gervase, with loneliness suddenly become intolerable.

"All in the past, you see," Lady Cleviss pointed out, in the homeward-bound coach. "You will have noticed that he did not even inquire about Kitty. The least he could do, one might think."

Fenella scarcely heeded her grandmother. For once again, she thought, she had escaped the imminent revelation of that evening in the Gardens. If the scene at Lady Heathcote's, in the full glare of public observation, led to such comminatory comments, then the pursuit of the unwilling Byron, in disguise as Caro was, without modesty or even decency, in the darkness must have set all of London on its ears.

But no word of the incident seemed to be current. If Lady Dorton were accurate, the details of Fenella's return home, on foot, unescorted, should have run through London society as swiftly as a summer grass fire.

Fenella's inexperience betrayed her. She could not think that Lady Dorton would falsify, for there was no clear purpose to be gained. It did not occur to Fenella that Lady Dorton simply did not want to receive Fenella again, for the burden of chaperonage lay too heavily upon her indolent nature.

"And that sister of his!" continued Lady Cleviss, ignoring her granddaughter's silence. "A sad want of character, I fear. I cannot like gossip."

"Nor I," retorted Fenella, "especially when the object is innocent of all wrongdoing."

"There is a lesson in this for you, Fenella. A reputation once lost cannot be regained."

Fenella did not respond. The words that sprang to her lips were totally ineligible to speak—too bad, she thought, to feel as guilty as she did and yet be innocent. One might almost wish to *do* some scandalous jape, simply so as not to waste such a heavy implication of guilt!

Instead, she said, "I liked Mr. Prentice. He seemed very kind. Imagine, he even tried to convince me that Gervase has a sense of humor!"

The coach turned in between the gates of Morland Manor. "Good humor," said Lady Cleviss, "is far more to be valued than a rakish attitude, or even frivolity, Fenella. You have sufficient lightness of spirit—one might say impulsive waywardness—to serve for two. But there, I do not mean to scold you. I simply wish you to stay clear of harm."

Until I am wed, thought Fenella. Then let Gervase deal with me!

"Passion," pronounced Lady Cleviss as the carriage drew up before the entrance and stopped, "is temporary. Like fireworks, Fenella. Brilliant for the moment, but leaving only acrid smoke behind."

"And," said Fenella, "the memory of a beautiful sight."

"Quite true. But my dear, scandal is forever. Look at Amelia Prentice. She has a firm grasp of damaging anecdotes, but I know that one or two of the tales she told happened five years since."

She allowed herself to be helped from the carriage, and went into the house, Fenella just behind her. In the hall she turned. "Fenella, the best thing in the world for you is to marry Huntley. Let him protect your good name. Always supposing such protection is necessary."

Fenella surprised herself. Tartly, she replied, "He is too stolid, too deliberate for any use along that line, ma'am. By the time he would address the problem, it would be all done with. You see how he deals with his dreadful mother? He is in no wise able to protect even himself!"

Lady Cleviss was in lively agreement, but she said, "A proper respect, after all. He is not so boorish as to be impertinent to his mother, you know. This speaks well for him."

Fenella, left standing in the hall alone, realized the afternoon was well advanced. A wasted three hours, she thought, spent in active dislike of the Dowager Lady Huntley. She must needs marry Gervase Wakeford, with all the disadvantages she conceived in such a match. But she was not wed yet, and there was still time—

First, she must ferret out the mystery of the highwayman's identity. The sooner the better, she believed.

16

The sooner the better.

How clever Caro was, thought Fenella, an hour later, picking her way through a thicket, well out of sight and sound of the Manor. Pantaloons were the ideal garb for such an expedition, but the pantaloons—as well as the expedition itself—were not quite the thing.

Although pantaloons might be appropriate, yet Fenella could not envision without a chuckle the spectacle of herself stealing through the shrubbery, dressed in scarlet and silver.

She stopped and looked back. All that could be seen were shrubs and a few saplings. All the rest was derelict, a no-man's-land where the land seemed too stony to farm with profit, and even sheep would tear their wool sadly in the underbrush.

The last hour had been active—Fenella had left Grandmama with Kitty to relate the afternoon's conversation, and changed into a simple morning gown of soft gray. She carried a shawl against the chill of the coming evening, and had sought out old Punthrop, behind the stables, sitting in the late rays of the sun.

Quite the oldest man Fenella had ever known, Punthrop had grown up at Morland Manor, served his active days, and now sought only comfort for his aching bones.

He did not seem quite aware of Fenella's name, but he was glad of any company. When she asked about the old smuggling road, he roused and opened his eyes. "Aye, in your granfer's day, or mayhap in *his* granfer's day—so long ago as makes no difference. Many's the keg of brandy, the roll of cloth smooth as new cream. All past now. Aye, the world's gone gray."

"The smugglers surely didn't come through here," suggested Fenella. "Wasn't there an old smuggling road?"

"Aye it was. Up yonder, past the lightning tree. But you, young missy, best stay away. 'Tis said they be ha'nts up there."

She asked a few more questions. Then she assured him that she would not go so far as to be lost, or to be in danger from the haunts. Now, almost an hour after she left Punthrop, she stood in the midst of encircling bushes, and had no clear idea of where she was.

Freeing her skirt from the last of the beggars' lice, she went back in her mind over what she had learned from Punthrop. The smugglers used to bring their boats into Cogges Cove, an easy climb off the shingle onto the land above high tide. Now the outlaws had moved their operations to the north. It was likely that the establishment of the coast guard station close to Cogges Cove had been the cause. While it was dangerous to catch sight of the smugglers' train against the full moon—as her Dorset nurse had often told her—it was dangerous for the smugglers to bring in their booty under the very noses of the riding officers.

Now she caught sight of what Punthrop had called the lightning tree. A giant of the old forest, perhaps even of the days when deep woods covered England from Land's End to John o'Groats, so it was said, now only a whitened stump, taller than the tallest man, but barkless and without the major part of its trunk. Lightning in some long-ago storm had felled the tree, obviously the last of its kind.

She must be standing on the bank of the road that was. Before her she could discern the sunken track as of old wagon wheels passing heavy-laden from the sea. It had been many years, she believed, since even a farm cart had gone this way.

She was relieved to remember that no smugglers would catch her here, for they had all gone "north, Naze way." But she was not after smugglers, after all.

She was disappointed. The road was grown over, and it was clear that no one had been this way. The rumor that the highwayman made use of the smugglers' road had been just that—an unfounded rumor. She would have to think of another way to ferret out Hereward's secret.

If Hereward were the highwayman.

Here in the quiet evening, when belated rooks sped overhead to their nests, far-off a sheep bell tinkled, it was impossible to believe in highwaymen, or even in anything but her own misguided folly in coming here.

She looked behind her. The track she had made was still detectable. She must hurry back before darkness descended to obliterate the path.

She turned, and something grabbed at her skirt. Her heart pounded. She looked down—only a bramble. She stooped to pull it off, and then she saw it.

A tiny track went off from the spot where she stood and vanished in the knee-high grass. She followed it with her eyes, and then turned to trace it in the opposite direction.

A thin thread of a path—disappearing in each direction, as though a single horse—not a smuggler's train!—had traveled this road, leaving only the track of flattened grass and small twigs broken.

Surely someone had recently used this old abandoned road. She could almost hear her nurse's voice in her ear—Cut a throat, they would, sooner'n look at ye!

But she was still on Morland land, wasn't she? And no one would dare touch her. She ought to go home, just the same. She moved, then, away from the Manor, to her left, following the faint path. She was not sure how she would get home again, for darkness was approaching. But she could no more have ignored the beckoning trail than she could have perched atop the lightning-struck oak.

She lost track of time, but the way was surprisingly easy to follow. Just when she thought she must be reaching the outskirts of Edinborough, or more likely Witham, she debouched into a small clearing. The grass was short, there were no encumbering bushes, and across the small clearing stood a ruined chapel.

Holding her breath in surprise, she became aware of a strange harsh sound. Fearfully, she traced down the noise—only a horse cropping grass! That was why the clearing appeared so neatly cared for.

But it was a fine-appearing horse, she noticed, sorrel with two white front feet. The animal was no lost plow horse, that was certain.

The chapel stood across the irregular clearing, but she had no interest in exploring it. Its roof had fallen in, so it seemed from the light showing through the broken windows. She was no foolish Ratcliffe heroine, to linger where she was not invited, to explore a ruin where the slightest breeze might dislodge a stone on her head——

How glad she was to remember that the days of smuggling at least here were long past. The moonlight trade was an illegal venture at best, but—as she had been told—the laws and economic necessity of the time required daring remedies.

But some doubtless enjoyed the danger for itself alone—
and the throat-cutting as well. She was grateful that the latter was long past, as well.

Then, without warning, an arm encircled her throat from
behind, and her scream was cut short——

She sagged in sheer surprise, and felt a very solid body at
her back. Desperately, she kicked backward, but her slippers
were soft-soled, and her captor only laughed softly.

"My dear girl," said Hereward, "you are sadly armed for
combat!"

"You!" she breathed. "Let me go!"

Abruptly he released her and she nearly fell. "Your
slightest wish, ma'am!"

"Then I was right. You are the highwayman!" she cried,
rashly.

He did not look in the least abashed, to her surprise. Instead, his eyes glinted in a distinctly devilish way, and suddenly she believed she should fear her future brother-in-law
more than any cut-throat smuggler she would ever meet.

"You recognized me, then," said Hereward. "Somehow, I
fancied you might. I should be a poor stick if I did not leave
an impression on a fair lady, wouldn't I?"

"You need not fear I shall betray you," she said, calmly
enough, though her heart pounded.

"No, strangely, I do not expect betrayal. Not from you, at
any rate. For I remember a certain kiss—aha, I see you recall
it too. With pleasure, I trust? At least, I have not heard you
rail against the liberties the outlaw took."

"You're laughing at me."

"Quite true. For you are such a delight—"

Her cheeks felt warm. She dared not let him continue in
that vein. In fact, her presence here in an abandoned clearing
with him was far more reprehensible than strolling with Caro
Lamb in the gardens.

"Why do you do this?" she wondered. "You surely are not
penniless."

"No one but a dormouse could live on the pittance that my
father saw fit to leave me!"

"But surely Gervase—?"

"Give me leave to point out that you know Gervase not at
all well. He is not a penny miser, but he has for some reason
the intention of keeping me on short rations—as I suppose
his army friends might say." Eyes narrowed, Hereward

changed his tactics. "Too bad, my dear, that your undoubted charm will be cast to the winds."

"I d–don't understand."

"Gervase will transform you. You will, within a year, I wager, be as dull as he is."

Fenella protested. "That is not true! He is very kind."

"And dull, don't deny it. Stodgy, dull, nearly without wit—"

"But—"

"You've heard him prose on and on about his sheep! Mutton for breakfast, I have no doubt!"

She caught, then, the hidden mocking laughter in his voice. Reluctantly, she was forced to smile. Gervase *did* carry on about his farming project. Yet she was conscious of a sense of disloyalty in her that she did not like.

Hereward, on the other hand, was much pleased with the way he was managing this interview. He had been nearly as startled as Fenella when he came upon her. He had not thought that anyone in the world knew of his lair. Of all intruders, he wished least to receive Fenella. But now he had persuaded her not to run to Gervase with her discovery. The delightful way she tilted her head when lost in thought, the clear serenity of her heart-shaped face when baited spitefully by his mother—all had not passed unnoticed. Now the opportunity had fallen into his hand like an overripe greengage plum.

Not only would she maintain his secrecy, but if he were to play his cards right, he might do his despised brother a disfavor. He had no illusions as to the depth of Gervase's regard for his betrothed. He was at a loss to explain where they could have met before, or to account for Gervase's sudden devotion to her. But were Fenella to prefer Hereward, even for a short time, then Gervase would be sorely wounded.

"I'm glad," said Hereward, "that it was you in the carriage that night. Such sweet lips—I vow they linger in my dreams." His voice sounded suitably forlorn. He took her hands and pulled her gently to him. "Do you like me even a little? Sister?"

"Sister!" she cried. "Sir, your behavior is far too familiar—"

"Familiar is just what it should be," he protested. "For you are nearly one of the family—no matter how ill-advised an arrangement I consider it."

He did not let her go. He placed, with grave deliberation, a chaste kiss on her lips. Her eyes flew wide open. He read in them an innocence that gave rise to misgivings in his mind, but also—so he believed—an innocence surprised by desire.

He kissed her again, in a manner not quite so chaste as before. Belatedly, she recognized that she trembled, not unwillingly, on the brink of a misunderstanding at the very least, and a shameful lack of modesty, more than likely. She drew back, pulling her hands away.

Too fast, thought Hereward, but there is surely a vein worth mining here. He would find her an amusing diversion, one to make his enforced stay in Essex more endurable.

She stood a little apart, wishing to go home, fearful of making the long trip over the narrow, half-invisible track alone, and knowing that night would fall before she had traveled more than halfway to the Manor.

She gave vent to her fears. "I wish I were a man!" Then she wouldn't be so fearful.

Hereward said, softly, "I'm glad you're not."

"No matter what I say, you twist my words out of all meaning!" she complained. "I simply meant that men have a right to adventure, and ladies have to sit by, not even allowed to hear about such things lest they faint away."

Surprisingly, she had nearly forgotten Hereward. She had never put her thoughts into such words before. In truth, she had not known she owned such rebellion in her heart. But as she spoke, she was astonished to find that she was both convinced of the justice of her protest, and also fearful of where such rebellion might lead.

"I have never heard," said Hereward, judiciously, "of a lady highwayman. A contradiction in the heart of the matter, after all."

"Oh, no, I should not like that above half," she cried. "For I cannot think what Grandmama might say!"

"No more can I," said Hereward with humor. "Nor, more to the point, would Gervase find words sufficiently chastising."

"He is so different from you," mused Fenella.

She was more distressed even than she knew. She had discovered ideas within her that she had not suspected. She had almost forgot where she was—at dusk in a remote clearing with her only company a hunted outlaw—transported as she was in listening to the tumult of her inner voices.

"I should hope he was," Hereward agreed. "He has always kept me from doing what I wanted to."

"I, too," she murmured, "am hedged about by rules."

"He's always kept me short of money. I wanted to keep my end up with my friends, a lively bunch, but I never had enough of the ready, you know."

"Couldn't you ask him?"

"You don't know him. I wanted a little boat, but if he had known about my plans, he would not have allowed it."

"Too dangerous, I am persuaded."

"No. Too expensive. But I outfoxed him. I must take you aboard my *Naiad*. I can think of no more romantic setting than a yacht afloat on the sea."

With a jolt she returned to herself. For that other, wandering-minded rebel was not Fenella, she told herself firmly.

"But you have your yacht," she pointed out, "and Gervase was not able to prevent you after all."

A glint appeared in his eyes that told her he was not pleased. "I should hate to think that you would meddle in my affairs. I wonder—would it be like you, do you think, to carry all my secrets to my brother?"

"That is insulting," she said coldly. "I am no tattler. If you will step aside, sir, I shall be on my way home. I am persuaded my grandmother will be wondering where I am."

"And you will not wish to tell her precisely where you have been, nor with whom, no more than I wish Gervase to hear of my affairs. Agreed?"

There was no hope for it. She must overlook his crimes, for she was in no position to point a finger. "Agreed."

"Then I shall see you safe home."

No further conversation ensued between them, until they reached, in deep twilight, the edge of the lawn surrounding Morland Manor. Then, he simply touched her arm and said, in dulcet tones, *"A bientôt!"*

She thanked him for his escort in a word, and then hurried toward the side door, hidden almost in ivy of vigorous and venerable growth.

But she would not go that way, up to the smugglers' road again, she was determined!

17

The matter of Fenella's trousseau, though of little moment to the intended bride herself, was of some urgency for Lady Cleviss.

"I shall of course ask Miss Rindell to show me the patterns she thinks best. I have fixed this afternoon to drive in to Witham."

"Of course, Mama," said Kitty. "But wouldn't it be better to send for her to come to the Manor?"

"No, indeed," said Lady Cleviss. "I have too vivid a recollection of the weeks before Fenella went to London. The house in an uproar, the servants far more interested in the new gowns than in their work—no, I shall leave Miss Rindell in her proper rooms. More convenient for all, I dare say."

The chaise was ordered, and Lady Cleviss, her daughter, and her granddaughter, with Grimsby driving and Cates on the box, set out. There had been a question of taking one of the footmen as well, to carry parcels if the need arose, but Lady Cleviss decided against such a convenience.

"For we shall not purchase anything today. Not even a ribbon, Kitty, unless you have need?"

"No, Mama."

Miss Rindell, suitably prepared for the descent upon her of Lady Cleviss with wedding clothes for her granddaughter in mind, waited anxiously on her own doorstep. She much preferred to sew in the homes of her clients—for there were excellent meals in the servants' halls, and she need not go to the trouble of preparing them. Nor was she oblivious to the delights of constant interest of the staff in the work going forward. Sewing was a solitary undertaking, as a rule, and the company of interested maids was welcome.

But Lady Cleviss was not tight-fisted, and with a certain amount of attention to her business, Miss Rindell might do very well out of the commission.

Miss Rindell was prepared with patterns and samples of fabrics. Soon Lady Cleviss and Kitty were in close consultation with the seamstress, a vigorous discussion under way at once.

Only Fenella remained aloof. She answered dutifully when spoken to, but her thoughts were all on Hereward. He had completely woven a spell around her, she fancied, a magic born of the soft veiling twilight, the sense of a clearing far from the occupied world, only the chapel to show that men had ever set foot there—

She did not precisely like him. But she was bound to him in promise of secrecy, and in a way her own fate was in his keeping. For if he were to take it upon himself to cry out what he knew, where she had spent the evening, there were no depths deep enough to hide her from shame.

While she could respond in kind, yet she knew that the world would deal gently with Hereward, at the same time flogging her to the end of the world. It was not fair, but it was true, none the less.

Now, standing at the window of Miss Rindell's cottage, she saw with a sinking feeling her betrothed, riding across the triangular green. She thought he did not see her, and quickly withdrew from the window lest he catch her eye.

Her luck was out. An hour later, after their business had been concluded with satisfaction on both sides, they left Miss Rindell and prepared to mount into their chaise. But Gervase was waiting for them.

"I am in good fortune today," he told them. "I had not expected to find you until I caught sight of Fenella. I hope you will do me the honor of taking luncheon with me? I have sent my groom ahead to bespeak a parlor at the Blue Swan. I have been told that Mistress Penn has a flair for dealing with ham."

It was a delicious meal. Mistress Penn was pleased, though not overawed, by her guests. She was well aware of her own worth in the sphere of life to which she had been called, and she would not, to quote her own words, "trade places with ary person, no matter how fancy born!"

Gervase was an impeccable host. His manners were easy, his attention to Lady Cleviss was marked, and yet he found time to smile encouragingly at Fenella frequently. How could Gervase be a penny miser, as Hereward said he was, and never blanch at the reckoning of a meal which was generous in amount and superb in quality?

Toward the end of the meal, Gervase, anxious to bring a

smile to his betrothed's lips, asked, "Do you like to ride? I should like to offer you the pick of my stables. I imagine you might find a mount to suit you."

Lady Cleviss said, "A gentle mount, I insist upon it. Fenella rides very well indeed, but I am fearful every time I see her clearing the hedge behind the stable. I am thankful to say that since she has returned, she has not taken up the habit again."

"My old Thunder had to be put down, you know. I haven't had heart enough to ride another."

"I never understood why your father permitted you to ride such a horse as Thunder. It was most unsuitable for a lady's mount. He was big, you know," she added, turning to Gervase, "and black, and the spirit of the devil. But this bit of a child managed him."

"He liked me," said Fenella simply.

Gervase smiled. "I cannot doubt it."

"Your father, though," said Lady Cleviss, "had no judgment at all. From an infant, he was impulsive. Even rash. No one but a fool would have thought of driving to London in a bleak wind that was sure to bring snow. Of course, he did not succeed."

Gervase remembered the incident she spoke of. Someone, he did not now remember who, had written to him about other things, and had, in passing, mentioned the sad death of Fenella's parents, in an accident on a snowy road.

He now reached for Fenella's hand, beneath the cover of the table, and pressed it with sympathy. She was grateful, and allowed her fingers to curl over around his solid hand.

Aware of Miss Morland's sharp eyes. Gervase withdrew his comforting touch. Illogically, Fenella felt more alone than before.

They rose, replete, from the table. Just before he handed them into their chaise, he broached the subject of an outing. "I should think that these fine days would make a diversion delightful, perhaps a lunch *al fesco* at the seashore. Pray, say you will come."

His glance was impartially given to the three. But Lady Cleviss said, with a touch of grimness, "I shall not countenance such generosity on your part, until we at Morland Hall have entertained you in turn. A dinner for you and your guests, Lord Huntley, a week hence."

A gasp broke from Kitty, a protest that was not lost on

Gervase. Nor, as they drove out of town, had it escaped the attention of Lady Cleviss.

"I know I said I would not receive that young man," she said, "but I hope I know what is due to civility. We cannot let Gervase continue to entertain us without returning his hospitality. Besides, my dear, you will of necessity be thrown in his company sooner or later. I shall expect that you will behave as you ought." She laid her hand on Kitty's. "Believe me, I am most sympathetic."

Kitty forced her answer. "I know, Mama. And truly, he means nothing to me now."

In the event, as Lady Cleviss had planned, Kitty's mopes were forgotten in the planning for the dinner. Lady Cleviss insisted that Fenella learn all she could at Kitty's hands, for she would soon be mistress of her own establishment.

"Four large houses, I believe," said Kitty, "and how you are to go on, I shall not even think!"

"I'll insist that you come to help me," Fenella told her. "After all, if Gervase can call on his mother, then I surely can rely on my dearest aunt."

Kitty gave vent to a mischievous chuckle. "I think that Lady Huntley and I shall not suit!"

Encouraged by Kitty's returning good humor, Fenella plunged once again into the intricacies of planning three removes, an apricot trifle, and the wines from her grandfather's cellar which would do honor to the house.

If, in her attention to Kitty's instructions, Fenella had little time to think of Gervase, he was not so handicapped. He allowed the plans for Wakeford Hall to come to him as they would. He would do nothing to alter the building without Fenella's express approval, and had no fear of interference from his mother. He would allow her to return to her cronies at Bath or wherever, but he did not wish to see the Dowager again at Wakeford Hall.

He had other houses—Oakbury in Wiltshire, where his mother had been living recently, and the great house at West Wycombe. He rather thought the Dorset manors boasted a house fit to live in, although he had not seen it. A nuisance to have been away for five years, for he could have spent the time in learning more about his estates, instead of having it all to do at once.

But it was Wakeford Hall that seemed the kindliest of

houses, and he hoped that Fenella would not object too strenuously to making their home here.

It came to him, not for the first time, that he knew almost nothing of what went on in Fenella's thoughts. She was lovely and graceful, he knew, and her laugh bewitched him. But what she thought about politics, about her family—about *him*—he had no idea.

Touched by her clinging to his hand at the luncheon at the Blue Swan, he was encouraged to think she had consented to marry him voluntarily, if not ecstatically. But certain things puzzled him.

The Fenella he was learning to know here was innocent, sweet, eminently biddable, but also a far cry from the Fenella he had first seen felled to the ground in the darkness in the Gardens. He could not reconcile the two. There, in London, she was indiscretion itself, far from her friends, in company with the strange page who he now knew was Caroline Lamb.

He had heard enough about Caro Lamb and her mad pursuit of the lion of the moment, Lord Byron, to know that innocence had no affinity with them. He could only thank Providence that he had been at hand to rescue Fenella.

He had taken to walking over his fields and pastures, alone at times, often with Warrod. The new sheep from Saffron Walden had been purchased, upon Warrod's enthusiastic endorsement, and now stood placidly upon their new turf, munching steadily, their black faces turned as one toward their owner.

"Why doesn't she trust me?" he demanded of the nearest ram. "Why doesn't she confide in me about that night—does she think I'd cry off?"

The ram moved closer, but even the most devoted animal-lover could not detect sympathy on that bland, ovine face.

"If I should tell her I was the man who sent her home in my carriage," continued Gervase, "I don't know what she would do."

He had not heard Warrod approaching. "My lord, you were speaking to me?"

"Warrod, you startled me. How much a civilian I have become in only these few weeks! In the Peninsula, I could be dead by now, had you been French."

Warrod considered. "Aye, but then in the Wars you would have had naught on your mind but the war, so to speak. Here, if you please, there's much to think on."

"Yes, and I am at a loss as to how to settle some. But the sheep look fine, don't they? Did we lose any in getting them here?"

"Not a one. They're sturdy beasts."

"At least this experiment is turning out well," said Gervase. Suddenly he turned to his farm factor. "Warrod, tell me this. How did you go about courting your handsome wife?"

Warrod, until now, had prided himself that naught that came his way could surprise him, much. But now he had to admit that the earl had given him a facer. Trouble with the miss at the Manor, no doubt of it.

"Well, my lord, there were a mort of suitors for my Bess, mind. I had no more to offer than the next, but I studied on it, and I came up with this—she's bound to think of the man who treats her best." Warming to his theme, and aware that the earl was a fascinated listener, he continued. "All of us, d'ye see, had about the same prospects. I had the small holding of my old dad's, and the rest of them about the same. But it's only natural that a woman looks for the best life. So I— not saying a word of my intentions, you mind—gave her a posy I picked from the wayside, took her a handful of eggs, by times. A nice piece of ham on a Sunday, next to the bone."

"The others didn't give her presents?"

Warrod was pleased. "Ah, but they did—at what you might call the ordinary times. Easter, mayhap, or Lady's Day. When all the boys give their girls summat. But I let her know that I thought of her every day in the ordinary way, d'ye see."

"I see," said Gervase slowly. "Thanks." They talked on then about the livestock management, and did not speak again of Warrod's Bess. But Gervase, on his way home, pondered long.

Not that he would find a nice bit of ham for Fenella—but what worked for one swain might well work for his lord.

Would Fenella care for books? He could have sent down by carrier from London any volume he wished. But he had been so far out of touch, and that fool Byron so close to the heart of this knot, he feared he might well set a foot wrong there.

At length he decided on a small basket of peaches, not grown in his own conservatory, which had fallen into decay in recent years. Against all the dictates of custom, he himself took the small basket in hand and walked over to the manor. Buston, shocked to the core at the sight of the earl carrying his own parcel, was speechless, a fact that saved him from an unfortunate protest.

At the Manor, Gervase presented the peaches to Fenella, in the small salon. "I am persuaded that your conservatories here can produce peaches in quantity. Alas, mine must be built up again before they can be a satisfaction to us."

He spoke so kindly, so confidently of the future together when they would plan the conservatories, perhaps the landscaping of the neglected grounds, that she was in charity with him at once.

"You must tell me if you like them," he said, putting the basket into Worth's hands. "A new variety, I am informed, sent to me from London. If they please you, we shall try to find trees to plant."

"Then you plan to live here, at Wakeford Hall?"

"Yes, of course. The family seat in early days, you know. Shall you miss London?" He could have bit his tongue the moment the words were out. All his planning—vanished in a careless moment.

She saw him stiffen slightly. He surely was hoping she would settle down—a reprehensible phrase, reminiscent of earth over a new-dug grave!

"Shall you not like London?"

"I have seen very little of it," he replied in an excess of caution lest he say too much. "But if you like, we can spend a few weeks there occasionally."

Penny miser? Probably Hereward must be right, for all fit in, thought Fenella. She was fond of the country herself, but the vision of a life spent under Lady Huntley's supervision, either at hand or from a distance however remote, held no charm.

Gervase returned to the Hall, not entirely satisfied with his first essay into deliberate courtship. It had been a stiff business, and even more than before he wished, he believed it was time to tell her his previous intervention in her affairs, or, even better, that she would confess the whole, trusting him to understand.

When he next saw her, it was the occasion of the small dinner party given by Lady Cleviss. There were only eight at the table, so additional leaves had not been added. Kitty was in a state, alternately moaning that she was so ill she could not stand, or looking out of the window to catch the first glimpse of the expected coach.

"Tom—you said he was wounded? But—why didn't he—I can't believe—how does my hair look, Fenella? Too youthful, I think."

"My dear Kitty, you are not thinking at all," said Lady Cleviss, her gentle tone taking the sting out of her words. "All will go well, I promise you."

"Do what I do, Aunt Kitty. Just close your eyes and think—in three hours this will all be in the past."

"A rather desperate move for one so young," was Lady Cleviss's comment.

The coach arrived. Fenella, true to her philosophy, clung to the thought that in three hours they would all go away again. She recalled afterwards only small snatches of conversation, never the whole, until the end of the evening.

Before that, though, she saw that Kitty and Tom could not look at each other at first, and then—surprisingly—later could not take their eyes from the other.

Amelia in her best houseguest chatter accomplished at least the appearance of a lively gathering. Lady Huntley, upon entering the dining room, gave her opinion. "A nice little room."

Later, Gervase's mother announced, in tones of surprise, "This meat is very well dressed." It was her sole contribution to the table conversation.

The room was full of crosscurrents, none of them precisely put into words. There were lengthy silences, trying to the nerves, and even Amelia's game efforts could not entirely rout the uneasiness of the gathering.

She tried, at last, to rouse Hereward. "I shall not dare set foot outside for fear of highwaymen. Do you, cousin, make sure to stay beside me all the way home! You see I have worn my best necklace, and I should not like to lose it."

Hereward laughed lazily. "You've got two soldiers in your party, dear Amelia. Although I imagine my brother is better at a desk than with a pistol. Aren't you, Brother Gervase?" He laughed shortly. "How very monkish that sounds— Brother Gervase!" He glanced briefly at Fenella.

Tom was overwrought. He had never liked Hereward, thinking him a loosecap, and his own life had not been happy enough to provide him with a serenity of spirit sufficient to enable him to overlook fools. Which, he thought, scowling, Hereward certainly was.

"You are wrong, as usual," said Tom across the table.

"Wrong?" Hereward turned to Tom. "You mean—although I blush to think it—that Brother Gervase is far from being a monk? I shall not quite believe that, you know."

Lady Cleviss raised an eyebrow. This kind of talk was not accepted at her dinner table, and she should stop it at once. But Tom had the clear intention of taking Hereward down a peg, and she would not interfere with a worthy endeavor.

"You mistake Gervase. He is an outstanding soldier," said Tom doggedly. "Always in the front lines."

"Attached to Wellington? In the front lines?" echoed Hereward, mockingly. "In the rear of the fighting, I am persuaded."

Tom was very nearly angry. "Don't you believe it, Hereward. Didn't Gervase ever tell you how we met last?"

Gervase, stiff with embarrassment, began, "Tom—"

His protest went unheeded. Perhaps it was the rare glass of wine that loosened his tongue, and perhaps the bright admiring eyes of his lost Kitty, but more likely it was a simple sense of gratitude that urged Tom on. "Gervase was on his way back—*back*, mind you, Hereward—from the battlefront, where the Frenchies were headed back to France as fast as they could run, when he found me. I'd got mixed up in a skirmish, and was unlucky. I was near dead, when he came by. Singlehanded, he pulled me into the shade, he rounded up stretcher-bearers—he even took one handle himself, and we got out just before the French reinforcements returned and overran the place."

Tom was aware suddenly that his audience listened in total silence, except for a sob, once, from Kitty.

Gervase said, gently, "Thomas—"

Flushed with unwonted emotion, Tom added, stubbornly, "Gervase has always been sadly underrated. I owe him my life."

Lady Huntley was mercifully silent, but her glowering glance around the table spoke for her. Amelia, pale as the wax candles, whispered, "You never told me."

Her brother said, succinctly, "You never asked."

Hereward struggled to regain his ascendancy over the company. "Never mind, Thomas. Those of us who know him best rate him at his *true* value." His equivocal remark would have eased the tenseness around the table, but he could not refrain from adding, "Anyone can be brave once."

Tom had spent more energy than was at his command. He now gave very clear signs of imminent collapse, and Amelia, shaken to her core by her glimpse of a war she had not truly thought of, shot a glance of appeal at Gervase.

The party broke up early. Lady Cleviss was grimly philosophical, saying later, "One might have expected disaster when That Woman was at hand."

Lady Huntley herself was furious, although she could not have told why.

Gervase paused in the hall to say farewell to Fenella. "I wouldn't have had this happen for the world. Tom is a sensible man. I can't think what started him off on his misjudged defense of me."

"I am sure, sir, you need no defense."

"Do you think we should forego our outing to the shore? I had hoped that next week we might plan such a diversion."

Fenella, to her surprise, realized that she was being consulted and even though it was a matter of small importance, his thoughtfulness took her unaware. Her answer was earnest. "Pray don't let your cousin feel he has done aught amiss. Surely he would suspect that it is on his account that you canceled the expedition?"

"He might as well think it is the fault of Hereward," said Gervase grimly.

"But Tom must know that he has not forfeited our regard by his—his very clear partisanship!"

She had spoken not from design, but from the depth of her feelings. Now she felt some trepidation lest her betrothed think her too far forward, too lacking in modesty. She glanced up at him, and was immediately reassured.

He gave her his rare smile that transformed his unexceptionable features into an expression of sunlit charm. "Very well, then, I shall send to let you know when we have fixed a day."

18

The next day, the household at Morland Manor was not at its best. Fenella had slept at last, to dream, not of Gervase in battle, or of Hereward's mocking laugh, but of standing in the middle of a great field, knee-deep in grass, and not a soul, a house, or even a beast in sight.

There was no puzzling out such a lonely dream, she thought in the morning. It occurred to her, however, that she might have had a glimpse of her future—lonely, uneventful, monotonous.

What kind of man was Gervase? His cousin worshiped him, his brother scoffed at him, his mother despised him.

She herself did not know what to think. Hereward and Tom—why would either of them lie? And if they did not lie, then how could one reconcile the two Gervases into one?

She wandered downstairs in search of company. Kitty was still at breakfast. She had had nothing but coffee, apparently, and her puffy eyes told of a sleepless, weeping night.

"Good morning," said Fenella. She was appalled to see her simple greeting result in tears brimming and slipping down Kitty's cheeks. "Aunt Kitty, I'm so sorry! What did I say amiss?"

"Nothing, Fenella. It's just that—I didn't know he was wounded so sorely. He nearly died, did you know that? And no one would ever have told me! And he never married. He said—"

Whatever he had said brought a faint flush to her cheeks, and she said no more.

"It was only," she resumed more temperately, "that I did not *know*."

"Well, what will you do, now that you *do* know?"

"Do?" Kitty echoed blankly, setting down her cup. "What is there to do?" She blushed. "Oh, I know you have romantic fancies, Fenella, but—"

"Indeed I do not!" Fenella protested. "I am the least of romantic persons. You do not see me leaping into a romantic attachment. Not even a marriage of affection!"

She was not quite truthful in her last statement, she realized. She might, if Gervase were to smile at her in such a way, grow at least to like him a little. But she could not envision any kind of existence at Wakeford Hall, conscious of his mother's constant scrutiny, that would allow either of them to smile overmuch.

Lady Cleviss hastened in. "I could not sleep," she burst out. "What a dreadful evening! I have done my duty to my family now, but I tell you this, I shall not allow That Woman to come to Morland Manor again! A nice little room, indeed! Meat well dressed! What did she think, that we lived like ostlers?"

She glanced at Kitty. "My dear, do not, I beg you, turn into a watering pot! I shall look with disfavor upon anything—or anyone—who so distresses you."

Kitty managed a watery smile. "It's just that I didn't know!"

"Nor did any of us. Certainly I did not consider carefully. I wonder whether I have done the right thing, Fenella, getting you into *such* a family!" She allowed Fenella to pour her coffee. "But I have agreed, and there's an end to it."

After breakfast, Fenella wandered at loose ends. In the kitchen cook was unwontedly cross, blaming her fatigues of the past days. "It's not what I've been used to, and that's a fact, Miss Fenella, and that foolish Maria worse than no kitchen maid at all!"

Cook had not come to the end of the litany of woes, but Fenella had ceased to listen. She moved out of the house, across the lawn. She was too tired to think, she told herself, but the truth was that she hardly knew what to think. Who was right about Gervase? The answer was not to be found.

Aimlessly, she allowed her feet to take her where they would, and it was with some surprise that she found herself at the edge of the old smuggling road. The sun was higher this day, and suddenly she wished to look at the old chapel in full light. It was at the edge of Morland property, and she was not sure it did belong to the family. She had not grown up here, and there were many acres she had not yet explored. She turned to her left and much sooner than she expected found herself in the clearing again.

There was the sorrel horse, with two white feet, and this

time there was another, a big black that looked much like Thunder. The chapel, seen in daylight, was much less ominous than it had appeared. The roof had fallen in only over the altar, and while the windows were without glass, the walls seemed sound enough. She crossed the clearing.

At the door of the chapel, she halted. She was astonished at the interior of the ruin. Far from being covered with the debris of generations, the floor had been swept clean. There was on one side what seemed to be a pew, uprooted from the floor and carried to a spot against the wall, under the sound part of the roof. A saddle blanket covered the pew, and there were other signs of recent occupancy. Hereward must sometimes sleep here.

His voice, as though conjured up by her thoughts, spoke behind her. "No lady goes uninvited into a gentleman's rooms!" he laughed. "Shall you like an invitation?"

She whirled. "Certainly not!" She was distressed that he should find her here, appearing to pry into his business, but certainly this was better than watching Aunt Kitty cry over every word spoken to her, or listening to cook's moans.

Hereward reached his hand to help her down from the step. He did not let her go, but pulled her to him. His arm went around her, and his lips found hers. When at last he released her, she said waspishly, "No gentleman kisses a lady—without an invitation!"

"I fear that you would never invite me," he said with false affliction, "so—but then, Sister, what is a small kiss between members of the family? Although, to be perfectly frank, I should not consider kissing my cousin Amelia in such wise."

"I suppose I should be flattered," said Fenella crossly. She had once again found herself in a dubious position, without intending to, and she knew that her coming here was open to the most odious interpretations.

"Aren't you flattered, dear Fenella?"

She bit her lip.

"Why the two horses?" she asked, seizing at the diversion.

"My fine Beauty is becoming too well known in the neighborhood," he told her. "I have even heard talk on the streets about the sorrel with two white front feet. If you were to take to the road, dear Sister—and I might well think you might, as an antidote to deadly Gervase—remember that any mark of identity is fatal. Or can be."

He leaned back on his heels, watching her. How pretty she

was! And how very innocent, despite a Season in London. She might just be out of the schoolroom.

Yet he had the suspicion that her meekness was all on the surface. No schoolmiss of his acquaintance would be so daring as to come to a clearing, where a criminal spent his time, and expect no harm to come to her.

Fenella was surely asking for attention, and he would be able to give her some amusing times. But still he stayed his hand. The evening before had opened his eyes finally to what he had once merely suspected—that Gervase was a man to be reckoned with. Hereward had told their mother that Gervase must not be underrated, according to certain information he had heard in London, but he was in danger of falling into that trap himself.

He longed to damage Fenella in Gervase's eyes, as payment for years of insults that were very real to him, although not apparent to anyone else. But yet, he was not quite sure whether Gervase's revenge might not be too high a price to pay.

Fenella, just now, was looking at him with a perplexed expression in her green eyes. "Do you really live here? Don't they miss you at Wakeford Hall?"

"I stay here only infrequently. I shall not tell you when, for it would not suit me to wake up to find the squire and his minions surrounding me."

"I should not betray you!"

"No? I wish I could be sure of that." He appeared to consider. "Come, let me show you, then, my own nest."

He had made it habitable, even comfortable. He made her to sit on the pew, and sat down, not too near, beside her.

"What are you going to do," she ventured, "with all that you have—stolen?"

"My tastes are expensive."

"But how long can you do—all this!" She waved her hands vaguely.

He didn't answer for a moment. When he did, he was apparently on another subject. "Have you ever been to Italy?"

"What does that answer? No, I never have."

"It's warm there," he said dreamily. "Flowers, brilliant colors, not like this faded landscape of England. soft romantic nights, good red wine, and always music. And the people! None of this looking down the nose at the lower classes!"

He imitated a woman of advanced years peering with disgust at an inferior—it was too bad, thought Fenella, as humorous as the impression was, that it should so remind her of her grandmother, whose nearsightedness often gave just that effect.

Drily, Fenella pointed out, "You will not have much scope for your criminal tendencies there, I should think."

"How unkind! No, I shall pay as I go. And when I can go no farther, I may return to England to find another fat purse or two."

"A worthy objective," she mused.

He glared at her. "I suppose you find it more exciting to raise sheep? Fenella, I must tell you I do not like your tart comments. One might think that Tom Prentice's unfortunate gift of what I am sure he calls plain speaking has been passed on to you."

"Perhaps so. I do confess that my mind is in a good deal of bewilderment, so that I do not control my tongue as I ought. Grandmama would be most distressed with me."

Not the least cause of Lady Cleviss's distress, he reflected, would be her dear granddaughter's presence with that known rake, Hereward Wakeford, in what amounted to exceedingly compromising circumstances.

"I myself will be most distressed with you, do you continue to tell me what I do not wish to hear," he said with a touch of laughter. "But, unlike Grandmama, I have my own remedy for the situation."

He drew her again to him and kissed her, and this time she did not pull away as quickly. "Will you miss me, Fenella, when I am in Italy?"

She smoothed back her hair, and rose. "I have stayed long enough. But in truth—I do not know what to do."

"Marry Gervase, and fade as dry as an everlasting."

She said only, "I must get back."

Nettled at her departure, he called after her, "Don't come back tonight, for I shall not be here."

She stopped short. "You're going to Italy so soon?"

"Not quite. Not till I convince you to go with me. But tonight I must make an appearance at the Hall."

She turned toward the Manor and did not look back. He watched after her until she was out of sight, and then, with a shrug of his shoulders, went back into the chapel. He went to the place under the altar, where he hid his newfound gains. After counting it all once more, he whistled soundlessly.

Nearly the sum he had fixed in his mind as being sufficient for a year of carefree living in a sunny village he knew south of Naples.

It occurred to him that his hiding place would be the obvious one for anyone coming upon his retreat. He thought for long, and then transferred it to another spot, outside the chapel.

He did not think Fenella would deliberately betray him, but it was more than likely that her absence would be noted, and she could by ill chance drop a clue that would give him away.

He had not remained at large for so long without taking every precaution. He needed one more prize, and then he would be away from England at the next tide. He had no true intention of taking Fenella with him. For one thing, he liked to travel alone, and for another, he had not sufficient funds for them both.

Besides, he could not quite encompass the ruin of his brother's betrothed. It was likely that he might wish to come back to England, and it would be much more comfortable if he were accepted, if not welcomed, by his family.

But he could—and would—unsettle Fenella sufficiently so that either Gervase himself would cry off, or she would lead him a merry chase out of her own misery.

She would never love Gervase—of that he was convinced. No one could, was Hereward's settled opinion. But in the meantime, he must take steps to ensure that the next time he stood out in the road, masked and armed, the purse would be worth the taking.

Meanwhile, the vague and alluring hints that he had dropped for Fenella's edification were rising like yeast in July sun.

She was not in love with Hereward. At bottom, she knew him to be selfish and even cruel. But equally, she was not in love with Gervase, and to spend a lifetime with a man who was slow and dull, in spite of Tom's encomiums, was not in the least appealing. But what could she do?

It was of no help to remember that many another young lady of her quality had spent just such aimless hours, such sleepless, weary nights, contemplating without pleasure a marriage that must seem like a life sentence to dreariness.

Even Caroline Lamb, the celebrated Miss Ponsonby who

had a myriad of swains at her feet, fell into a dismal marriage. But Caro had made the best of it!

And with the bracing thought of Caro's ingenuity, of her embrace of whatever diverting came her way without regard of the consequences—which were, more often than not, bound to reverberate scandalously to the skies—Fenella made up her mind.

She had not the *panache* of Caro. She could not carry off a *tour de force* in style, especially in the face of countless horrified spectators, but she could at least enjoy herself privately for a while.

It was soon, then, that she made the trip again to the clearing. She was not quite sure in her mind of her purpose. She knew only that where Hereward was, there would be excitement and a bit of danger, of one kind or another. She did not consider that peril was as addictive a drug as opium, that, once tasted, induced a clamoring of the blood for ever stronger portions.

She stopped at the edge of the clearing. She had come this far without qualms, but now that she had arrived, she longed with all her heart to be back in her own room.

"You really must take instruction," said a voice from the clump of bushes at her right hand, "in how to approach without sound. One might think a herd of frightened horses was coming."

"You startled me!" she said.

"No more than you sent a shiver of alarm through me," he told her. "Why did you come?"

"I'm not sure."

"Well, I must leave you here, Fenella. I shall return, perhaps, before midnight."

"Oh, no! I cannot stay here alone!"

"Believe me," he said ironically, "you will be safer alone than with me. But I have no choice. I have a rendezvous with a fat purse on the Witham road before dark."

"Take me with you."

He stared at her, aghast. "You're an idiot!"

She waited, not arguing, for him to decide. She had no true feeling for Hereward himself. But she dreaded the arid life she saw ahead of her. Instinctively, she rebelled in the only way she knew.

"I can ride," she said at last, seeing his resolution waver in her favor, "and I'll be no trouble."

"You, my dear sister-to-be, are trouble the moment a man looks at you. Well, so be it. If you're an idiot, I'm a fool!"

He turned abruptly and entered the chapel. When he came out in a few minutes, he carried a spare saddle. "Can you ride the sorrel?"

She looked down at her skirts. She would simply have to hike up her petticoats. When she had been younger, still at home in Dorset, she had often ridden astride. She had no time to think then, for Hereward, every movement shouting his irritation with her, was waiting to help her mount.

"Go away," she said, "I can manage."

"Modesty has no place in the outlaw world," he told her, somewhat returned to his pleasant humor.

She followed as he rode the black horse along the trail she had noticed the other day. Her sorrel knew the way well enough, and she had only to hold a loose rein. The trail twisted, until she had no idea how far they had come.

Even if it had not been dusk, deepening into twilight, she would not have noticed, for she was prey to all the doubts she had successfully overcome when she decided to join Hereward in his forays.

Now, alone with too much time to think, she could see nothing but the monsters of her imagination. Suppose they were caught. Would she swing on the gallows? Could her family save her life, would they care, or would they pretend she were an imposter?

With these reflections to keep her bad company, the journey passed with leaden pace. At length, Hereward stopped, and dismounted. Tethering the black horse to a convenient limb of a tree, he came to her. Putting his hands around her waist, he helped her slide to the ground. "We'll wait until moonrise," he said. "The waiting may be tedious, but— perhaps not!"

They were in a glade close to the road. She could hear wheels squeaking nearby, and Hereward whispered in her ear, "Only a farm cart. Pay it no heed!"

He sat beside her on the grass. The only sound was the rise and fall of summer insect song, and the cropping of grass by the horses.

"How long till moonrise?" she ventured.

"Not long enough," he told her, slipping his arm around her waist. "I vow we shall hardly know how the time has gone. Will they miss you at home?"

"I went to bed with a headache," she said.

He was practiced in seduction, and she trembled as his fingers stroked her forehead—"Best treatment for headache!"—and slipped down to cup her chin. He kissed her, and though her mind told her she must not give in, yet her body refused to obey her.

It was as though she were no longer Fenella Morland, no longer a young lady of modesty and good sense—strangely, Caro's remark, about another man, came to her mind. "Bad, mad, and dangerous to know!"

She pushed him away then. To her surprise he seemed not to mind. I must go home! she told herself. But how? She had no idea even where she was. She surely could not take to the road, traveling skirts rucked up, through Witham and the long road to the Manor without losing every scrap of reputation she had.

Nor, truth to tell, could she stay here.

She turned to him, but to her mingled chagrin and relief, he did not heed her. His attention was entirely on the sound of approaching wheels. She could detect the difference in the sound of the two horses and vehicle now at hand from the farm cart she had heard before.

Hereward moved quickly. He pulled her to her feet to stand beside him. "Go mount the sorrel," he told her. "I'll have no time to spare afterwards."

"What if—what if something goes wrong?"

"Just give my horse his head, and follow."

She meant no more to him than that tree trunk, she thought, untying the reins and climbing into the saddle, to wait for him. She was glad that he had no true *tendre* for her, but also, she must confess, was a trifle piqued as well.

She waited. She could hear voices, an echo of the other occasion when she had been the victim in the coach, instead of risking everything she held of value.

In the middle of the night, at times, one reaches the lowest point of existence. Nothing is worth the candle, life is a desolate dryness stretching endlessly without reward. So it was now with Fenella. Never again would she put so much at hazard.

Hereward was back before she knew it. He vaulted into his saddle, and, without more than a word to her, set his horse back the way they had come.

The return was accomplished far more speedily—and far

more recklessly—than the leisurely journey to the glade. Fenella was an expert rider, else she would have been thrown almost at once. A wild, breakneck ride—and she exulted in every minute of it. No saunter in Hyde Park could be spoken of in the same breath as this plunging gallop through the dark.

At length, Hereward pulled up, turning in his saddle to speak to her. "Are you all right?"

"Wonderful!" she exclaimed, exhilarated.

"Well, then, I'll take you home another way. Just follow along."

She had no idea then where they were. Nor did she recognize any landmark on the sober trot home. Finally, he reined up, and came to help her down. She slid into his arms, but he set her on her feet at once.

"It's late," he said. "Time for a respectable miss to be in bed."

"Back there in the clearing," she told him, "I longed to be in bed. But now I am too excited to sleep. When can we go again?"

"Never!" he said. "Too dangerous."

He pointed out the beginning of the cart track that would take her to the lawn surrounding Morland Manor. Obediently, she took a few steps on it, and then turned. He was watching her, but a certain rigidity in his shoulders suggested that he was not best pleased with her.

She hurried toward home. She was not the same Fenella who had left the Manor only a few hours before. She reached the side door of the house, never locked as she knew, and slipped inside. Before she closed the door she looked behind her. The lawn stretched out, cream-colored and ebony in the light of the rising moon, now topping the great trees of the home park.

She closed the door behind her and stealthily climbed the stairs. She reached her own room, and latched the door.

She was safe!

19

The day of the proposed outing, Gervase's attempt to entertain his guests, as well as Fenella, dawned clear and bright.

Lady Huntley, being made aware of the day's plans, refused to consider attending. "It will be far too hot," she pointed out.

Amelia said, brightly, "But there will be a breeze near the sea. Gervase, we are going to the sea, are we not?"

"Yes. I seem to remember that there are several coves along the stretch from St. Osyth to Bradwell, sheltered from the worst of the gales."

Surprisingly, Tom spoke. He had been for the most part silent since he had renewed his acquaintance with Kitty, and Gervase was curious to know what old desires moved behind his stolid features. "An island stretches off shore," he said. "I remember it well."

"I am sending our lunch ahead," said Gervase, pleasantly. "Ma'am, you need have no fear. I shall not expect you to disarrange your own comfort for an outing like this."

For a moment, Lady Huntley seemed to tremble on the verge of telling them she would go, after all, but the rigors of a day *alfresco* would indeed be a sacrifice of her comfort.

Hereward informed them, "I should be most happy to go with you, but——"

"Then," interrupted Gervase, "it is settled. I really cannot do without you, Hereward."

"You can't? I am surprised."

"Tom must ride in the coach, with Amelia and Fenella. The ladies would find it too far to ride, I am persuaded."

Hereward had a quick recollection of Fenella, a veritable Amazon, galloping behind him through the night. The memory did much to reconcile him to the day's activities.

But when he and Gervase were alone, a short time later, he had a second thought about making one of the party. "I do not like outings like this, Brother," he said, "and I must cry off. You will do very well without me."

"Perhaps I don't enjoy an outing like this, either," observed Gervase. "But we must provide diversion for Tom and Amelia, you know."

"And Fenella? Is this not a diversion for her? Or do you place her lower in your esteem than our cousins?"

It was not so much the words as the tone of voice that was meant to irritate. Gervase gave no evidence that Hereward's taunt had struck home.

"Fenella is my charge, you know, not yours."

Hereward did not try to hide his derisive smile.

"We will leave at ten, to pick up our guests at Morland Manor. Will you want to ride your bay, or shall you select another from the stable? I am sorry that I have not been able to find time to buy the cattle I shall want, but you are welcome to any I have."

Hereward said, "I am not going. Did I not make myself clear on that head?"

The earl raised an eyebrow. He had been thinking about Hereward, over the past weeks since he had come to Wakeford Hall, and his thoughts did not please him. He had not yet decided, however, on his best course of action, so he simply said, "Nevertheless, courtesy demands your attendance."

He turned away, but Hereward moved to intercept him. "Or, dear Brother, it it only you who demands and demands?" Hereward was prone to impulsiveness, but often, so Gervase considered, at the wrong times. "Just because you hold the purse strings!" said Hereward, clearly angry now.

Gervase smiled pleasantly. "I'm relieved to know that you are aware of that fact."

Hereward, having failed to carry the day by bluster, retreated, fighting a rearguard action. "I'm not one of your miserable troopers, you know, to order around."

"A pity."

"But I shall not go."

Gervase considered him. "If you insist upon discourtesy to our guests, you know, I shall have to bend my thoughts toward discerning the reason for your decision."

He walked away, not nearly as confident as he appeared that his request—a veritable command, in truth—would be honored.

Hereward, for his part, was puzzled. He became aware that a new force had entered his heretofore untrammeled life. Gervase had altered. It was as though, he thought with rare imagination, an enormous boulder had come to rest athwart his path, an obstacle he could not overcome but must, somehow, find a way around.

Perhaps it was Gervase's army command that had changed him so. Hereward did not like the new Gervase, no matter the cause. But reflection told him that he would be a fool indeed to rush his fences. He had more at stake than Gervase dreamed of. He was not stupid enough to defy openly a "request" that truly was only inconvenient to him, and not catastrophic.

He must temporize, until he could get away free and clear. The *Naiad* would anchor, one day soon, at Maldon, and whatever Gervase wished, from that day on, would be of no avail as far as Hereward was concerned.

On his way upstairs to change his clothing to something more suitable to a day in the open by the sea, he stopped at his mother's door.

"Come in, my dear," cried Lady Huntley. "Have you ever heard of such foolishness as to take an invalid bouncing over the roads just for a meal in the open air? I vow I have not."

"I shall tell you all about it when I return."

"You are surely not going!"

"Surely I am. My dear brother has commanded me."

"Nonsense!"

"Not at all. I should shrink from giving you counsel, dear ma'am, but I truly believe you do not perceive how he has altered."

"No matter, Hereward, for I am still his mother. He cannot alter that, and I well know how to deal with him."

"But you see he does plan to marry the Morland girl. Did I not understand you rightly? It was my belief that you were going to stop the marriage plans."

"I wonder at you, Hereward. He is not yet wed, is he?" Nonetheless, Hereward thought he detected an uneasiness in his mother's expression that he had never seen before. Was it possible that old Gervase had indeed kicked over the traces?

"You will see, my dear," said Lady Huntley. "I will see to it that the little minx never marries Gervase. I promise you this!"

The Wakeford Hall coach, containing Tom propped up with comfortable cushions supporting his helpless arm, and Amelia, trundled up the drive to Morland Manor.

Fenella waited with some trepidation. The night escapade

with Hereward filled her thoughts to the exclusion of all else. She recalled in detail every change of heart, every exhilarating moment, several times a day.

Lady Cleviss had pointed out that she was abstracted to the point of idiocy, but misread the cause as the ordinary reaction of a young girl on the verge of her wedding.

If Fenella had been as wise as her grandmother, she would have recognized her seeking for excitement as being of the same Morland strain that had led Fenella's father to set out for London in the teeth of a dangerous storm. But Fenella simply knew that she had enjoyed even her fears and misgivings that night with Hereward.

Kitty joined her to wait on the step for the coach which they could hear coming up the graveled drive. "I have resigned myself to seeing Tom," she informed Fenella, "for we cannot be neighbors, and even connected, after your marriage, and refuse to speak."

"I thought him very nice," said Fenella, encouragingly.

"But he is not interested in me anymore," Kitty said calmly. "I understand that."

Fenella's attention was of short duration. She lapsed into her own dreams, thinking, What I could write to Caro Lamb! But then, Caro would not be interested, since she cared only for the events that revolved around herself.

"Will he be coming?"

Thoughts full of Hereward, Fenella answered, "Of course."

Kitty, her brave show of serenity faltering, said, "I shall not enjoy the day."

"I shall."

"But of course you're betrothed to him."

Fenella burst out, "I wasn't thinking of—" She bit her lip. She almost betrayed herself. The coach arrived before Kitty could ask unwished-for questions.

At last they arrived at their destination. The coach turned off the narrow road that passed along the highest point of the land, and, flanked by Gervase and Hereward on horseback, followed by two grooms, came to a halt a little way from the road.

Fenella stepped down from the coach and looked around her.

"What a lovely prospect!"

It was, indeed. The land sloped down from the road that paralleled the shore, gently, grass-covered, until it arrived at the high-tide mark. From there to the water, the shingle was still wet from the withdrawing sea. The tide was not high here, for the large expanse of Mersea Island altered the rhythm of the open sea.

The sea wind, which was strong on the upland, here was reduced to a whisper. The marquee, erected by Gervase's servants sent on ahead, provided shelter for the invalid, and he was shortly settled in an arm chair.

Gervase stood beside Fenella. "Are you pleased with this?" He waved his hand vaguely.

"It is lovely. The air is so fresh. I had not thought that Morland Manor was so far inland that we were not influenced by the sea, but this is so different!"

Her eyes glowed with pleasure, and Gervase was conscious of a strong desire to seize her and plant passionate kisses on her cheeks, her lips——

He said, calmly, "You see that small building far to the north? If I am not much mistaken, that is a Riding Officer post. To watch the coast, you know, against contraband."

"Smugglers, you mean? I thought that there was no smuggling here now. Punthrop said——"

"Punthrop?"

"One of my grandmother's pensioners. He said there used to be—'in my granfer's time,' he said, 'or in his granfer's time!' I think Punthrop was fuddled in his wits!"

"Most likely. I suppose that there are fashions in smuggling as in all else."

She looked earnestly at the building Gervase had pointed out. She could see no sign of activity. Perhaps it had been abandoned now that the danger of invasion from France was past.

Gervase on the other hand was trying to recall Cogges Cove. He may have known it when he visited here, but it was such a long time ago that his memory was blank.

Their conversation was interrupted by a call from the marquee. Amelia told them, "Come! After this long ride, I am peckish in the extreme!"

They joined the others around the table under the marquee. Already, Fenella noted, Tom Prentice looked much better than he had on his arrival at Wakeford Hall.

Amelia, away from the overwhelming presence of Lady Huntley, was altogether different. She seemed younger, gayer, less brittle. She and Hereward engaged in a series of verbal ripostes, amusing them all, and they came to the grapes and peaches in great good humor.

"Gervase," said Amelia, "I must confess you are a perfect host. Never have I been so content." She was suddenly solemn. "I owe you more than I can say," she added in an undertone.

"Not at all," said Gervase, bewildered.

Glancing at the others, she returned to her gay mood. "Now, dear cousin, I must tell you that this visit is completely delightful. I only wish that you were able to provide us with a view of a ruined abbey. All the best novels have one. Can you not show us some frightening scene?"

Fenella opened her lips to refute Amelia's claim that the region possessed no interesting ruins, but remembered in time. She would never make a conspirator! she realized. She was too innocent in the ways of deviousness.

Hereward exclaimed, "Only a henwit would think of it!"

But while he looked at Amelia, Fenella felt that his words were directed at her. She glanced guiltily at Gervase.

He seemed to be watching Tom and Kitty, sitting together, exchanging only a word now and then but exuding a kind of peace with each other, but suddenly Fenella was convinced that he missed very little of what transpired around him. A kind Providence must insure that he not read her own mind!

Tom, replete and relatively without pain, closed his eyes. The servants on Gervase's direction worked quietly to remove the broken meal, and Fenella strolled over the grass to the edge of the shingle, gazing at the ever-changing water.

Gervase took Amelia away, so that Tom and Kitty might be alone. Now that he knew about times past for them, he wished them well.

He and Amelia wandered without purpose along the shore, his thoughts filled with Fenella. He was acutely aware that Hereward had joined Fenella, and said something amusing, for he could hear Fenella's laugh, the innocent sound like water chuckling over stones that had captured his fancy at the start.

How open Fenella was! he thought. But yet, he knew of that one escapade she had never told anyone, so far as he knew. Did she remember her rescuer? It did not escape his attention that, if she had not revealed that incident, there might be others locked away behind that innocently candid face. How would he know? He longed for her to tell him—no secrets between them, ever, was his ardent wish.

Fenella was no longer amused by Hereward. Gervase could not hear from where he stood exactly what caused the change in her, but she became unwontedly sober. He would not have enjoyed Hereward's words, had he heard them.

"See how well Lord Bountiful arranges this," Hereward was saying, "as though he were Deity!"

"It was simply a pleasant luncheon," protested Fenella. She did not like Hereward in this mood.

"He has put Kitty and Tom together, isolated in their private marquee. Don't tell me you had not noticed that? Tongue-tied they are, though, not a word this past half hour! But Gervase knows best, and doubtless all will come right!"

"You cannot deny Gervase is kind!" She glanced toward Gervase, relieved to see he was too far away to overhear. But the simple look in his direction told him far more than she knew. They were talking about him, the earl was convinced, and, even worse, laughing. He had no illusions about Hereward's opinion of him, but Fenella's glance was like a sword thrust. He frowned.

Strangely, seeing Gervase glance gravely in her direction did not rouse defiance in her, but only humiliation. It was excessively ill-bred to speak ill of her host, even if she could not quite be happy with him as her future husband. Hereward had led her astray! But she could not escape the strong feeling of guilt that filled her.

Kitty, when they had all gathered again at the marquee, smothered a delicate yawn.

Gervase rallied her gently. "I am afraid our outing has been not exciting enough? My apologies, Miss Morland."

"Not at all," she disclaimed. "But I do not sleep well." Upon being pressed, she confessed that several nights before, she thought she saw a man crossing the lawn.

"A man! A stranger?"

"I am not even sure it was a man," said Kitty, embarrassed at the unwonted attention. "But I have given orders that all the doors be locked at night. Even the small one that gives onto the kitchen wing. But yet I am anxious."

Fenella was dismayed. She had almost been discovered! And she had thought she was safely away from the danger of that night, that all had gone well. Now, not only was Aunt

Kitty alerted to watch from her window, but the doors would be locked against her!

Tom, for his part, grew angry. "I should—" He did not finish. He had meant to promise to stand guard, but he remembered his uselessness. He pressed his lips together to hide his despair.

Kitty said, gently, "No need to worry. I am persuaded there is no danger."

Sobered by the thought of Kitty's intruder, they prepared to begin their homeward journey. Hereward spoke sharply. "What's this fellow want?"

They turned to see a man, dressed in a rough kind of uniform, approaching. "The Riding Officer," said Gervase, in a low tone.

The newcomer passed Hereward without a glance and addressed Gervase. "Lord Huntley?"

"Yes, officer," said Gervase. "Is there trouble?"

"No, not as I know of. But I thought to make myself known to you, my lord, as long as you were this close."

They exchanged a few remarks. Then Gervase asked, "Is there much smuggling here?"

"No, not here, my lord. Up the coast, Naze way, they've got some, but this coast is mostly quiet."

Gervase looked at him thoughtfully. "But there is something amiss, I am persuaded."

Reluctantly glancing at the others, the officer told him. "Signs of summat going on along the old smuggling road, my lord. Since that goes right alongside your lordship's land, I thought it best to mention it."

"Quite right. But, if not smuggling, and I believe you do not think it, then what?"

The Riding Officer, whose name he had told them was Smith, shifted his feet. "I don't rightly know, my lord, and that's what troubles me. That's the fairest I can say. Something is wrong, that's all I know."

"Well," said Gervase at last, "you were quite right to inform me. I shall warn my men to keep their eyes open."

Expressing thanks, Smith left them. The others were in the coach. Only Fenella lingered. "I shall hope that Smith is wrong," said Gervase slowly.

Hereward had been shaken by the revelation of the Riding Officer, but he had concealed it well. Now he said, "I swear to you, as head of our family, dear Brother, that I am in no way involved in smuggling."

After a few moments, Gervase nodded. "I believe you. But I must warn you that I shall not tolerate any stain on the name of Wakeford."

Hereward smiled. "Don't worry. Wakeford will never be known for aught but sheep and haymaking! I'm sure you have had all the danger you want—from the vantage point of the general's tent!"

Gervase was aware of a surge of anger that recommended, quite simply, that he throttle his brother. The struggle was uneven, of course, but he turned away until he mastered his expression.

A little apart, Fenella took Hereward to task. "You're not fair. You heard what Tom said about his courage in battle!"

Hereward was surprised, and not well pleased. "Don't tell me you see a spark of liveliness in the stern lord of the manor!"

Fenella was troubled. "I don't know what to think."

Gervase heard none of this, but he knew that his brother was intent on taunting him. He would not be baited. Never had he descended to such a level as sniping. He held his temper, until he had made his decision—he had learned this lesson well over the past years. Then, once decided on the best course, he made his move. A simple, logical progression of thought and action—and he could not so far betray himself as to become what he was not.

Not even were he to lose Fenella.

The coach regained the road, headed for home. Hereward and the grooms followed close behind.

Gervase put his horse at a slow lope, staying behind out of the dust, and followed the picnic party home. He was a very lonely man.

20

The day after the outing found Gervase at loose ends. Not that he could not have found tasks to set his hand to, not at all. There were a number of items in the accounting sheets Paston had left for him that puzzled him. Surely his mother could not have required an additional ten thousand pounds a year, beyond her household needs which were otherwise provided for.

The only answer he could think of was that the Dowager had fallen in with gamblers. He must deal with it, of course, but at least here at Wakeford Hall she was under his eye. Now that he was back from the wars, and no longer under trusteeship, there would be no expenses that he himself did not authorize.

There were repairs to tenant houses, there was a matter of sheds to house his new sheep, there were a myriad of questions to be answered on the estate. But his thoughts refused to consider any of them.

He was about to lose Fenella—there was the nub of it. He knew well, of course, that contracts had been signed, and Fenella would never cry off, not without overwhelming cause. He was sure she would go through with the marriage. But it was losing her regard that gnawed at him. How could he live a loveless marriage, as his father had done?

Hereward loomed in his mind, not least because of his marked attentions to Fenella the day before. His brother had sworn he was no smuggler, and Gervase believed him. But who then was traveling, at times, the old smugglers' road? He could not recall whether the old road lay on Morland land or Wakeford's. No doubt it was a sort of wasteland, or common land, between the two. He must look into this problem, too, in due time.

Just now he was studying how best to please Fenella. He knew he cut no fine figure as Hereward did. He was not gifted in the small exchange of conversation. Even Warrod knew better how to win a maid than he did. But he could not adopt Warrod's ways, for they were alien to him. He must go his own way with Fenella. There was a way to her heart—there had to be. But he had not the slightest idea of how to find it.

He knew he would do better without his nearest of kin at hand but after the wedding, all would be changed. Lady Huntley would depart in haste for her purlieus in Bath, and Hereward would vanish at the snap of a finger.

His was not the only unquiet mind under the roof of Wakeford Hall. The Dowager Lady Huntley had been more alarmed by Hereward's hints than she had admitted. She had no doubt that she could, in the end, lead Gervase in the ways she wished him to go, but the struggle might be more arduous than she expected. At any rate, she believed, it was best to have all settled at once.

She had no wish to remain here at Wakeford Hall. She longed to return to the busy whirl of the valetudinarians at Bath, or to the country visits that made such a large part of her life at Oakbury.

But a letter from her old ally Paston reposed in her pocket, a letter that contained such disturbing news that she had nearly swooned away when she read it. Even now, she could not believe what he had written. The marriage, especially on such terms as Paston had outlined, must be halted. She dared not wait.

To decide was, with Lady Huntley, to act. She found Gervase moodily staring from the windows of the west parlor. The dejected set of his shoulders might have suggested that she defer her requests until later, but, never one to cater to another's mood, she spoke as soon as she entered the room.

"Gervase, I am relieved to find you alone. I wish to talk to you." When he did not turn to greet her, she added on a note of rising irritation, "What do you find of interest on the lawn? I see nothing at all. Not even a well-kept flower bed."

"I think," said Gervase meditatively, "the new wing will go best just here."

"*What*? What new wing?"

"The house is too dark. I daresay you have not noted the lack of sunshine—"

"I have not," said the Dowager ominously.

"But in the winter months, don't you see, the sun will come in at an angle, and give a cheerful effect to all these rooms."

Lady Huntley, intending to speak disparagingly of the house in favor of a family removal to, say, Oakbury or even West Wycombe, abruptly veered course. "This is a very fine house, Gervase. Your father and I always intended to live here, except for his untimely death. There is no need to alter the rooms in any way. I believe I made my opinion clear in the matter of the bricking up of the windows in the dining room?"

He ignored her, an action not likely to calm her indignation. "On the Peninsula, you know, they close up their houses against the sun, which is really quite strong in those parts. But here we must open up to take advantage of it. I imagine that tall windows to the south would be most effective."

Lady Huntley so far forgot herself as to stamp her foot. "Gervase, I shall not give my approval to any such arrangement."

She had, to say truth, not thought out the implications of his plans. Whether a new wing, or tall windows, would be an advantage or not had no relevance. It was only her lifelong principle of opposing Gervase, honed to a fine point now by the subtle alteration she found in him. Her dearest Hereward had mentioned such a change, but now was the first moment she accepted the possibility that Gervase would not be quite as malleable as before. She still, however, had no fear that she could win out in the long run. She dug in, as she supposed the military phrase went, for a long battle.

Gervase seemed unaware of her objections. He moved to the side, to consider another angle of view. "Yes, this must be the place. None of the large trees will have to be taken, and the expanse of park slopes gently enough."

In a minatory tone, Lady Huntley said, "Gervase, you will be good enough to give me your attention."

He turned. "Of course, ma'am. I am at your service."

His back was to the light, and she could not see his features. Nor, to do her justice, would she have been set off balance by anything she might read there.

"I know you are merely talking idly about changes in the house, for you must know that I am pleased with it as it is."

"But I am not."

The Dowager gave vent to her genuine shock. "Gervase!"

"I am persuaded," he told her mildly, "that, since any changes I make in the house will not affect you, you are of strong enough mind to dismiss all thoughts of objecting."

"What is this, Gervase? You are not yourself. I cannot think you have truly considered. To say I am not affected is wide of the mark. You cannot—"

A steely note entered Gervase's voice. "I cannot what?"

She saw then that she was riding breakneck for a fall. She must adopt more subtle means to her ends. But she could not refrain from playing her trump card at the first. "You will not have funds enough to take out a brick, to say nothing of building a wing, after the marriage settlement you contemplate."

His features, set darkly as they were now, would have boded ill to anyone familiar with him. His mother saw only her own injustices.

"On that flighty miss, besides! Gervase, you are more of a fool even than I thought if you think she'll suit!"

The earl, shaken by the struggle to contain his bitter thoughts, turned his back to her.

Lady Huntley had never yet cut short her conversation until it suited her to do so. "A totally unheard-of arrangement! Paston tells me you did not even know the girl before you came down to the Hall!"

Her son turned, deliberately. She had never seen him so calm, so unruffled, so deadly. "*Paston* tells you—Pray inform me."

She took a step backward. "Gervase, I had every right—I simply—"

Gervase did not move. Yet suddenly, he seemed larger. "Let us have it all, ma'am."

Well, she told herself, she had nothing to be ashamed of. She would tell him the whole, and he would see that he couldn't deceive her, his own mother! Then, let him crawl to her!

"I wrote Paston. I had certain bills I wished him to pay for me. He has always done this, you know. And—and I asked him for a certain sum in hand."

She fell silent.

"And he said?" encouraged Gervase, still in that mild voice that for a reason she could not understand was almost frightening.

"He simply suggested that I reduce my expenses for a bit. Until, he said, the settlement was worked out, and you would see your way clearer."

"Was that all he said?"

She fidgeted before answering. "He did say that I still had my own money. But that's a mere pittance! Gervase, I shall not endure such treatment!"

"I see." He reflected for what seemed to her a long time, before he added, "I shall wish, ma'am, to see your bills myself before you send again to Paston."

Lady Huntley's eyes blazed. "B–but—"

He continued, "I suggest you listen to Paston, at least as far as spending money is concerned."

Lady Huntley felt her advantage slipping away. Her maternal influence, wielded as a club until now, had somehow given signs of shattering at the next blow. "Gervase, you are not suggesting—"

"I suggest only this, ma'am. Write to Paston if you wish. I make no recommendation about the best way to handle your own affairs. But Paston will not be handling my business from this moment on."

"He had every right to tell me!"

Firmly, Gervase said, "He has only the rights I give him. Now let there be an end to this matter, shall we?" He gave her his rare, winning smile. "Come, ma'am, surely this is no Cheltenham tragedy?"

She sat abruptly in a nearby chair. Her features were set as in stone, and she refused to see the hand he stretched out to her. After a moment, he left the room. She sat a long time without moving, only thinking. He had indeed altered. Always she had managed him before by direct orders. Anxious to please her, he would have done anything she wished. She could see now that those days had gone by.

But what could she do to counteract such a calamity? Paston, so it seemed, would no longer be in a position to send her money, or even pay her bills. All he could do for her was to hold in trust her own money, the dowry with which she came to marry Gervase's father. The small pittance, she called it, and the shabby house in Yorkshire!

Well, she decided, she would not endure this ramshackle treatment by her own son! Besides her own discomfort, she must remember that Paston had been most obliging in advancing sums that went directly to Hereward. If that source of income were cut off, her younger son might well fall into evil ways.

She must meet fire with fire, there was no hope else. But the direct route to Gervase no longer served. She must find more devious means to look out for Hereward, and herself as well.

She cast her mind over certain friends in London, those who would be in a position to know anything of discredit to the Morland girl. She would phrase her inquiry so that her purpose was clear.

By the time she had sent the letter—she dared not ask Gervase to frank it—she felt pleased at a job well done. A few days only, and she would have another weapon in her hand.

There was no harm in waiting a few days.

But Hereward sought her out, and unwittingly burst her bubble of satisfaction. "What maggot does my dear brother have in his head now? He looks murderous. You don't suppose he is, do you? Although—no. I doubt he ever killed even a Frenchman."

Lady Huntley said, oppressively, "He wishes to add a new wing."

"Here? Then he intends to live here?"

"He's gone totally mad!" She was determined not to confide Hereward on the subject of a possible lessening in the flow of funds to him. She had no illusions, for his affection for her could accurately be described as "honeypot love."

"He's really going to marry her then," said Hereward. "I thought she might cry off."

"You know something of moment?"

He shook his head. He knew better than to relay his secrets to such a rattlepate as his mother. "Not at all. But I truly expected that by now you would have wrecked the marriage."

"I shall not allow it."

Hereward laughed derisively. "I don't believe you can stop him."

All her anger with Gervase, all the fear that he had instilled in her about her penurious future, all the indignation that filled her at sight of his clear defiance of her, came together and boiled over. "I shall stop him, have no fear of that."

"Best do it quickly then. I'll be leaving England if she marries him."

"Don't tell me you're hanging after that minx!"

"If you say so," said Hereward mockingly, "I shan't tell you so."

It was true, however, he reflected. He had started out simply to make Gervase jealous, or to present him with an unhappy marriage. But he had fallen into the snare himself. While the Fenella who danced through his dreams was of a different aspect than the sweet innocent who came to Gervase in his visions, yet Hereward would be most reluctant to take his leave of her.

He bowed to his mother and left her. She was miserable. All had gone awry this day, and to think that only this morning she had been in total command of her world.

Now, she was clutched by fear and anger. "Wretched!" she muttered. "A wretched business at best."

She rose to her feet, and started to the door, tottering a few steps until she gained control of her emotions. She was wretched, indeed. And when Lady Huntley was unhappy, no one in her sphere could hope to escape.

21

Hereward was sincere about leaving England. What he had not seen fit to tell his mother was that his departure did not depend upon Gervase's generosity. His plan had from the beginning been to leave the misty climate of England behind him in favor of warmer climes.

His goal, while clear and fixed in his mind, had been on a basis of a time in the future. Now, circumstances were closing in on him, and he believed he must finish up his endeavors in England quickly before it was too late.

The next few days would see the culmination of his efforts. Gervase had gone to Colchester the afternoon of his interview with Lady Huntley, no doubt to escape—Hereward judged—the fury of the aroused Dowager.

But a word Gervase had let drop in the past days had struck a certain alarm note in Hereward's ears. *Investigation,* the earl had said. The old smugglers' road would no longer be safe. But Hereward had until Gervase's return, he thought, to close out his affairs.

Late in the day, he mounted his big black horse and made his way, seemingly without set purpose, toward Witham, and the Blue Swan. He threw the reins to an ostler, and sought the cool taproom.

"Ah, there, sir," said Penn from behind the bar. "What's your pleasure?"

"Naught you can furnish me with, landlord," said Hereward. "Not unless you can fill my purse with guineas!"

"A tall order, sir," said Penn. He glanced around. "I might be able—" He left his hint dangling in the air.

Hereward caught it up. "Know of a mark, then?"

"You and me've done business afore, sir, and you've never had cause to be dissatisfied. But this time, mind me, is best of all."

Leaning on the bar, his eyes on the street, Hereward said, "How soon?"

"This night, sir. Fair toward Thaxted. Lots of selling livestock and whatever. A certain man I know—" The conversation turned upon technical considerations with the intent of identifying the owner of the fat purse expected to come down Witham road hastening to arrive safely home by dark.

"He'll stop here for a pint of my best," said Penn, "and I doubt he'll be going on as fast as he thinks. Might well be full dark before he sets out again. No matter, 'tis just after full moon."

So it was settled. He stopped on his way out as a thought struck home. "Did my brother pass through here on his way to Colchester?" He had spoken of making inquiries about the old smuggling road. He could well have begun at the Blue Swan.

"He did pass through," said Penn, scratching his bald head in the effort to remember. "But he didn't go Colchester way."

"No?"

"Not that I seen. He went—" Penn's brow cleared. "I mind it now. He went Thaxted way, doubtless looking for more of them fancy sheep."

Hereward would have thought it odd that the earl, without Warrod, would have set himself in the way to purchase livestock. But Penn might well be wrong.

None the less, Hereward's feeling of urgency pressed him harder. Instead of returning to Wakeford, as he had planned, there were things to do at the old chapel, tasks that could not be deferred.

He paused before moving into the clearing, looking carefully around. He saw no signs of intrusion, a lack that pleased him. So far, he was in the clear. He had half expected Fenella to be waiting for him, even though she had no idea of his plans. Nor, to be honest, had he.

His thoughts of Fenella were of two aspects. He wanted—how he wanted!—to take her with him, the two of them against the world. She had bewitched him, in spite of himself, and he believed she was more than willing to respond to his advances. But he did know her kind—ready to brave the devil today, but sunk with remorse tomorrow.

He dismounted, and tied the black next to the white-footed sorrel. He started toward the chapel, and then remembered that he had removed the cache to a place less obvious. When he had his leather pouch in his hands, he considered prying the gems from their settings. Easier to carry, of course, and he still had the sacks of gold coins to put in his saddlebag. But there would be loss of precious time, prying out the gems. He might well do better with them still in their settings. Old family jewels, he could call them, and sell them privately.

He would have to come back in daylight to make sure he had missed nothing of value. But he could feel the hot breath of pursuit almost as though it were already at his shoulder.

He was badly shaken, both by his unexpected interest in Fenella, and by the clear alteration in his brother. If he were to wager on the outcome, the odds would not be with his mother.

He stopped short, in the act of pulling together the thongs on his washleather pouch, and listened. Yes, he decided, someone was indeed approaching. Not silently, either—precisely as he believed a riding officer with clumping boots might sound.

He drew his pistol and leaped to one side of the clearing, seeking refuge behind a growth of young oak. The intruder came nearer, and now he could detect an attempt at stealth. That damned Smith! He cocked his pistol and aimed it at the precise spot where the man must emerge. He waited.

The sun was setting, and in only moments the clearing would be in such obscure light that he would likely have only one shot at the officer.

But the figure that, at length, tiptoed into the clearing was slim, of smallish height, and dressed in skirts.

Breathing, "Good God," he came into the open, thrusting his pistol into his belt.

"Fenella, you idiot!" he burst out, angry in his relief. "You could have been killed!"

She said, "But you always said you recognized me when I came, a herd of frightened horses, I think you said?"

"But this was different! Oh, never mind why. What are you doing here?"

She had, while he was speaking, glanced around the clearing, noting his small store of treasure heaped together, and come to the right conclusion. "You're leaving."

"You sound desolate," said Hereward, again in control of himself. "Will you miss me?"

"Yes, I believe I shall."

She was not entirely clear in her mind. She would miss the excitement of stealing out secretly, of outwitting her aunt and grandmother as though she were still a schoolroom miss escaping from her studies.

Her need for excitement, for stimulation to enliven her days, was filled by Hereward and the deliciously clandestine meetings in the clearing by the chapel. She understood only that she wished for Hereward's company, for the simple reason that he demanded nothing of her—except, perhaps, an occasional kiss. She need not watch her every word, as she did in Gervase's presence, or dread opening her mouth lest the Dowager Lady Huntley pounce on her and reduce her to a whimpering shred.

To be fair, Lady Huntley had not yet ventured to criticize her directly, but if ever the opportunity came, Fenella was sure Gervase's mother would be prepared, and more than ready.

"I shall think of you too," said Hereward. "The bitter winds off the sea in the winter, chilling you to the bone—and you muffled to your pretty little nose in furs! Do not be concerned. Gervase will see that you're as well wrapped against the cold as one of his prize ewes."

"That's insulting," she told him, without spirit.

"I intended it to be," he retorted. "You have surely discerned by now that my feeling for my brother is far from kindly. He has taken from me everything I hold precious from the very start. But this is too much for me to endure."

"You're talking fustian!"

"You think my feeling for you is worth nothing?" Hereward no longer knew whether he was playing out a practiced line with bait sure to net him his prize, or whether his regard for Fenella, grown out of bounds, would in truth lead him into some great folly.

She could have thrown herself on him, she thought, simply to feel a kindly arm around her. She felt more than ordinarily lonely. She feared Lady Huntley, she was averse to the thought of living with Gervase forever, but all doors were closing behind her, and while she would have fought against any coercion by force, the persuasions that captured her were silken, but inexorable.

Hereward was seized by a conscience he would have denied owning. He seized her arm. "Go home!" he ordered harshly, tightening his fingers deliberately.

"Nobody knows I am out of the house. I went to bed pleading a headache."

"We've been simply playing games like children up to this point," he said, soberly. "We've done with foolishness, Fenella. You have your way to go, and mine is far different." With a genuine sense of sadness, he added, "The game is much too serious now."

Whether he meant his own involved feelings for her, or simply the dangerous mission he was resolved upon accomplishing in the next hour, he was not himself sure. But seeing that she did not move, he was led into a blunder. "This business tonight is dangerous. You don't have nerve enough to see it through——"

"I do too!" She shook his hold on her.

"I shall not take you with me!"

"You can't leave me behind!"

She clutched his sleeve. "Hereward, you cannot go without me!"

He was truly angry, she knew, but she dared not even contemplate staying in the clearing alone, the ruined chapel brooding silently in the moonlight. Nor, and with more reason, could she agree to make her own way home in the dark.

He pulled away. "Fenella, you're in my way!" The scene had delayed his planning, and it was nearly time for the moon to rise. He would be angry indeed, and nigh desperate, if the fat purse Penn had mentioned had already passed by on a safe journey home.

He crossed to saddle his black horse. She picked up her skirts and ran to his side. "Hereward, I want to go with you! I must!"

He looked down at her, his eyes glittering. "Go on back,"

he said harshly, "back to your safe little life, and get out of mine!"

He leaped into his saddle, and pulled at the reins savagely. The horse whinnied in protest, but Hereward hardly noticed. "You could come with me to Italy, you know. But you'll have to decide. This little hole-in-corner escapade of robbing fat merchants on the road, is only the beginning. Dangerous, but exciting too. Think about it! I'll send for you!"

His laugh rang out in the clearing, sharp to her ears, mocking. But though her cheeks stung from the lash of his insults, she had not so far lost her wits as not to see that he was indeed leaving her alone in the darkening clearing.

She ran to the sorrel and untied the reins. Hitching her skirts high about her knees, she grabbed a handful of mane, and pulled herself up. There was no time to find a saddle. Nor would it have helped much, she thought in a few moments. Before, when she had followed Hereward through the thickets, he had been just ahead, and the sorrel had been willing enough to keep its place.

But now, the black was so far ahead that the sorrel was afflicted with the same degree of panic as Fenella. Her mount, uncontrollable for the moment, plunged madly after the other horse, now out of sight.

Hereward had, in fact, thought better of his actions. He recognized that his feeling for his brother's betrothed had gone far beyond a simple wish to rouse Gervase's jealousy. He could even, with some degree of equanimity, contemplate taking her with him, though it would mean ruin for them both. He could never bring her back to England, nor in truth could he himself return, in safety, alone.

Her company would mean a certain amount of sacrifice, for his gains, however large, would not suffice to support two in luxury. And he would never descend to the species of boardinghouse favored by Englishmen of little funds on the Continent.

His hatred of his brother had grown in the past weeks of proximity. While Gervase was on the Peninsula, Hereward could speak of his brother's tyrannies without rancor, for they were in truth not seriously hampering. Hereward was able to diddle his mother into obtaining estate funds for his use, and he had lived comfortably enough.

But living in the same house with Gervase, even for a short time, had proved a revelation. Gervase had become a very real obstacle to his continued ease. It would be difficult to overestimate the threat that Gervase posed to him, thought Hereward, his reluctant respect overlaid by fear, and a long-cherished jealousy.

But when he reined up to listen, he could hear the sorrel's frightened passage through the breaking branches of shrubbery, and he thought with misgivings, All is going awry tonight. I shall endeavor not to believe it an omen!

"Hereward——" Fenella squeaked when she came up with him.

"Of course," he said, more easily than he felt. "Did you think I would truly leave you behind?"

She had indeed thought he would. But she was too proud to confess how frightened she had been. Fortunately, he said only, "We must hurry, if we're not already too late!"

They moved ahead on the road that she had traveled before. But instead of stopping in the place she remembered, they continued. At length they came to a spot that Hereward must have marked in some way, she thought, for she could detect no difference between this great tree and the little space around it, and half a dozen others they had passed just like it.

He came to help her down. His lips brushed her forehead, but his mind clearly was on the events to come.

"Where are we?" she whispered.

"South of Witham." That was all he dared tell her. He intended to break, after his encounter with the farmer, toward Maldon, where his small yacht lay at anchor. He had told Gervase the yacht was coming to Cogges Cove, a gambit intended to focus his brother's attention in a harmless direction.

He helped her tie the sorrel, and taking her hand drew her with him toward the road's edge.

Her ride had this time not proved exhilarating. She was aware of a small doubt creeping in at the edge of her mind, as though an imp danced there shouting, What are you doing here?

There were small sticks caught in her skirts, and one particularly sharp twig had worked its way under her petticoats to stab her with every step, most uncomfortably.

What indeed was she doing here? Deceiving her grandmother, who had shown her nothing but kindness, except in the matter of her betrothal, running a grave risk of discovery in an escapade which truly meant less than a jot to her. She

did not share the loot, nor would she have touched a penny
of Hereward's illicit gains.

All for what? A small rebellion, that was all, and one without purpose or cause. Had she fallen in desperate love with
Hereward, she might have had some excuse, she knew. She
was well aware that Hereward would be a broken reed, no
pillar to lean on in trouble.

Some small sound must have escaped her, for Hereward
stopped, and casually slipped his arm around her waist.
"Peril, my dear, is its own intoxication. Do you not feel it,
like a drug that gets into the blood?"

His question came too closely on the heels of her own reflections. "No," she said sharply. Then, to palliate her denial,
she added, in an attempt at lightness, "Only a stick that I
swear is drawing blood—that's all I feel!"

"Would you be happy living like this?" His tone was rally-
ing, but she fancied she could hear an undertone of gravity in
his voice.

She was saved from replying, for suddenly the muscles in
his arm tensed and he lifted his head in an attitude of listening. After a moment she too could hear the unmistakable
sound of wheels on the old Roman road, and the smart clop-
clop of a well-paced pair.

"Ah, my luck is in!" breathed Hereward, and, leaving Fenella to stand where she was, he gave her a last pat on the
shoulder, and crept forward, toward the road.

His luck, however, having been out all day, had not yet returned. It was perhaps the divided mind that he carried with
him, the image of Fenella still hovering in his thoughts, that
wreaked the havoc.

He hovered, in the shadows, listening to the approaching
vehicle. A curricle, judging by the sound of it. A wealthy
farmer indeed! He was aware that the moon, rising the color
of a gold crown, was already tipping the trees on the other
side of the road, and while not strong, still there was light
enough to see outlines and shapes, and the illumination was
growing steadily.

At last, near enough!

Hereward stepped to the side of the road. He drew his pistol from his belt, and shouted the time-honored cry of the
highwayman, "Stand and deliver!"

From that point, his fortunes failed. In the act of stepping
forward as he cried out his command, his foot mistook the

edge of the road, the crushed stone of the metaling unstable beneath his foot. His ankle turned.

In the unexpectedness of the accident, his finger tightened convulsively on the trigger. The bullet sped harmlessly past the ears of the driver of the curricle, a sound unmistakably familiar to him, even though unexpected in this country.

The latter, surprised less than were his horses, spent a few moments of intense effort controlling the plunging animals before he could turn his attention to the unfortunate highwayman.

The robber was sprawled on the ground rubbing his ankle and making small sounds of pain. He was for it, he knew, for he could not escape recognition at this point, unless the farmer were too terrified for his gold to stay.

Hereward's luck had entirely deserted him. The driver, holding his pair under easy control now, allowed a sour smile to touch his lips, and waited, for the moment he dreaded.

It came. Hereward struggled to his feet, and looked for the first time into the face of his intended victim. The shock was considerable.

"Gervase!"

"It is indeed. I must tell you that I am somewhat gratified to observe that your activities do not run to smuggling, but I confess that robbing on the King's Highways is outside of enough."

"Read me no sermons, Brother!" snarled Hereward.

"I shouldn't think of it. A waste of breath, I am quite aware."

Suddenly the great injustice of life swept over Hereward. He had no fat purse, his already garnered wealth lay back at the chapel on the step, where he had left it inadvertently, and his brother now looked at him with a level gaze that told him he had lost everything.

In a sudden frenzy, he threw the empty pistol at Gervase's head, and turned to run, limping, into the underbrush.

Gervase listened with trained ears. He could follow Hereward's progress as though he could see it. All caution had fled from Hereward's actions. He crashed through the shrubs, apparently to where his horse was waiting. There was a quick word to someone. Gervase's eyebrows rose. He expected his brother to work alone, but he had a confederate, it was clear.

Hereward said roughly, "All's gone wrong, Fenella."

Her fearful voice rose, unrecognizable to the man in the curricle. "Will you come back?"

The only answer was the thunderous sound of the pounding hooves of Hereward's black horse, followed shortly by another set of hooves fading into the distance. Clearly the confederate had fled, as well.

Gervase saw no reason to linger, and yet his instincts, honed in five years of constant warfare, told him that the woods were not yet uninhabited. He waited.

He had a fairly sound idea of where Hereward would be heading for. The earl had gone off, ostensibly to Colchester, but instead, alone, to pursue some inquiries he had in mind. The *Naiad* was not at Cogges Cove, as Hereward said, nor had men along the coast north heard of it. Hereward was drawing him on a false scent, and Gervase wondered to what purpose.

He had found the *Naiad* at last, nearly concealed in a hidden indentation in the coast near Maldon. He could set the authorities to tracking down their felon, his brother, but the Wakeford name deserved no such stain on it, and he, Gervase, would do all he could to protect it.

He wished with all his heart that he did not know what he knew. But knowledge, once gained, cannot be easily forgotten.

There had been no sound from the direction in which Hereward had escaped into the woods. But yet, Gervase would have sworn there was still someone nearby. Stealthily, he slid to the ground. He looped the reins over a convenient limb, and drew out his pistol. Cocking it—for a pistol unready to use is without purpose—he set out in search of the owner of that second voice.

His unsuspecting quarry was sitting on the ground not far away, unable to think what to do. The key to the side door, always locked now by Aunt Kitty's orders, was pinned safely into her pocket, but what good was the key when she didn't even know which direction the house lay?

All turned to ashes on her tongue. Hereward, fleeing as though the devil himself were in pursuit, gave unmistakable signs that he would not return for her.

She was numb. She had, in her wildest dreams, never envisioned such a coil. She listened to the silence. She would count twenty, and if there were still no sounds around her, she would move. The question crossed her mind—what would Caro do? There was no answer. She wished she had never heard of Caro Lamb!

There was nothing else to do. Home lay somewhere beyond Witham, and Witham, judging from the general direction they had come, lay some miles to the right. Perhaps she could beg a ride on a farm cart as morning approached.

Certainly she had no hope of coming home in a coach, as she had from that dreadful night at Vauxhall Gardens.

She stepped out of the brush, going quietly but hearing each breaking twig sounding like a cannon. At last she emerged, an eternity, so it seemed, later, onto the road, praying it were empty.

It was not.

Gervase, whose acute hearing had marked her coming, recognized the fragile, frightened figure stumbling into sight. His surprise was unbounded, but his calm demeanor gave no sign of the wild surmise rioting in his thoughts.

He lowered his pistol and stretched out his hand to Fenella.

"Well, my dear, may I escort you home?"

22

Lady Huntley, contrary to her habit, spent a perfectly wretched night. Not prone to think overmuch during the day, except to make sure that her comfort was assured, she now found herself compelled to reflect upon her future.

Until now, she had been comfortable enough. Her marriage, while not happy, had not been miserable as a certain few she knew of, and even though the older son, the heir, was too much a Wakeford to interest her, the second son was entirely to her taste.

She had never bothered to conceal her clear preference for Hereward, and considered that Gervase, having all the perquisites of the heir, was far better off even without his mother's affection.

She had always found London to be too crowded for her taste, which was essentially indolent and unambitious.

Oakbury in Wiltshire was indeed her favorite of all the Wakeford manors, for its amenities, its staff long used to cosseting her, and for its proximity to the parlors at Bath.

Now, in the space of only a few weeks, she was beset by doubt and unnamed fears for her future. Hereward, far from being a comfort, daily provided her with new anxieties on the head of his brother's intentions. Even the company of Amelia and Tom, if Gervase had meant them to provide diversion for her, failed in their purpose.

Amelia had begun well enough, a fount of all manner of mischievous and most entertaining anecdotes, but of a sudden she too had altered. Worried about Tom, she claimed, but Lady Huntley was not deceived. And Tom himself seemed to disappear just when she might have wished to talk to him. Long walks, he said, were good for him. She would not have been overly pleased had she known that more often than not the walks took him in the direction of Morland Manor.

Lady Huntley, in exasperation, tossed back the covers and left her bed. Perhaps the cool air might send her drowsy. She wrapped her warm robe around her against the maleficent night air, and stood at the window.

She was lost in unpleasant thoughts, and did not know how long she had stood there when she saw movement on the lawn below. Smothering an exclamation, she peered intently. One of the servants, doubtless, stealing home after a forbidden night away from the Hall. She would see who it was, and lodge a complaint. There was not a servant here who wouldn't be better, she deemed, for a sharp setdown.

She watched the unknown with close attention. He approached, limping badly, his progress somewhat crablike, and slow. As he neared the building, he looked directly up at the windows. To her dismay, she recognized the nightwalker. "Hereward!" she breathed. "And hurt!"

She opened the casement and called hurriedly. "Come up, Hereward. Can you get in?" He nodded briefly, and she closed the window. Her first impulse was to call her maid, but something in the untoward circumstances bade her wait and see what was amiss. It might well be that Hereward would not wish the servants made aware of his condition.

She took the poker and stirred up the fire. Unused to dealing with ordinary tasks, she finally found wood to put on the embers, and by the time Hereward arrived she had quite a good blaze going.

He came in and all but fell into a chair. He laid his head back, and closed his eyes. He was very near exhaustion. The bad luck that had dogged him all day had not left, even presenting him with the appalling knowledge that of all persons in the world to meet on the road, the last, and least desired, was Gervase, who had not even seemed overly surprised at seeing his brother masked and threatening.

"I should have killed him!" muttered Hereward. "If I'd had my wits!" Even as he spoke he knew that Fenella, bold and dashing as she wished to appear, would not have held her tongue if Gervase had been murdered in the course of the robbery.

"What happened?" his mother was demanding, for the third time.

"My horse threw me," said Hereward, relating the story he had concocted in his journey from the clearing where he had left Fenella. And what kind of story would she tell when she got home? He knew he had played a coward when he fled, leaving her there, but it was her own fault. He had not wanted her to come with him in the first place, he argued to himself.

"You, Hereward? I thought you could ride the devil's horse!"

"It would be more to the point, ma'am, were you to fix me up, instead of quizzing me like a judge in Old Bailey." The tone of his voice was one she had not heard before. He was in a fiendish temper, and she began to experience a vague queasiness somewhere near the pit of her stomach. What had he gotten into? She dared not ask, for in a way she feared to know the answer.

Hereward tugged at his boot. It would not come off. "Damned ankle! Should have cut it off before."

"Cut it off?" his mother squealed.

He ignored her, finding in his pocket a knife of some sort, and clenching his teeth, slit the leather. When the boot at last came away, his mother drew in her breath. "Broken, is it?"

"I think not, for you know I have walked for some miles on it. Damned horse threw me."

He did not tell her how he had savaged the horse's mouth, in his reckless need to be gone out of Gervase's sight, until the beast, never patient, rebelled. Intending to stop at the chapel and pick up his gold, he found himself afoot miles from home. It did not occur to him that, somewhere behind him, Fenella would be in just such a predicament herself.

His only thought then, mile after mile, was to get to some place of safety. It was too far, then, to travel to Maldon, where the *Naiad* waited. But now, he had a rudimentary plan which, while not perfect, yet would serve.

He told his mother how to dress his ankle, binding it tightly enough so he could walk on it. When she insisted upon knowing more details than he wished to confide, he told her only his fixed conviction. "It was Gervase's fault. He deceived me, saying he was going to Colchester for three days."

At length, abandoning the attempt to learn the events of the past hours, Lady Huntley exclaimed, "I wish we had never left Wiltshire. Hereward, let us return to Oakbury, and be done with this foolish affair. Gervase will come to us, as he should. I am persuaded that is the best solution."

"Too late, ma'am," he told her. "I have a bit of unfinished business here, and then I'm off to the Continent."

She was stricken. "I cannot let you go! What will I do without you? Hereward, I beg of you—"

All her pleas were in vain. Hereward was determined to be gone before Gervase returned. He could not understand where his brother had got to, for it seemed hours that he had himself been walking. But the moonlight slanting in through the window told him that the night was scarcely half gone.

There was no time to waste, if he were to escape. Gervase's return would be bad enough. But suppose he brought the bailiffs with him?

He stood, testing his ankle. It would serve. He would find a horse in the stable, and be gone. "I've got to hurry."

It had been borne in on his mother that this was no minor escapade. Hereward's danger was clear in his white face, the fixed glare of his eyes, the very set of his shoulders.

"What have you done?"

"It doesn't matter now."

"Where will you go?"

"It is better that you don't know, ma'am, for then Gervase cannot force the information from you."

She was overcome. She sank into a chair and covered her face with her hands. Fearing hysterics, he set himself to calm her, in his way. "Come, now, ma'am, I promise you I'll send word in a day or two. I rely on you, my dear Mother, to protect my interests."

He limped out. He would go to earth somewhere, he planned, until he could get back to pick up his loot from the chapel steps where he had left it. It was a grim prospect which awaited him. And all Gervase's fault! If he had not lied to him about going to Colchester!

Lady Huntley was left with a great void in her life. Not to see her dear son again, not to be charmed by his base flattery of her. It was not to be supported. There must be a way to alter events.

By morning she had made her plans. If Gervase had returned home the night before, he had left again before her belated appearance at the breakfast table. Buston, in response to her query, answered woodenly, "I couldn't say, ma'am. His lordship did not inform me."

Buston was suspicious indeed. There were goings-on that he could in no way approve—forays in the night, young Wakeford limping home. Buston had seen too much to believe that Hereward was up to any good. Not a question of the village girls either, he knew that, for he had made inquiries.

Lady Huntley, avoiding Amelia for once, knew what she must do. It was almost a trust, she considered, a high mission to protect her dearest Hereward from the injustices of the heir. She ordered the carriage.

When she arrived at Morland Manor, she had her lines ready to speak. She would tell Lady Cleviss that Gervase had sent her with a private message for his betrothed. She knew her device was faulty, but she had been able to think of none better.

Fortunately, Lady Cleviss was not receiving. "Then I shall speak with Miss Fenella," said Lady Huntley.

When Fenella was told that a visitor awaited her in the salon, she was elated. Gervase had come to call, once more, and this time she was most pleased. She had not, last night, been able to summon sufficient words of gratitude for his rescue.

He had been the soul of kindness, driving the curricle slowly enough so that she was able to compose herself before they reached Morland Manor. He had, without questions, set her down at the opening of the little cart road that led to the edge of the lawn. But he had tied his horse and walked with her, helping her over the rough ruts, and standing at the edge of the lawn until he saw that she was safely inside. There truly had been no one she had rather seen than Gervase.

And never a word of reproach. Not even a question as to what had brought her into such straits!

She entered the salon, a smile for Gervase on her lips. The smile vanished when she recognized Lady Huntley.

"Close the door," said the visitor. "I wish to be private with you." Fenella obeyed. "You know why I am here?"

"Perhaps you will be so good as to inform me?" Fenella answered, not giving an inch. She would not make the interview easier. At the first meeting, she had been tremblingly in awe of the Dowager. So would she be now, except for the strong notion that after today she would need to see her no more.

Would she miss Hereward? Not after last night, she told herself. But she had become aware in the last few hours that she might well miss the earl for the rest of her life. He had been so kind, so considerate—more so than any other gentleman of her acquaintance.

She was darkly aware that his like might not cross her path again. It was not a consoling thought. Suddenly she was aware that Lady Huntley wore a look of stern expectancy on her coarse features. Clearly she had asked a question, but Fenella had not heard it.

"I am certain you understand me," said Lady Huntley with heavy emphasis.

Fenella reddened. "I am sorry."

"Any girl of right mind must see the proper thing to do, and of course I shall insist."

Fenella suddenly suspected that a hive of bees had swarmed inside her head. She passed a hand over her forehead. "Pray, Lady Huntley, excuse me. I did not sleep last night, and my wits are not sharp."

Neither had Lady Huntley slept, and her temper was much the worse for it. No matter her own feelings on this score, she reflected, no one should be saddled with a witless creature like this one!

"Very well, I shall put the matter in the plainest terms possible. I have come to extricate my son from the most grievous mistake he has ever contemplated."

Fenella's thoughts flew to Hereward. If ever a misguided man existed, he was the one. Casting aside the advantages of birth and position, in order to stand in the middle of a road frightening honest merchants, Hereward was beyond understanding. And far from being the dashing hero he wished to appear, at the first sign of trouble he had run home to shelter behind his mother's skirts.

Her voice was tinged with scorn as she assured her visitor, "You may rest easy on that head, Lady Huntley. I shall say nothing."

She had clearly misread the Dowager's thoughts, for the expression of astonishment that spread over Lady Huntley's features was surely genuine. But perhaps what she had expected was that Fenella might attest to his innocence before the magistrate! Not even for Gervase would she so perjure herself.

She did not care overmuch what happened to Hereward. He had fled incontinently, leaving her to the mercies of wild beasts and villains. It was only her great good fortune that Gervase was so kind, and so near at hand.

Lady Huntley lost no time in setting Fenella straight. "Say nothing! I cannot think what your scheme might be, but I tell you I shall not allow it. Simply because Gervase feels sorry for you, he must not be permitted to ruin his life."

At last she had hit home, she realized. Fenella's face blanched and she swayed.

"S—sorry? For me? But—"

Lady Huntley pressed her advantage. "He is now aware of his mistake. I confess I was concerned when he entered into this contract in such haste. I myself was acquainted with my late husband above six months before allowing him to speak to my father."

"But he did not—he said nothing—"

"He confides, most naturally, in his mother before all others," said Lady Huntley, with a hint of a smirk. She should have come to this point long before, she believed, for the matter was proving so easily accomplished.

"And he told you?" Fenella's tear-bright eyes were fixed on the Dowager. She disliked her above all others, and to have the fatal blow dealt, as it were, by proxy, and especially by this hated woman, was beyond all believing.

"Wh—what did he tell you?"

Best have it over with at once. "He said he feared you wouldn't suit."

Fenella's courage was returning. She was puzzled, she was so sorely disappointed she wished only to go up to her room and sob, but, also, she had the pride of the Morlands. To be jilted was a disaster. But to have the man's *mother* come to carry his message!

"When did he tell you this?"

Lady Huntley thought quickly. She was positive the betrothal was not of long standing. There had, quite simply, been no time for Gervase to become well acquainted with this minx. And she herself had kept an eye on them whenever she saw them together. She could not detect any strong affection on either side. But then, she was not a noticing woman, she knew, and in addition she was prepared to trample on a love as strong as that of Tristan for Isolde.

Lady Huntley did not know quite how to answer, lest she set a foot wrong. Chance advised her—"Last night."

For once, chance had veered to the side of Lady Huntley. No answer could have been more telling, more wounding, than the one that came to her out of the very air.

Fenella covered her face with her hands. She had lost everything. She had thought that last night had marked a turning point in her own feelings, for Gervase was proving himself an absolute paragon of all the virtues. So understanding that he had not pressed her on the question of how she came to be alone in the woods into which a notorious highwayman had recently vanished. He had helped her into his curricle, and left her to her thoughts for the most part. He had tucked in his robe around her knees, and smiled so sweetly at her when he said, "You must not take cold."

And all the time—*all the time!*—he had been thinking how best to tell her he did not wish to marry her. Oh! how could she endure such a shameful thing!

"So you see," pressed Lady Huntley, "the way is clear before you. You know what you must do."

She contemplated the bowed auburn head with satisfaction. She had accomplished her mission. It had been more trouble than she liked, but since Gervase was not responding quickly enough, she must do all herself.

She moved toward the door. "I shall expect to hear at once that Gervase's mind may be set at ease."

A note, perhaps of triumph, in her opponent's voice roused Fenella. This was shabby treatment indeed, and she did not like it.

"Why didn't he come to tell me?"

Lady Huntley paused in her progress toward the door. "He

is too much a gentleman to cry off. Even you," she added contemptuously, "should be able to see that!"

"But not too much of a gentleman to send his mother to carry his distasteful messages?"

Lady Huntley's eyes glittered. "I had not thought you so shameless."

Fenella whirled to face her. "Shameless!"

The guilty flee, she thought, even when no man pursueth. How much worse it is to have a heavily-laden conscience!

But Lady Huntley did not know that Gervase had been tender and gracious, only the night before. Fenella could not reconcile that Gervase with the one Lady Huntley spoke for.

The Dowager added, cunningly, "You must see how irretrievably you would be ruined, if you persist in an arrangement that is doomed to unhappiness."

"No—no," whispered Fenella, disjointed visions of bailiffs and gallows fleeing through her mind.

Lady Huntley bored inexorably on. "If you do not inform my son that you are setting him free, then I warn you, you will be dealing with me. I have no such tender feelings as Gervase does for your reputation."

"Why do you say such things to me?" Fenella cried out.

"Because Gervase will not."

"You are mistaken!"

"I? Not I! Don't forget, I am his mother. I know what is in his heart. I know what is best for him." She warmed to her peroration, not hampered in the least by any foolish regard for truth. "He is sensitive. How often would he be shamed in the future by ramshackle behavior of a miss scarcely out of the schoolroom! He cannot allow the Wakeford name to be tarnished by any madcap wife!"

"Ramshackle!" protested Fenella, with returning resentment. "You cannot—"

Lady Huntley, if not intelligent, was shrewd. She detected some reservation in the manner of this chit of a girl, some guilt perhaps that was of no more moment than stealing chocolates from the governess's private table drawer. But no matter how small, it was a rift quite susceptible to being widened. "I see that you understand me," she continued.

But I don't, thought Fenella. How could Gervase have gone straight home, after kissing my hand and watching to see that I reached the house safely, and confided such an overwhelming burden of doubts to this—this unfeeling monster?

"I think—" Fenella began.

"No matter," interrupted Lady Huntley. "It no longer matters, if it ever did, what you think. Gervase is too tender to tell you the straight of the matter. It's up to you."

Then, suddenly, Fenella felt an influx of stiff pride. It was almost as though Lady Cleviss herself stood beside her, hand reassuringly on her shoulder. Grandmama would never allow that Woman to carry the day!

"I must thank you, Lady Huntley, for your great kindness in coming." Fenella spoke automatically, without irony. "But I shall wish to hear Gervase's decision from Gervase himself. Pray tell him that I shall as always abide by his wishes."

The transformation in Lady Huntley was notable. Her face grew dark, her eyes were lost within their ugly folds. She was furious.

"Then you brazenly refuse. I tell you, I have no intention of being as tolerant of a daughter-in-law's behavior as is Lady Melbourne!"

She vented some of her rage in stalking stiffly to the door. Her hand on the latch, she turned to fire her last, and disabling, salvo.

"I shall take steps myself to stop this marriage! Whatever happens, the blame is all on your head!"

23

Fenella scarcely knew where she walked the rest of the morning. After Lady Huntley's carriage rolled down the graveled drive, Fenella sought relief for her pounding headache in the rose arbor, in the herb garden, in the coppice where a small stream rose from a spring and trickled away into the dead leaves.

Too restless to stay in one place, she wandered aimlessly until she found she had returned to the small door set in the ivy-covered wall, the door whose key she had carried in her pocket, the door from which she had turned to wave at Gervase, watching in the shadows.

And now, the safe comfort of remembering was shorn from her by the realization that all the tenderness of Gervase's care for her the night before was false. He had not wanted to protect his future wife. He had only wished—so her fevered thoughts told her—to get her home as a distasteful task, and then be done with her.

The realization that Gervase wished to be rid of her was more than lowering. She would have resented such a revulsion on his part, of course, but now, when she was beginning to value him as she never would another, the blow was doubly devastating.

She looked up at the stout walls of Morland Manor. The ivy was thick, evidence of generations of Morlands who had lived and died in this country house, content with their lives. Loving, perhaps, and grieving—they lived through their troubles, and so would she. Comfortless, but not swinging on the gallows had the mischancy encounter on the road been with one other than Gervase.

She went inside. If she had been less wrapped in her own overwhelming troubles, she might have noticed as she proceeded an unaccustomed buoyancy in the very air of the hall. She was at first not even aware of the excited voices beyond the closed door of Lady Cleviss's sitting room.

"My dear," Lady Cleviss had said, a short time before, "must you hum that tune? I yield to no one in my admiration for music, but 'Amazing Grace' wears on one after the twentieth time."

"Twentieth, Mama? Surely not?"

"I did not exaggerate," her mother told her. She eyed her daughter with a mixture of fondness and exasperation. Kitty was surely altered in some way. Lady Cleviss was not given to fancy, but it occurred to her that Kitty's attitude was much as though she were listening, fascinated, to strains of faraway music.

"I must say I am gratified that your glooms over the arrival of the Prentice man have dissipated."

"Oh, yes, Mama!" cried Kitty, setting down her embroidery. "I do have something to tell you." She smiled happily. "Mama, Tom is going to call on you."

Lady Cleviss drew a deep breath. "So. You have forgiven him everything? His spineless flight into the army, his failure to write, and now, so handicapped that he cannot do for himself, his intention to claim your sympathy? You forgive him all?"

Kitty flushed deeply. "I thought, Mama, that you would at least be pleased. For I am happy, you know. I have always had a strong regard for him."

"But my dear, you have seen so little of him. Are you simply nourishing your affection from your memories?"

Kitty found a stitch of great interest in her embroidery, and studied it long, before she answered. "I must tell you, Mama, that I have been seeing much of him."

"Kitty!"

"I know it was wrong, Mama, but you see he must take walks to build up his strength. Every day he goes farther, you know, and—"

"And all roads lead to Morland Manor." Kitty's expression was sufficient answer. "Well, then, I shall not stand in your way, my dear. But I trust he has sufficiently explained his lapses?"

"His father told him I had written, telling him I did not wish to see him again."

"I always thought him a scoundrel," said Lady Cleviss. After a bit she gave Kitty one of her rare smiles. "All mended at last, then. Well, I shall not object."

"Oh, Mama!" Kitty burst into tears. Not until she had buried her face in her mother's lap, and felt the calming effect of loving caresses on her hair, did she recover. "It's been so long, Mama!" she explained. "But I shall hate to leave you alone."

"Better than having a gloomy companion all my days!"

She thought for a long time, conscious of mixed emotions. Tom Prentice would have only a competence, she was sure. She did not wish to allow Kitty to live in happy penury, for it was her own belief that the terms were contradictory. At length, she said, "Well, Kitty, I should like to ask one small favor."

"Dear Mama, of course!"

"Let me get this child off my hands. Gervase wishes the wedding to take place very soon, and I confess I shall be glad to put her into his hands. I always wonder what she will think of to do, for her mother was a mischievous darling."

"And my brother was not the staidest of fathers for her, either," commented Kitty.

"Well, so far, so good," summed up Lady Cleviss. "The wedding will be before month-end, I expect, and then, Kitty, I shall give my attention to you. Do you think that little house beyond Oak Knoll would be suitable? A pleasant prospect, I always considered it. And not more than a half hour by carriage."

Kitty was overwhelmed, but not so much so that her tongue failed to move. She was aware of only one doubt, however. "Will Tom think that I am taking charge of his affairs?"

Lady Cleviss thought, He might well consider it so, but, undaunted, she said, "Leave that to me. I shall make it agreeable to him." After a moment, she continued, "Will you feel that Fenella has much the best of it? For Huntley is vastly wealthy, you know."

Kitty laughed outright. "No, Mama, I shall not feel it so. Oak Knoll presents itself to me as the proper size for us. For there will be no room for Amelia, do you see? But Lady Huntley can always be accomodated at Wakeford Hall, or Oakbury."

"Or West Wycombe, or wherever she wishes," finished Lady Cleviss. "I cannot like That Woman."

Kitty and her mother spent the next hour most agreeably. They were truly devoted to each other, and sympathetic as well in disposition. Kitty was vastly relieved that she would not be taken far away from Morland Manor, and in truth felt a bit sorry for Fenella, soon to be so wealthy that she could, likely as not, never do as she wished.

"First," said Lady Cleviss, folding her work and placing it neatly in her basket, "we must deal with Fenella's wedding."

Fenella's hand clutched at the rail. She was halfway up the stairs, when she heard the voices from the sitting room, and distinguished the words.

Her grandmother's voice came clearly to her. "We must deal with Fenella's wedding!"

She could easily set Grandmama at ease, thought Fenella. There would be no wedding. It would be best to break the news now, for then the seamstress could be stopped, and the cook's frantic planning could be eased—

But Fenella was more stubborn than she knew. If Lady Huntley were right in assessing Gervase's wishes, if Gervase had indeed asked his dreadful mother to inform Fenella she was no longer his choice, then Fenella would of course be decently acquiescent.

But how she wished this had all come about a fortnight ago! Or even last week, before she had begun to slip irrevocably into love with him.

Gervase must come to her himself, and tell her his wish. For she could not quite believe he would be so lost to the proper thing as to delegate Lady Huntley for the purpose.

She climbed the stairs and sought the solace of her room. Her haven for all the years to come, she thought desolately, throwing herself on the bed.

She went over every word that Lady Huntley had spoken, every alteration in expression, and found no more meaning now than at the time the conversation had occurred. But it was her own conscience, at last, that dealt her the final blow. The reference to Lady Melbourne's tolerance could mean only one thing—the scandalous conduct of Caro Lamb was known as far afield as Essex. And if that were the case, then—so Lady Dorton had hinted—Fenella's friendship, however slight, with Caro Lamb would redound greatly to her discredit.

Perhaps Fenella should cry off. Should she burden Gervase with a wife whose reputation, while not precisely tarnished, yet did not gleam white as new snow?

To say nothing of last night's dreadful episode. She could not believe now, that she had been so bold, so lost to propriety, as to seek out a highwayman's lair, and, even worse, go with him on his criminal outing. She buried her face in the pillow. She was sunk in remorse. How could she have done so?

It was of no help to recall that Gervase had not scolded. Indeed—and this was puzzling to her—he had almost seemed to expect such wild behavior from her.

Should she cry off? Or should she wait to hear from Gervase?

She had still not decided her best course, when she fell asleep, exhausted. She was awakened, an hour later, by Agnes. "Lord Huntley's come, Miss Fenella."

When Gervase was announced, she was caught unprepared. She had not yet found her way out of the obscuring underbrush of her muddled thoughts.

She entered the salon. He was standing by the far window,

appearing unusually tall and solid. She advanced into the room some little way before he heard her step.

He turned, too soon to erase the frown on his face that seemed always to accompany his thoughts of Hereward. And his brother was indeed much in his thoughts.

"Gervase?" she said.

"My dear," he came to her, holding his hand out to take her small one and press it before releasing it. "I trust you are well? You did not take cold?"

"N–no." How unkind of him to remind her of her folly! She began to think that Lady Huntley had the right of it. But at least, Gervase had come himself to make the break with her final.

Fenella knew she must speak first. "Gervase, I know why you have come."

He raised his eyebrows. "I was not sure whether I should speak to you on the subject or not." He believed that Hereward was his own responsibility, and wished not to burden Fenella with decisions in which she might have too emotional an interest. But, in all fairness, he had come to clarify certain obscure points that troubled him.

"I should certainly expect you to," she said. "But I must tell you that I have given great consideration to the question, and I have made up my mind."

Slowly, his eyes never leaving her face, he said, "I shall be glad to hear your conclusions."

"I wish—" She swallowed hard. "I wish not to marry you."

Her words were so far afield from his own expectations that for a moment his jaw dropped. Then, recovering himself, he strove to conceal the wound she had dealt him.

He was stunned, he believed, but yet, on reflection, he should not have been too surprised. He could not give her the excitement that Hereward could. He had thought, on their way home last night, that she had looked at him with growing liking, and he had been more than encouraged.

Tact deserted him. "I do not believe you."

She cried out, "Don't make this too hard for me, Gervase. Please, just accept what I say."

"I see," he said gravely. "But I shall need to know the reasons, my dear, before I shall be satisfied."

She turned away. She had not expected her refusal to be thrown back, nor had she believed it would be more than ordinarily difficult to look into his eyes, the color of the North

Sea, and simply say she had changed her mind about marrying him.

She read in his eyes a concern for her that quite overwhelmed her. She covered her face with her hands.

He came to stand beside her. He did not touch her, but she was as aware of his presence as though he had seized her in his arms.

"Why have you changed your mind?"

The words she found bore no resemblance to those she had rehearsed in her confused attempt to decide what was best to do. "I'm too flighty," she said, the words barely intelligible through her fingers. "Too unworthy——"

He pulled her hands away from her face, and held them tightly. "Look at me, Fenella. That's better. Now tell me again."

"I c–can't."

"Fenella!"

"I am simply too wayward, too impulsive—too—"

She pulled at her hands, but he did not release her. "This is for me to say, isn't it?"

She opened her eyes wide. "But you—you already have!" His mother had told her so, claiming to know the secret workings of her son's mind.

"You're not making sense!" he said, startled out of his calm.

She pulled her hands away and collapsed into a chair. Now, since it no longer made any difference, she let the sobs come. If he thought her a watering pot, a hysterical female, such opinions were far better than those his mother might voice.

He came to stand over her. "Fenella, I shall not allow this. Tell me what under heaven has got into you?"

Her words were not audible, except that he thought he heard the word *tarnished.*

He felt a cold hand clutch at his heart. In his worst imaginings, he had not plumbed these depths.

"If Hereward touched you," he said with icy deliberation, "I shall quite simply kill him!"

Fenella looked up, startled. "Touched me! Oh, no, Gervase, how could you think that of him?"

"I could readily believe him capable of anything!" he said. "But I confess I should not think you were a willing victim."

She hiccuped, "I should hope not!"

He waited, but she said nothing more, of a coherent nature at least. "I think we must talk again on this, Fenella."

"Oh, no, no, I could not bear it," she cried. She had spent all her determination to put an end to their betrothal, but if it were all to do again, she did not think she could survive it without losing her wits. "Just please—please *go!*"

He paused, letting his hand drop fleetingly on her shoulder, and feeling her flinch beneath his touch, tightening his lips grimly, he strode to the door. He looked back, feeling his heart lurch at the sight of the frail figure bowed in such distress, and then swiftly left the room.

Worth, that estimable man, was aware of crosscurrents in the house. He knew that Miss Morland had been slipping out like any lovelorn kitchen maid to meet her soldier in the lanes and byways of the neighborhood. As much respect as he had for Miss Morland, and as brave a soldier as was her young man, yet he could not entirely approve of such goings-on.

Also, he had hovered, only this morning, just outside the salon while Lady Huntley had talked for some time with Miss Fenella, and left with a ferocious glower on her ugly countenance. Miss Fenella had given her more than she got, Worth believed. But now, here was the earl, a favorite of Worth's in just a short time for he was a true gentleman, through and through, looking blue deviled as though he had wagered his fortune and lost the lot.

There was something greatly amiss here, thought Worth. He hurried now to open the door, thinking furiously. He swung the door wide, and said, "I trust Lady Huntley arrived home safely?"

It was an idiotic thing to say, Worth thought later, but he had had too little time to frame his remark. No matter, it did the trick, he believed, for Lord Huntley stopped short and stared at him.

"My mother, Worth?"

"Yes, my lord," said the butler blandly, "this morning it was. My lady was not receiving, but I know Miss Fenella saw her."

Gervase reflected. If his mother had been here this morning, she meant nothing but mischief. Coupled with this knowledge, he could readily believe that Fenella's outburst was directly connected with the morning call. There was more to this than was readily apparent.

"Thank you, Worth," said Gervase at last. He strode off down the driveway in a manner that brought Worth great satisfaction.

"Now there's a man," Worth said to the empty hall, "that's bound to get to the bottom of it, I'll wager a crown on it."

24

The day after the fateful conversations at Morland Manor, Lady Stover, the Squire's wife, prepared to answer the call of duty, no matter how distasteful it might be to her.

The previous afternoon, she had been favored with a visit from the Dowager Countess, a visit which had shocked her to the core.

Not with the Countess, of course, she reflected. But Lady Huntley had sought her out—so Lady Huntley had said—for the sole purpose of confiding certain information she had. "Knowing," said Lady Huntley, "that of all my new acquaintance here, I find you most sympathetic to me."

That the compliment might be considered two-edged did not occur to Lady Stover.

Lady Huntley had said she was relieved to get away from Wakeford Hall. "I am too troubled to abide there in peace, although I must be at the service, you know, of my son."

Lady Stover poured tea, and murmured, encouragingly, "Troubled?"

The squire's lady, preening herself on being selected as an intimate of the great lady, cast all judgment to the winds and settled down to a good gossip. She was not disappointed.

Now, after a night's mulling on the things she had been told in the strictest confidence, she was driving into Witham, buoyed by the certain conviction that she acted as the arm of stern duty.

She owed much, she thought, to the neighborhood, as an example of rectitude, and as—on the distaff side—a supporter of moral law and order as her husband dealt with legal affairs.

She swung her pony cart between the gates of the vicarage,

hoping that the Vicar's wife had not taken it into her head to hare off on some errand of mercy.

But Lady Stover was in luck, for Mrs. Watling herself opened the door to her. There was no conversation of moment until the tea had half cooled in their cups.

Mrs. Watling spoke valiantly of the weather, of what she had heard of the crops of the area—"harvesting well, I am told, with the first cutting of hay already in the ricks"—and cudgeled her brain to find other innocuous topics. For she knew Lady Stover well. She eyed her now with misgivings, for her visitor looked near to bursting with news. Unpleasant news, too, thought Mrs. Watling, from the look of things.

She was not wrong.

"I must tell you," said Lady Stover, "what I have heard on the best authority."

"Must you, indeed?" murmured the Vicar's wife. "I shall not wish to hear it, I am persuaded."

"But you must," insisted Lady Stover. "You in your position must be the first to know that we have in this community a loose woman."

Mrs. Watling cast her mind over Maggie Tench, the blacksmith's daughter, and the Semple girl, and one or two others whose behavior, especially on Fair nights, was not unexceptionable. "More than one," she said with an attempt at lightness.

"I am not speaking of the lower classes," said Lady Stover oppressively. "I mean—" She lowered her voice—"One of us."

Mrs. Watling sighed. There was little else to do but to hear her visitor out, for Lady Stover's verbosity was well known. She need not listen more than superficially, she decided, and set herself to thinking of the state of her larder, and the need to teach her new maid Betty a simpler method of making butter.

But her attention was caught with Lady Stover's first words. "Fenella Morland!"

Mrs. Watling's reaction was all that Lady Stover could have wished for. "Fenella! I shall not believe it!"

"On the best authority," beamed Lady Stover.

Mrs. Watling moved her hand aimlessly. There was no help for it. "Tell it all to me," she said, resigned. "I cannot help but think there is a grave error somewhere."

"There is, and it is Fenella Morland's. I shall not tell you who informed me of the danger in our midst. I shall for one not wish to have any daughter of mine consort with such an irresponsible woman!"

Since Lady Stover had no children at all, the remark passed unnoticed.

"You must know that Caroline Ponsonby, Lady Bessborough's daughter, has done the most frightful things. Even her husband, young William Lamb, you know, can do nothing with her!"

There followed, to Mrs. Watling's bewilderment, a full relation of Caro Lamb's pursuit of Lord Byron, her attempt at suicide at Lady Heathcote's rout, and "I know for a fact, that last summer she sent him a curl of hair from a Certain Area!" Lady Stover pursed her lips. "A lot of good it did her!"

"But," protested Mrs. Watling, puzzled, "what has all this to do with Fenella?"

"I told you!"

"You didn't even mention her name," said Mrs. Watling, becoming more than a little disgusted with her visitor. "Nor did you mention the name of the gossipmonger who told you all these little tattles!"

"I had not thought you to be so nitpicking!" said Lady Stover, disappointed.

"And besides," said Mrs. Watling, "how can you know for a fact what Caroline Lamb has done? I should imagine that you have never seen the young lady."

"Nor do I need to," sniffed Lady Stover. "It is sufficient for me that Lady Huntley—who is appalled, I should tell you, at the idea of having such a woman for a daughter-in-law—told me that Fenella Morland was the Lamb woman's companion." She thought for a moment and added, "*Constant* companion."

Mrs. Watling raised her hand to the bellpull to summon her husband. But he would be sorely distressed, and she would be wrong to upset him with a matter she felt quite capable of dealing with herself.

"What Lady Cleviss could be thinking of," said Lady Stover, "raising Fenella in such a way. And I must confess that my opinion of her has plummeted—simply *plummeted*—to the lowest depths."

Mrs. Watling thought furiously. Absently, she said, "Lady Cleviss did not raise her, you know." Then, with spirit, she added, "I cannot—indeed, I *will* not—believe that Fenella has had any part in Caroline Lamb's shameful behavior. I think you have not given sufficient attention to the motives that Lady Huntley may have——"

"Certainly our Vicar's wife," said Lady Stover, "should be the first to maintain our standards of morality. I thought you of all people would lead us in our crusade to uphold the standards we all hold dear."

"Fustian!" muttered Mrs. Watling, but it was not clear whether her visitor heard her or not.

Lady Stover swept on. "How we can call ourselves Christians, and overlook such a maleficent influence in our midst—"

Mrs. Watling was quite as wellborn as Lady Stover, and, in the event, far better-bred. Besides her inborn assurance, she was now quite angry. She rose from her chair and fixed Lady Stover with a baleful eye. Lady Stover rose, as well.

"I think, Lady Stover," said Mrs. Watling in clear accents, "if you were as well-read in your Bible as a *Christian* should be, you would find numerous references to charity as a virtue to be cultivated. I suggest the thirteenth chapter of Saint Paul's first letter to his friends at Corinth as a start."

She said much more, but later, try as she might, she could not remember a word. She watched Lady Stover leave in a fury, white with mingled humiliation and rage. Mrs. Watling was still standing in the center of her parlor, when her husband came in.

"I saw her leave!" he said without preliminaries. "*What* on earth possessed her?"

"You may well ask!" his wife retorted with vigor. "Earth it was, not heaven!"

Still more than ruffled, she told him in general terms the burden of Lady Stover's visit. As she was speaking, her husband, with a murmured apology—"I must see that she does not carry away the gatepost on her way out!"—moved to the window. Thus he was in a position to see the next episode in the unhappy tale.

"Look at that!"

She hurried to his side. "It's Fenella!" she said.

Fenella had come in to Miss Rindell's for a fitting of her wedding clothes, and Kitty, of course, had come with her. Kitty's fingers had moved over some of the fabrics, seeing

herself in them, for she would set Miss Rindell to making her
own bridal clothes as soon as Fenella's were finished.

Fenella had left Miss Rindell and Kitty a moment since,
and was now approaching the chaise. She was not aware of
Lady Stover, sitting in her pony cart in the Vicar's drive, her
face dark with anger at what she considered the unnecessary
insults of the Vicar's wife. She had been humiliated, had
Lady Stover, and disappointed. She decided, now, that if the
proper persons to lead a crusade against sin refused to do so,
then she, Lady Stover, would carry on. Duty lay heavily on
her, even though it now was mingled with resentment and
spite.

As Fenella climbed into the chaise, she came face to face
with Lady Stover, emerging from the vicarage drive. Lady
Stover perceived the opportunity presented to her, and took
full advantage of it.

She looked full at Fenella, staring coldly at her. Fenella
smiled a greeting. Lady Stover, features set in stony disapproval, turned and looked straight ahead, whipping up her
pony. The "cut direct——" Fenella turned white, and then
dull red.

Mrs. Watling clutched her husband's arm, and gave an
inarticulate cry of protest.

"How could she?" she moaned.

"Quite easily, I think," said the Vicar. "She is an evil
woman." After a moment, he added, "But I think we have
not seen the last of this, my dear. We are not the only
witnesses."

He indicated the elegant figure of the gentleman standing
on the Vicarage side of the street, just opposite Miss Rindell's
small cottage.

"I myself would hesitate long before incurring the wrath of
that young man," mused the Vicar. "Lord Huntley could be a
dangerous enemy."

Kitty came out of the seamstress's then, having spoken privately to Miss Rindell about her own needs, and, bemused
with thoughts of Tom, did not notice that Fenella was abstracted. Kitty picked up the reins and soon the street was
clear, except for Lord Huntley, who having watched the Morlands out of sight, came now along to the vicarage.

He seemed calm enough when he joined the Watlings in
their small parlor, refused the offer of tea, and accepted their
invitation to sit down.

"You may not remember, Mr. Watling," began Gervase, "but at some gathering—I forget just where—I seem to have heard you refer to a leak in the vicarage roof. Or was it the church?"

"The vicarage," said Mrs. Watling, "just over the spare bedroom."

"It is not a bad leak," said the Vicar, valiantly keeping up the trivial conversation while his mind longed to explore the implications of the scene in the street.

"Bad enough so that no one dares sleep there. I must send Betty home at night, and she's such a slugabed that she hardly comes before noon."

"Well, don't worry," said Gervase. "I'll send someone from the Hall to fix it. I shall ask him to consult with you, Mrs. Watling, as to what needs to be done. Pray don't hesitate to mention any other repairs you need as well."

They thanked him for his trouble.

"Not at all," said Gervase, "but I warn you I shall expect some recompense." He smiled, but Mrs. Watling failed to detect any amusement in him.

"Anything!" said Mrs. Watling.

The Vicar, more cautious, said, "I shall be glad to hear what we could do for you."

"Then," said the earl, his voice suddenly harsher, "pray tell me what is going on here?"

To their credit, neither the Vicar nor his wife pretended not to know his meaning. The Vicar fumbled his words, protesting that he was not quite sure——

"I am quite sure," said Mrs. Watling. "And it's time that this idiotic mess was placed in your hands, Lord Huntley, for it is more than I can think how to go on with."

Gervase nodded encouragement. Mrs. Watling scarcely needed it, for she was convinced that the sooner a stop was put to such vicious gossip, the better all would be mended.

"Lady Stover was just here," she began, "with a wild tale—"

When she finished, Gervase did not speak for a moment. He had not interrupted her once, during her narrative, but she was sure he had not missed a syllable.

"Dear me," he said at last. Heavy on his mind was the recollection of Fenella and Caro Lamb wending through the byways of a twilit garden of resort, until Byron and his fellows stood their ground and repelled momentarily the pursuing Caro. There was enough of truth in Lady Stover's tale to give him pause. But he failed to understand how rumor could have picked up that incident and enlarged it so.

"Did the voluble Lady Stover tell you where she heard this calumny?"

Mrs. Watling's reaction surprised him. She blushed, and for once appeared tongue-tied. She turned for support from her husband, who by no perceptible sign yet instructed her in the way she should go. She shook her head.

"I see," said the earl, "that she did. I shall not wish to importune you unduly, but perhaps you could bring yourself to tell me this—would I be far off the mark were I to consider the source of this slander to be Wakeford Hall?"

The Vicar suggested, "You must remember, Lord Huntley, that Lady Stover is the only source of whom we are sure."

"Of course, you are right," Gervase agreed. "And we must not ourselves indulge in foolish conjecture, else we descend to a level we scorn."

He gave them a winning smile as he took his leave, without referring again to what he had learned from them. They watched him out of sight. The Vicar laid his arm companionably around his wife's shoulders. "We're well out of it now," he told her with satisfaction. "But I would not count on getting the roof fixed, my dear, for he will not remember his promise."

She retorted, "I'll wager the roof is fixed within the week!"

In the end, she was proved right, even though Gervase's thoughts as he drove slowly home did not dwell on the vicarage repairs.

He needed time to think. He had sufficient to worry him, and he must sort it all out. His mother had gone to see Fenella, and Fenella, later that day, had cried off from their marriage. Now, Lady Stover cut Fenella in a public street, and the Watlings had as good as shouted that his mother was quoted by Lady Stover as the source of the ugly gossip.

He came at last to the fork in the road which led, one way, to Morland Manor, and on the left to Wakeford Hall. He longed to rush to Fenella and hold her close, protecting her against the arrows of the world, telling her he would mow down all her enemies.

He hesitated long at the fork, weighing his desires against the proper course to take. At length, he turned to the left, toward home.

Miss Morland had been with Fenella in town. Whether Kitty noticed Lady Stover's snub or not, yet Fenella was not alone. His own comforting must, to Fenella, sound hollow just now.

His face settled into grim lines. By the time he reached Wakeford Hall, he was settled on his course of action. He inquired of Buston the whereabouts of his mother, and found her, in the salon.

He stood in the doorway. Would his old desire to please, to curry favor, play him false now? Strangely enough, he was no longer in awe of her. He looked across the room and saw her as though with the eyes of a stranger. As, indeed, he thought, he was.

The two women in the room looked up at him, startled. Amelia was sorting out embroidery silks for Lady Huntley, a futile exercise, for the delineation of birds in a tree had been work in progress for a dozen years.

He caught Amelia's eye. Wearing an indescribable expression, she set the silks aside and in one smooth movement was out of the room. The soul of tact, she closed the door quietly behind her.

"Gervase," said Lady Huntley with an indefinable air of triumph, "I have been wondering where you have got to. I am persuaded that your father would not be so taken up with his landlord duties—"

She caught sight of the expression on his face, and allowed her voice to die away. He looked much the same, she believed, but still she was aware of ringing as of a far-off alarm bell.

"Now, ma'am," Gervase, ignoring her remark, "I wish to tell you that at last you have tried my patience beyond enduring."

She sat very still. Then, she ventured, "I do not know what you mean."

"I think you are aware of my meaning. I confess I had not expected you to give vent to such malice. I know that you consider my wishes not at all, but perhaps it is time for us to come to an understanding."

"I understand you, Gervase," she said nastily.

"Not at all, ma'am," he retorted, still in his easy manner, "for you would not otherwise believe I could allow such spite to go uncorrected."

"Spite! Gervase, I warn you not to use such terms in connection with me. I think you forget what you owe to your mother."

"Don't add to my vexation by lying, ma'am."

"Lying!" She caught herself up, realizing that it would do no good simply to echo his accusations. She must do more than deny. "How can you think, Gervase, of setting up that chit of a girl in my place here?"

"What girl?"

"That Morland minx—Fenella."

"Then," said Gervase, his eyes glittering, "you do understand what we are talking about. I had not mentioned Miss Fenella Morland, you know, and yet you are instantly aware of the nub of the matter. I suppose you feel justified in spreading such vile rumors abroad? You cannot have thought that Lady Stover was a suitable repository for secrets!"

She brushed his taunts aside, for in truth she had no answers for him. Instead, she repeated, "How dare you put the Morland girl in my place here?"

"There is no question of that," he told her.

She was winning, she thought. He backed off, she crowed to herself.

And indeed he had veered to another subject, apparently. "Where is Hereward?"

"I do not know."

"Ma'am, I am persuaded you do know. How else will he be able to secure funds, if not from you?"

"What do you want of him?"

"The question does not arise at this time, ma'am. I simply wish to know where he is."

She began to cry then, not the simple tears of vexation which often proved of such value to her, but instead real sobs.

"You leave me unmoved, ma'am," said Gervase after a bit. "I see I shall have to find my brother myself."

"What for? To kill him?"

Gervase paused, as though considering the validity of her sob-strangled question. "No, I think not. I shall wish him to serve as your escort to Yorkshire."

The sobs stopped. "Yorkshire?" Lady Huntley shrieked. "I think not!" Indignation rounded her tones into full, clarion sounds. "I shall go to Oakbury. I did not wish to leave Wiltshire at the outset, nor would I expect that you were too selfish to come to me there. Instead, I hastened here to do your bidding—"

Smoothly, he interposed, "As you will now, ma'am. Oakbury is out of the question. I shall wish to live there at least a few months of the year."

Grasping at straws, she said, "Only part of the time? I shall not mind that."

She caught her son's eyes on her. They were cold as the North Sea in winter storm. Her protest died on her lips. This was a Gervase she had never seen, nor did he resemble his tolerant father, in any degree.

"You do not perfectly understand, ma'am. You will retire within the fortnight to your dower house in Yorkshire. Paston will consult with you as to how you wish your income paid to you."

He turned to leave. The interview had proven far more distasteful than he feared. But he was no longer the pliable son, hoping for affection from his indifferent mother. He was a man of responsibility and authority, with a large number of tenants and, soon, a wife to look out for. He would take no chances on future brangles to mar the peace he had come home to find.

He reached the door, before she called out, "Amelia! It's all her fault, you know."

"Amelia?" he repeated, startled.

"She must needs gossip about all her friends in London!"

Contempt routed the last of the lingering reluctance he had for his task. She could not even take her own blame. "I am obliged to you, ma'am, for reminding me. I shall persuade Amelia to keep you company on the road north. *My* staff will be sufficient to care for Tom's needs."

He bowed punctiliously, and left the room. He sought refuge from the tumult of his feelings behind the large desk that had been his grandfather's. Propping his elbows on the desk, he held his head in his hands for a long time.

It had to be done. He couldn't go on without cutting his mother out of his life. And, curiously, though he had expected to feel remorse, filial guilt, the compunction of a painful conscience, he felt only the liberation of relief.

Still one loose end to deal with, and then he would go again to Fenella. He was more than certain his regard was returned. She would not be allowed to cry off!

25

The Blue Swan in Witham was proud of the amenities it could furnish to wayfarers, especially outstanding in a town the size of Witham. Travelers were more likely to stop at Chelmsford, where the Assizes were held, or at the Red Lion in Colchester to the north.

Mistress Penn of the Swan set an excellent table, and the inn was in the highest degree respectable. So she believed.

But she was troubled now, and not the least of her vexations was that she did not know precisely what was amiss. Whether it was an unusually abstracted air in Penn himself, or simply the brangles among the guests in the taproom the night before, she could not say. The talk had been all of the dashing highwayman, the gentleman of the road who had not robbed at random for the most part, but only took fat purses, almost as though he knew aforehand which held gold crowns and which might be empty.

She lingered overlong upstairs, airing the rooms, unaccountably not her brisk self. Thus it was that she happened to be standing at the window of the second-best room, overlooking the stableyard, when she saw Penn, acting strangely indeed.

Without thinking she moved into the shadow of the window frame, and watched. "Forevermore," she muttered, "he's got one of my good dishes. What's the man doing with that? Going to feed the horses, I don't think!" Going toward the stable, he certainly was. "And my best linen covering whatever is on that plate!"

She hurried down the stairs and out the back door. She caught sight of her husband just as he vanished beyond the stable.

She started to follow him, and then caught sight of the stable boy Rulf, and one of their overnight patrons, and decided that, whatever quarrel she had with Penn, she would have it indoors in privacy.

She waited, not patiently, until he came back. He slipped in, closing the door carefully behind him, putting the back corridor in shadows. He did not see her until she spoke to him.

"Where's my best platter, Penn?"

He started like a shying horse. "I didn't see you. Why do you have to scare the devil out of me? Spying on me?"

"Don't think you can change the subject on me, Penn. Where's my platter?"

"Out yonder."

She took a step toward him. The light from the kitchen fell on his face, then, and she surprised on his face a look she had seen before. When she had caught him watering the brandy, that's when it was!

"Who's in the stable, Penn? I warn you, I'll not take any excuse. I'll call the bailiffs first before I let you ruin my inn!"

"Your inn! I'll thank you to remember—"

"Where's my platter?"

He could see she'd never give over pestering him, and in truth it would be a relief to tell her. He was tired of this sneaking around, and while he did not consider that he shirked his duty by laying all on her shoulders, yet she had learning and he had none.

"Out in the stable," he answered, "I suppose you've got to know. Won't give me no peace till you do."

She eyed him, waiting. "Who's out there?"

"The highwayman."

"Lord have mercy!"

"Got to feed him," Penn explained reasonably.

"Why? I thought the dog took the roast yesterday, and beat him soundly. Now you tell me you took it!"

"Well, I couldn't do aught else, you see."

"Why are we sheltering a felon, Penn?"

"Not so loud!" He looked around hastily.

Mistress Penn was far from stupid. She knew her husband far better than he suspected, and now, judging from his manner, she saw the truth of it. "You've been tipping him!" His expression told her she was right. "But who is he, then?"

"Better you don't know."

"I'll tell you this, Penn. Better you get him out of here by nightfall."

"He'll never go by day," said Penn, exasperated. The highwayman who had come, limping, to demand shelter three days before would not depart until he was good and ready. Penn was aware that the worst had happened—he was caught between his wife and his fellow criminal. It was not a comfortable position.

"Then by daybreak," warned his wife. "I suppose he's best fitted to travel by night. But, Penn, mark you this. By tomorrow morning, I call the bailiffs!"

The object of the acrimonious conversation between the Penns was at this moment sitting in the small room at the back of the stable, devouring a plate of ham, biscuits, and honey.

Hereward was in a dilemma. He knew he could not leave the shelter of the Blue Swan's stable, lest he fall prey to the forces of law. Nor could he stay, comfortable enough but expecting every footfall outside his door to be the heavy boottread of bailiffs.

His nerves were screaming now with apprehension. His ankle was better. He could stand now, and even walk without discomfort. But he had had too much time to think in the last three days. His thoughts revolved around his brother. Had it not been Gervase on the road that night, he would now be free, wealthy, and beginning to enjoy his life on the Continent.

Instead, he was forced to live in dirty straw, eating when it pleased Penn, and his escape in the highest degree improbable.

He could not travel as far as Maldon, where the *Naiad* rode at anchor, a substantial hoard under the floorboard. He must get to the chapel, obtain his pouches of gold and jewels that he had left behind, and then reach the yacht.

He had mentioned his yacht's captain to Gervase, a harmless bit of pomposity, for the man was only an old mariner who, for a coin or two, moved the yacht from one anchorage to another, as Hereward bade him.

The plan that had burgeoned during Hereward's forced inactivity was now full-blown. He would escape, this very night, and England need not look for him any longer. But he would not leave Gervase unscathed to enjoy his righteous life!

Obtaining materials from Penn, he composed two notes, to his satisfaction. The first, to the boatman, directed him to bring the *Naiad* from Maldon to Cogges Cove. The second, far more carefully worded, was addressed to Fenella.

He summoned the stableboy. "Here, you. I've a job for you."

Rulf stood before him without speaking. Ordinarily slow of speech, not burdened with a sharp mind, Rulf had the reputation of being a mute.

Hereward gave him his instructions. "Understand?" Rulf nodded. "I'll give you a coin when you get back and tell me what you've done."

Rulf took an old nag from the stables, rope-haltered him, and climbed on his back. He left the Blue Swan behind him and set out toward Maldon. Slow to contemplate, yet in the end Rulf arrived at a conclusion. He had dealt with Hereward before. Payment when he got back, was it? Somehow the gentleman was never there when Rulf returned. Rulf had no hope of payment this time, either.

There was no use in looking at the messages, for Rulf did not know his letters. But one of them was for the sailor, so that meant boats. And boats meant—more likely than not—Riding Officers, so he'd heard tell. And maybe there might be a coin or two from the men along the coast. 'Twould do no harm to see, he thought, and turned his nag's head toward the station at Cogges Cove.

Smith was more than welcoming. He fingered the note to the mariner, and overcoming his own reluctance to pry, opened and read it. "That's just what I need!" he said to Rulf. "Now there's no need to tell anyone you were here, boy!"

"I'd be afeered to," said Rulf, speaking for the first time that day. "Penn'll skin me."

A coin changed hands. "Find another place to sleep if you need to. I'll keep this note, but you can deliver the other."

Rulf nodded, and set out on his slow progress toward Morland Manor.

At the Manor, Fenella's noisy thoughts turned her world upside down. Two days ago, in Witham, Lady Stover—merely a squire's wife—had deliberately snubbed Fenella Morland, great-granddaughter of a duke, betrothed to an earl. Fenella was sunk in despair.

She had never even seen a cut delivered. Now, to her intense mortification, she had herself received it. The death knell of her reputation, a disaster of the first water! Now, Fenella realized, too late, that Lady Huntley had not been tilting with words. She was possessed of stronger weapons than any Fenella might find to wield in defense.

Lady Huntley had warned her. "I will stop this marriage by any means required."

And Fenella's deepest wounds were inflicted by herself. She had deceived—for the most innocent reasons!—everyone she knew. Lady Dorton at the start, Grandmother, Gervase—and, even herself. For she had longed for excitement to keep at bay her dislike for her betrothed, and now she realized that she had developed more than a *tendre* for him. She was falling ever more deeply in love with him, for his kindness, his concern—there were so many ways in which he was far more than she deserved!

She had told Gervase, two days before, that she did not wish to marry him. His response had not been satisfactory—he had not seemed convinced, but on the other hand, he had not come back to her.

Tom had told Kitty that Gervase had gone to London for a day, and Hereward had vanished.

She dared not tell her grandmother about the incident at Witham. Kitty was too happy for Fenella to wish to cause her any unhappiness. Gervase had departed without telling her where he was going. And Hereward had totally deserted her.

She was wretched, and alone.

By the time Rulf reached the Manor, Fenella was considering seriously whether it would be better to throw herself from a cliff, or simply refuse to eat until she was dead.

Hereward's note jolted her. There *was* a way, then! "Meet me at chapel," so read the note, "we go abroad tonight. No luggage. Don't fail me."

This very night! She must pack, she must leave a note—there was no time—At last, she forced herself to settle down and consider.

She did not want to flee with Hereward. The life ahead with him would be unpleasant, how unpleasant she had no way of knowing, but no matter how ugly the future, it could be no worse than staying here, watching her grandmother sink into disillusion and hurt, maybe even causing Tom to cry off, deserting Kitty a second time.

It helped, she discovered, to think of far-off things, as her hands chose, folded, and stacked clothes, only to reconsider them and begin again to pack. At length, an hour before dark, she tied the corners of her shawl together, enclosing the items she thought indispensable. She set the note she had written on the dressing table. It had been hard to write, but at length she had managed, except for the one splotch where she could not restrain her tears.

Hereward was waiting when she arrived at the clearing. Even in the half dark she could see that he was furious.

"What did you do with them?" he said, voice cold and cutting.

"Wh—what?"

"The pouches—I left them on the step the other night. Thanks to you, I was late. You came back here, didn't you?"

His accusations were the last straw. Fighting back tears, she retorted angrily, from anxiety and fear, "You bungled, and left me behind, Hereward. Don't blame me for your own follies!"

"Feeling sorry for yourself?" he scoffed. His own nerves were quivering. "You like danger, don't deny it. And I gave it to you. You were safe enough, all the time, for nobody would blame that sweet innocent face. Is that what you believe?"

She looked away, lest he see the tears brimming. She had struggled so with her decision to come and he berated her so scorchingly that she could no longer pretend to be brave.

This was so much fun in London, she reflected. To dance gaily on the edge of propriety, knowing that a wrong step could lead to misfortune had been stimulating. And while she had protested her innocence to Lady Dorton of any wrongdoing, she was aware that she enjoyed the titillation of recklessness more than she should.

But why wasn't it fun now?

The memory came unbidden of the last, and most dangerous, escapade, in Vauxhall Gardens, a coil into which she had been drawn in spite of her good resolutions. She would give her life, now, if the knight-errant who had come to her rescue then might be just now on the gallop to save her again.

Her former rescuer was indeed galloping at that moment, but not precisely to her deliverance. While Fenella had been making her determined way toward the clearing, Kitty, simply because she was now so quietly happy, had somewhat belatedly realized that Fenella's mood could be termed at best miserable. She had been in the mopes for two days, and Kitty, blaming herself for her insensitiveness, made her way to Fenella's room to offer comfort or at least a listener.

Upon receiving no answer to her knock, she entered, and in moments held Fenella's note in her hand. With a strangled cry, she rushed to Lady Cleviss.

"Dear Grandmama—" Lady Cleviss read, her face turning gray and her eyes looking upon disaster. "She's gone, Kitty."

"Where, Mama? Can I send the men to search?"

"No, no. If I could only keep my wits—we must not let the servants know. Kitty, get me someone to take this message to Wakeford Hall. Let us hope that Huntley is back from London!"

Huntley had in fact just returned from the city where he had taken care of a few distressing arrangements. Handed Lady Cleviss's note even before he drew off his driving gloves, he frowned.

His fastest horse saddled, his caped driving cloak set aside, he was on his way to the Manor at the gallop. He could not think why he was summoned in such haste, unless Fenella— an accident? Thrown from her horse? Taken ill with the plague?

"I came at once, Lady Cleviss," he said, eying the somber Morlands with grave misgivings. "Fortunately, I was at home."

He read the note Lady Cleviss handed him. Fenella was off with Hereward, then! His own fault, for he should have come to reassure her before he went to London. Instead, even though he might have surmised the agony of mind she was experiencing, he had yielded to his own wish to have all settled before he saw her again.

Now, for his great folly, he must retrieve his error. God help Hereward if he were too late!

"Pray, Lady Cleviss, do not give way to forebodings. I know how to deal with this. I shall have Fenella back in your hands before morning." He sounded more confident than he felt.

After he left them alone, Lady Cleviss said, "I shall send the servants to bed, Kitty. When he brings her back, we shall not wish the circumstances to be trumpeted far and wide."

His smile, as he had left, was most reassuring to Lady Cleviss. She was suddenly reminded of a painting she had seen once—a tiger, in Indian jungles, powerful—and ruthless. Fenella was as good as home.

However, on the heath above Cogges Cove, Fenella wept silently, convinced she would never see her home again. Nor could she face Grandmama, were she to bolt this moment for Morland Manor.

At the moment when Gervase strode out of Morland Manor, Fenella was lying face down in the prickly gorse. They had abandoned the horses half an hour since. Hereward, a short distance away, in a furious temper, snarled, "Riding Officers all over the place. You didn't leave a note, did you?"

Fenella weighed her answer. Finally, resolving that this would be the last lie she would ever tell, she answered, "No."

Hereward was no longer enchanted with Fenella's charms. She had been transformed, almost before his eyes, into a species of insurance against capture. He was not sure whether to suggest she divert the Riding Officers while he dashed the short distance to the water, swam out to the yacht, and fled, or whether to wait until he was captured, and trade her reputation for his freedom.

The *Naiad* was waiting for him. He had seen as much from a height above the slope to the water. He was thus convinced that his note to the mariner had reached him, and he was at a loss to explain the unexpected traffic along the shore.

Fenella scarcely heard her companion's grumbling. She was at last exhausted. Her natural resiliency had brought her through until now, but the last mad dash from the clearing, Hereward frantic over the unexplained theft of his wash-leather pouches—some meddling bailiff, likely enough, he said—and desperate in haste to reach the safety of his boat before the Law Officers intercepted him.

She lay trembling on the ground. She knew she should be feeling remorse over her ruined life, but she was, quite simply, too tired.

She was hardly aware, even, of footsteps approaching, even of voices at hand.

"I'm Riding Officer Smith," one voice said, "and I have a warrant for your arrest."

Hereward snarled, "Not me! You have no grounds. I advise you not to make a fool of yourself."

Fenella roused sufficiently to know that boots approached. A man shouted, "Look here!"

"A woman," said Smith. Having read Hereward's mail earlier in the day, he had an accurate idea of the identity of the woman that Sergeant Drockett had discovered. Now he was for it, for he had hoped the lady would refuse to run off with the villain he now held firmly by the arm.

"You don't dare to arrest us!" shouted Hereward. "My brother will have your hide for this!"

An urbane voice cut across the hot exchange. "Assisting the officers are you, Hereward?"

Fenella whispered, "Gervase!"

The earl only gave her a speaking glance before he stepped forward, and addressed Officer Smith. "What have you found?"

"My men 've been following him, my lord."

"And found him doing?"

"Well, my lord, nothing, come to that. But a pouch full of jewels—and there's the sorrel with the white feet. Identified more than once, you know. The—" He swallowed. He was in awe of the earl, but he had principles, and he would stand his ground. "The young lady there was riding with him."

"I see," said Gervase slowly. "Well, Hereward? You have something to say for yourself?"

"Go to hell!"

"You may be right." Gervase reached to hold Fenella's wrist. His hand was warm, and comforting, and very solid. She could count on this man to the end of the world.

"What will happen to my brother, Officer?"

Slowly, Smith commented, "Depends on judge." If the judge were in the earl's pocket——

Gervase understood him. "I have no judge in my pocket, Officer. Is this a prison offence?"

"Likely so, my lord," Smith's answer was stronger now, for he had taken the earl's measure.

"Suppose my young brother were to leave England?"

Smith nodded slowly. "It could be that we lost him in the dark, my lord. If that would suit?"

"Fools!" cried Hereward, aware only that Gervase was once again vanquishing him. "You have no proof of anything!"

Smith stiffened. "Best watch your tongue!"

Gervase smiled slightly. "You see, Hereward, you are not yet in the clear. Officer, perhaps you would wish to call your men back from their patrols?"

"Of course, my lord." He saluted smartly, and the three were left alone, in the dark.

"You interfering nuisance!"

Gervase, still holding to Fenella, said, in a radically altered manner, "My inclination, Hereward, is to let you languish in gaol for a few nights, or even weeks. Then we might be able to come to a mutual agreement on our best course of action."

Hereward's comment was unintelligible.

"So? Well, then, since it is clearly ineligible for you to stand trial, I see no point in allowing you to suffer unduly. For my own reputation, Hereward."

"So you are letting me go? I should have known you didn't have bottom enough to see a thing through. Wait till word about Fenella gets out!"

Suddenly, Hereward took a backward step. Gervase seemed to grow larger, more formidable.

"I shall expect you to make your home somewhere on the Continent, Hereward."

"Suppose I don't?"

"It is of no moment to me. I am prepared to allow you the sum of money that our father thought proper. If I learn of your setting foot in England, at any time, then my agent will inform me and there will be no more money. Do you understand me?"

"Oh, I understand you, all right. Old moneybags, throwing your weight around—All for gold. Never fear, Gervase. Paston will find a way—"

"Ah, do you think so? Perhaps I should inform you, although it is truly not your affair, that Paston is no longer handling Wakeford business. And don't look to your mother for assistance, either, for within the fortnight she will be settling down in Yorkshire."

Hereward laughed shortly. "You *did* it. I told her to watch out, but she knew best, she said. I hate the air you breathe, Brother, but I've got to admire you."

When Officer Smith returned, Gervase suggested that he or his men escort the *Naiad* to a port in The Netherlands. And then he was alone with Fenella.

"What will happen to him?" she murmured.

"Does it matter so much to you?"

"No," she said truthfully. "I never want to see him again."

"You will not need to, for you are in my custody now."

"What will you do with me?"

"Cherish you. Protect you." She looked up quickly. She began to tremble. "Adore you."

"But I thought—Oh, Gervase, I was so wretched!"

"My dear."

He pulled her into the safe circle of his arms, and for a little space there was a lack of coherent remarks, but neither of them seemed to notice.

"We'll be married within the week," he told her after a bit. "My mother should attend, for convention's sake. Believe me, she will not trouble you."

For a moment, he toyed with the thought of telling her where he had first seen her. But he noticed, in the growing moonlight, there were circles under her eyes that he had not seen before. Now was not the time.

"Your grandmother will be anxious," he told her, and, his arm still around her waist, drew her away from the seashore.

He would tell her, sometime, but in the meantime he could anticipate with pleasure the expression on his love's face when he would assure her that she had never deceived him—not even from the very beginning!

About the Author

VANESSA GRAY grew up in Oak Park, Illinois, and graduated from the University of Chicago. She currently lives in the farm country of northeastern Indiana, where she pursues her interest in the history of Georgian England and the Middle Ages. She is the author of a number of bestselling Regencies—THE MASKED HEIRESS, THE LONELY EARL, THE WICKED GUARDIAN, THE WAYWARD GOVERNESS, and THE DUTIFUL DAUGHTER —available in Signet editions.

More Bestsellers from SIGNET

☐ **THE PASSIONATE SAVAGE by Constance Gluyas.**
(#E9195—$2.50)*

☐ **MADAM TUDOR by Constance Gluyas.** (#J9053—$1.95)*

☐ **THE HOUSE ON TWYFORD STREET by Constance Gluyas.**
(#E8924—$2.25)*

☐ **FLAME OF THE SOUTH by Constance Gluyas.**
(#E8648—$2.50)

☐ **WOMAN OF FURY by Constance Gluyas.** (#E8075—$2.25)*

☐ **ROGUE'S MISTRESS by Constance Gluyas.** (#E8339—$2.25)

☐ **SAVAGE EDEN by Constance Gluyas.** (#E9285—$2.50)

☐ **HARVEST OF DESTINY by Erica Lindley.** (#J8919—$1.95)*

☐ **BELOVED CAPTIVE by Catherine Dillon.** (#E8921—$2.25)*

☐ **REAP THE BITTER WINDS by June Lund Shiplett.**
(#E9517—$2.50)*

☐ **THE RAGING WINDS OF HEAVEN by June Lund Shiplett.**
(#E9439—$2.50)

☐ **THE WILD STORMS OF HEAVEN by June Lund Shiplett.**
(#E9063—$2.50)*

☐ **DEFY THE SAVAGE WINDS by June Lund Shiplett.**
(#E9337—$2.50)*

☐ **MOMENTS OF MEANING by Charlotte Vale Allen.**
(#J8817—$1.95)*

☐ **FURY'S SUN, PASSION'S MOON by Gimone Hall.**
(#E8748—$2.50)*

* Price slightly higher in Canada

Buy them at your local bookstore or use this convenient coupon for ordering.

THE NEW AMERICAN LIBRARY, INC.
P.O. Box 999, Bergenfield, New Jersey 07621

Please send me the SIGNET BOOKS I have checked above. I am enclosing
$_____(please add 50¢ to this order to cover postage and
handling). Send check or money order—no cash or C.O.D.'s. Prices and numbers
are subject to change without notice.

Name _____

Address _____

City_____ State_____ Zip Code_____
Allow 4-6 weeks for delivery.
This offer is subject to withdrawal without notice.